One True North

One True North

Georgina Templar

Bold Fish Publishing

For my beautiful family and my wider soul group—thank you for your unwavering support and love

What is it that calls me there
And implores me to venture forth,
Neither south nor east nor west to bear
But towards my One True North?

1

The light flooded through the crack in the curtain, illuminating the room and reminding her exactly where she was. A hotel room. Again.

Maya's life from the outside looked favourable, particularly in the current economic climate—she had the well-paid job, the BMW, the farmhouse in a rural part of the country. Inside, though, something felt wrong, like a chocolate egg that was missing the googly praline filling, the waterfall that was missing the expanse of pureness crashing over the rocks, or the mountain that was too steep to climb you couldn't reach the beautiful views.

'Ohhh,' she groaned and willed her thoughts to turn more positive. Slowly she peeled herself from the bed and went about her morning routine: shower, gym, office.

'Coffee?' enquired Leia, jerking her out of a million thoughts of what Zidan and Amy needed when she got home, why her husband had yet again failed to take them to their evening clubs, and other such annoying things on the endless list that was on repeat around her head.

'Sure,' Maya responded, 'but no chocolate. My arse is growing again, I just know it!'

'Nah it's not,' Leia laughed, while hitting the copier next to her desk, trying to print off the finance figures ahead of the board meeting.

'Bloody thing's not working again,' she grumbled. 'I'm pretty sure *my* butt's growing, though,' she joked.

Maya turned to look at the spreadsheet she'd been working on for the last three hours. Her job as a Sales Director at a healthcare company involved days in the office hundreds of miles away from her home and frequent visits to hospitals all over the world to sell the company's products and services. Contrary to her husband's belief she did not in fact drink champagne and eat caviar while away from home, Maya's work life was a never-ending array of dull hotels, often arriving exhausted after long days and constantly wondering what the point of it all really was. Oh yes, it's to earn a good salary for her family and have a nice car and house, right?

'Hey!' Ben waved as he came round the corner. Ben, her work husband, always nagging her, no sexual tension at all but he often had her back and for that she was grateful.

'Anna wants to see you. She's got her war face on, so be warned,' he said, stuffing peanuts into his mouth and waving his over-target achievement printout in front of her face.

'Brilliant,' Maya sighed, 'and there's me thinking I was about to sneak off early and get a head start on the traffic.'

Maya pushed her chair back and, standing up, she felt a sinking feeling in her stomach. She just could not connect with Anna. She didn't feel any emotion coming from her.

With most other people she could find some common ground or at least get an understanding of where they were coming from, whether it be fear, frustration or ego, but Anna was a closed book. Maya took pride in supporting and coaching her team in a way she felt helped them evolve as human beings and not just corporate slaves, but Anna didn't see the value of such sentiment. She all but rolled her eyes when Maya spoke about it and was always pushing to discipline sales personnel who missed their targets, even if they had been great performers the year before. She thought back to her last discussion about Brian, who had achieved one hundred and fifty per cent of his target last year but had, through a series of challenges beyond his control, slipped to sixty-seven per cent this year. Maya felt he had acted professionally, and ensured that problems with the drug he was selling were handled sensitively and ethically with the customers in his hospitals, but Anna had different ideas and had made them decidedly clear. Bottom line with her was, the sales were not coming in.

Maya passed by the 'WE CARE' slogan on the wall as she walked towards Anna's office and internally rolled her eyes. Yes, the company cared, but on condition that sales were met and patients took their drugs.

She knocked on the door, intending to wait until Anna called her in, but the door suddenly swung open and she almost fell face first into the room. It seemed Anna had been waiting for her.

'Maya, how are you?' Anna asked, floating back to the other side of her desk. 'Please sit down.'

She gestured to the large black chair at the other side of the desk. Anna's room was positioned in the corner of the building, with large windows that overlooked the frantic cars and the people scurrying back and forth on the road outside. Today it seemed to capture the mood in the office well—stressed, rushed and mostly pointless.

Anna appeared to have a dark cloud around her, well more than usual, and Maya sensed an unsettling feeling creep into her stomach. She had long suspected that she could feel other people's emotions, however she couldn't work out in that moment if that was Anna's, hers, or both of them feeling the discomfort.

'Maya,' Anna started with a serious look on her face. 'I was in a meeting earlier today with Bill, who is my boss' boss, as I'm sure you know, and I was told you'd been pressing Medical Affairs to escalate a complaint that one of your reps took from a hospital about a patient after they received our drug?'

She paused, looking for recognition that Maya knew what she was talking about.

'That's correct,' Maya answered curtly. 'The patient passed away only a few days after the drug was administered and, given our product is still fairly new to market, I feel it needs to be looked into and escalated as quickly as possible. Is there a problem?'

'Well, yes!' Anna barked, fussing with the front of her shirt. 'Of course, we must ensure we're following company and industry guidelines, however you need to focus on what *you* are employed to do, which is to coach your reps and sell the products. The Medical Affairs team can handle it from here.'

Anna shifted in her chair as she finished, a stiff stance

spreading across the upper half of her body. Her eyes had darkened and Maya knew she was talking to someone completely unable to access any human empathy.

'Oh,' Maya responded coolly, as she felt her frustration rise and her heartbeat quicken. 'Well, I feel I *am* doing my job by following our ethics statement, you know, the one that says Every Patient Matters? Given that the death of a young woman straight after taking our drug aligns with Principle Three: Patients' Safety and Principle Five: Reputation is Key, I thought you'd be supportive of this action?' she quipped, raising an eyebrow at Anna.

The room seemed to still and a cold air crept over Maya's arms and up through her neck. Anna's face darkened further, the edges of her eyes creasing in an attempt to control what was clearly bubbling up under the surface.

'It's very nice that you have such high standards, Maya, but I assure you this is under control. I don't want you involved in this any more and you are to focus on the job at hand. Our drugs have been through clinical trials and are deemed safe for the market. It is not your job to challenge that,' Anna continued.

Maya felt herself tense. That wasn't what she was doing, she thought. Anna was taking this out of context and loading blame and guilt back onto Maya. But then the voice of doubt came in. Was she sticking her nose in where it wasn't necessary and making a rod for her own back? Surely the company wouldn't purposely try to cover up the death of a patient if they suspected it was the drug that caused it? Maya felt a sickening feeling and a cloud of confusion roll over her. The drug in question still had a black triangle associated with it and, as such, was still under specialised safety monitoring, therefore Anna's statement was not wholly true, she concluded. Anna and many others in healthcare always seemed to deal in absolutes—is it black or is it white?—whereas Maya viewed the world as grey, depending on the situation, an approach she found better suited to the complexity of life.

Anna sat staring at Maya, clearly expecting more push-back. Maya paused, mulling over whether to say any more, but she felt her conscience prick at her heart. This was wrong, all wrong, and it wasn't the first time she'd felt like this. The company seemed more and more to be putting profits before people. She thought back to the literature just released on another product she'd been working on, and remembered thinking that the statistics had been manipulated to make them look better. When she enquired with the marketing team about it, they excitedly informed her, 'Yes we got our new full time statistician to play with them. It looks great, doesn't it?'

Evidently no one else could see the problem with playing with efficacy figures on a drug with strong side effects and hiring a full time statistician to make the figures look better, despite the fact it didn't reflect the full truth and certainly gave no consideration to the risk-benefit ratio. No, she decided she had to speak up.

'Anna.' She started by angling her next point around profits to soothe Anna's now clearly frayed nerves. 'The hospital where this happened has a target of four hundred thousand pounds this year. If we don't handle this clearly and transparently with them it'll affect our reputation.'

Anna looked up from the pen she had been rolling through her fingers. 'It's one hospital, Maya, and not well-connected internationally. We're not too worried about contagion, and we have our public relations team well-briefed. I know you care about your team, but we can make sure they're not unfairly penalised financially for this, if that's what you're worried about.'

Maya felt tears prick in her eyes. She felt so unbelievably frustrated and angry and she knew that this conversation was somehow bringing together her growing unease that had been building over the last two years in the whole healthcare industry and the things she was witnessing. Did she really want to be part of this any more? In times like these, the critic in her head reminded her she needed to provide for her family and so the loop went round again in her brain, a never-ending circle of thinking how she wanted to leave and then how that would negatively impact her family and her whole life. She pursed her lips, desperate not to let Anna see the tears in her eyes.

'Well,' Anna said, raising her voice to the level of fake interest, 'I'm glad that's clear. What have you planned for the weekend when it comes? Anything nice?'

Maya shrugged. 'I don't know yet,' she replied honestly.

'Well, don't forget the meeting tomorrow, although I know you're joining online—something I wouldn't have allowed, of course, but my predecessor seems to see fit to approve you being out of the office on a Friday and I will honour that.'

She paused, seemingly to wait for an 'Oh, thank you, you are so kind' type of comment that would never come. Maya got up from her chair, calmly stating that Joan, her former boss, was a woman who saw the value in a work-life balance.

'As do I!' Anna exclaimed, clearly enraged by Maya's dig. 'As I've suggested before, if you moved down south, closer to the office, you'd have a much better quality of life full stop.'

Maya turned with one hand on the doorknob.

'No,' she said defiantly. 'I would not.'

She wanted to say more, wanted to say how the south felt devoid of any human emotion any more—it was all about cars, money and titles. How the air was thick with pollution, how more and more phone towers made her head hurt from the EMF radiation and everyone felt fake or were lying to themselves that they lived a happy fairytale life. She much preferred her homeland of the north, even if the same infliction was creeping into all areas there now, too. However, she reasoned with herself, Anna would never understand that and it would only give her more reasons to get on her case.

She turned to leave and, as she opened the door, the Medical Director breezed past her—or rather *slimed* past her. He made Maya's skin crawl. He was only interested in himself and what he could gain and exploit out of any situation. She pitied the patients he still saw in his clinic when he wasn't here acting like King of the World. Maya knew he was aware what she and Anna had been discussing, judging by the sly look he gave Anna while smiling a hello to Maya. She felt sick just being near him. Her stomach clenched in objection. Dark one, that one, she thought as she made her hurried departure.

She headed straight for the toilet, closing the door and sitting down so she could let the tears flow. She felt so hopeless. How can these people not see the bigger picture? When she first started in the healthcare industry, she felt that she genuinely was able to help clinicians understand which medicines might help people. Maybe that was true or maybe she was naïve—either way, today's industry shoved medicines at everyone. They had lost sight of the risk-versus-benefit balance in favour of chasing ever more profits. The regulations ensured individual reps were persecuted within an inch of their lives and had the fear of God put into them, while those at the top could carry out orders without punishment. Here she was, stuck in the middle—literally a middle manager—and she knew in her heart that something had to give. But how?

'Euck, maybe I just care too much,' she growled at herself, wiping away the tears and leaving the cubicle.

Ben was waiting outside. He took one look at her and rolled his eyes.

'Let me guess,' he said, 'you were doing the green thing again and it backfired.' Ben loved the personality colour training so much that it was now a permanent part of his vocabulary. Apparently, Maya was part green—all caring and fluffy—and part red—fiery and driven—an unusual combination, she was told by the tutor running the class. There had been knowing looks around the room that day when he said that, like she was a problem-child for having a fire in her heart and a strong moral compass.

'Yeah, something like that,' she sighed, looking at Ben.

'Look, Maya,' he said softly. 'I think you're a wonderful woman and I admire your strength, but you're going to burn out. Just let stuff go, okay? It's not your battle to have.'

'So why do I feel like it is?' she asked, trying to avoid the glances of Natalie and Graham behind her, who clearly thought some office romance was in the making.

'I don't know,' he said, taking her arm and steering her out the door. 'But I do know you should get yourself off. You have a long drive and you'll have plenty of time to reflect on that, stuck on the M1,' he said, chuckling.

'Yeah, great. Thanks, mate,' she shoved him gently.

Ben was one of the few people she knew that could show empathy and kindness, but he was very guarded as to when and how he did so. It was like his true self was under cover and the rest of the time he was the face the company wanted to see: professional, balanced, obedient. Maya could do that too. It's just lately, every time she put that face on, it felt like something inside her was dying. Emotion bubbled up once more and, worried that she would start crying again, she said a speedy goodbye to Ben, signed out and jumped in her car.

'Three miles!' she huffed twenty minutes later. 'I got three miles onto the M1 before hitting this traffic jam.' She howled with frustration and threw her head onto the steering wheel, scaring the small boy in the car next to her and causing a knowing smirk from his father. Her phone buzzed with work emails and messages from the children and her husband Jacob, containing varying demands and questions, including whether she was going to be home in time to pick their eldest daughter up from the disco.

'Shit,' she cursed, remembering she had promised to do that. Well, that's out the window now. Bad Mum award again, she thought. 'Oh, give me a break,' she said to nobody in particular.

Maya stared out the window, now partly obscured by condensation, and tried to think about anything except this cursed traffic jam. She was jolted out of her thoughts by the sound of an approaching helicopter. It passed overhead and landed in front of the queue of cars. As she watched it fade from view, slowly sinking to the ground up ahead, she felt a terrible pain in her chest, followed by blind confusion and dark, swirling raw fear. Anxiety rose up her throat and her head throbbed. It took her breath away and she clutched the door handle in an effort to stabilize her breathing. Slowly coming back to herself, she realised with a sense of dread these weren't *her* feelings—they were coming from the scene ahead. Someone was clutching onto life, as people were frantically trying to save the poor soul.

Perspective, she heard clear as day in her head.

She spun around—where did that come from? Was it a thought? No, it somehow felt louder than her thoughts and further away.

'I'm losing it. Great, I'm actually losing it now.'

She started laughing, despite the fear in her chest, and the laughter gave way to some kind of deep understanding that it didn't matter—the worries in her head, the madness of the world around her—she was here safe in her car and up ahead someone's life was slipping away; she could feel it. Her eyes brimmed with tears and she sat back in her seat, letting out a huge breath. She felt down to her heart and sent an energy of love and care back to wherever the feeling came from, hoping it provided just a bit of relief for the stranger she had never met but could feel in their hour of need. The heaviness in her chest remained and Maya wondered how she could stop this if she didn't know why she felt people's emotions in the first place. It didn't make sense, any of it.

The tightness in her chest rose, threatening to pull her into a panic attack, and just as she sensed herself losing control, she became aware of a soft feeling, almost like a hand placed on her shoulder, and a warm liquid sensation spreading throughout her body.

Shortly after, she became aware that the anxiety in her chest had lessened and her breathing had calmed again. Baffled by the experience, she turned, half in fear, half in anticipation, expecting to see someone sitting behind her, but nothing was there, just the back seat piled messily with papers and clothes. Weird, she thought, turning back to face the road, relieved to feel her anxiety settling some more.

Above her car a slither of light made its way through the car roof and over the traffic queue towards the scene of the accident.

Finally, the queue started moving and an hour later, after chatting with two of her team and her husband and ticking a few to-do things mentally off her list, she pulled into the services to relieve her aching bladder and her thirst for caffeine. The line for coffee was long but she decided she needed the fix to keep her awake. As she waited in line, her eyes were drawn to the cashier who was working almost frantically making coffee. The waitress who had 'Sam' on a badge pinned on the front of her tunic looked up and caught Maya's eye, as she steamed some milk, shaking it every now and then to stir up the froth. She smiled at Maya but the smile never reached the eyes and there was something under the surface that made Maya feel sad and uncomfortable.

As she observed further, she saw that Sam was taking in short sharp breaths, and a sense of nervousness and stress flooded Maya. It took her a few seconds to register her change in emotion. She wasn't feeling stressed a minute ago. Or was she? She'd had a tough day, she mused. Suddenly she felt herself welling up and she just wanted to get out of there. Maya turned on her heel, exited the line and sped back to her car, apologising for knocking into a well-suited gentlemen on the way out. She sat down, pulled the car door shut and closed her eyes until the feeling had all but gone. God, I just need to get home and start again tomorrow, she thought, starting the engine.

Ten minutes later, her sister rang and interrupted one of her favourite songs of all time, as Cyndi Lauper's *True Colours* was belting out from the radio.

'May as well listen to someone else's traumas other than my own,' she chuckled, pressing the answer button. Maya's sister Freya was always in the midst of a drama and often Maya could go a full ten minutes saying nothing while Freya ranted down the phone about the most pressing current anguish, which, if Maya recalled correctly, was the on/off boyfriend last time they spoke.

'Hey,' Maya said, trying to sound upbeat so she didn't get an interrogation as to what was wrong. She just didn't feel like she could talk about the day right now.

'Are you on your way home?' Freya asked.

'Yes. Why, what's up?'

'Steve just called me from work,' she answered. 'He said there was a huge jam on the A1 North—lorry overturned and it was likely going to be shut for hours.'

'Oh, great!' Maya said, feeling frustration rise again. 'Why can't I just catch a break today?'

She went on to tell Freya about missing the pick-up time for Faith from the disco and that she had nothing better to do now than to sit in a five-hour traffic jam. That last comment was dripping in sarcasm.

'Hey,' Freya butted in, 'why don't you come stay at mine? Dee is coming over to do a tarot card reading. You could join us, it'll be fun.'

Maya paused to think before answering. She supposed there was nothing she could do about getting home so late now, and it might be nice to see Freya and decamp the day before arriving back at the madhouse.

'Okay,' she said decidedly. 'My ETA is about an hour. Get the wine in the fridge. I'll bring chocolate!'

2

Maya pulled the bronze-coloured BMW through the arch-way into the parking area of her sister's block of flats. She cut the engine and groaned as she eased herself stiffly out of the car, flicking her long brown hair over her shoulder and having a good stretch. Her joints seemed to have started aching recently, no doubt made worse by long hours sitting at the wheel. She scooped up her overnight bag and the large bar of chocolate on the front seat and made her way over to Freya's door.

Maya found the door open and, as she pushed inside, balancing her laptop which was now threatening to fall out of her travel bag, she was greeted by the customary cacophony of two yapping dogs. The small, furry animals jumped up at her, clawing at her calves while she addressed them in her usual affectionate way of 'Hi, you little rats' as she pushed through into the living room. The larger of the two continued to bark, apparently trying to appear menacing.

'This thing thinks it's a husky,' she laughed, rolling him

over with a flick of her wrist and rubbing his tummy to quieten him.

'Ah, leave my puppy alone,' Freya said, floating into the living room in a usual haze of mild panic and swirling chaotic energy.

'No, no!' she shrieked, seeing where Maya had deposited the items she'd brought in. 'You can't put your shit there. Dee will be here soon and I'm so behind tidying up. Go put it in the bedroom. And straighten out your boots in the hall as well.'

Maya dutifully followed her sister's orders, then returned to the living room and fell back onto the sofa, asking with a cocked eyebrow if she was allowed to sit there, or would that be deemed too messy?

'I'm just so stressed,' Freya gasped, scooping up dog toys and clothes.

'Situation normal, then,' Maya remarked, pulling a dog chew from underneath herself, only to roll onto another one as she did so.

'How the hell do two little rats need this many chews?'

Her tights felt itchy and Maya stood again.

'I need to get changed. I hate these work clothes. They're so uncomfortable,' she informed Freya. 'Can I come to the reading in my pyjamas?'

'NO!' shrieked Freya, spinning around with her hands on her hips.

'I don't have anything else to wear that's clean,' Maya protested.

Freya dramatically rolled her eyes and pointed to the cupboard in her hallway.

'Get the blue tracksuit bottoms from out of there. I'll allow that,' she offered, before barking, 'but put them back afterwards!'

Just as Maya had finished changing into the tracksuit bottoms in Freya's small bedroom, her mobile phone rang. As she fished it out of her now discarded skirt pocket, she saw Faith's name flash up on the screen. She inhaled deeply and answered, 'Hey, sweetheart.'

'MUM!' Faith cried. 'I can't believe you aren't going to pick me up. It's bad enough you're not here to do my makeup. It's gone all wrong!' she shouted, and started to cry down the phone.

'I'm sorry, sweetheart,' Maya said, feeling the guilt crawling across her heart space. 'I'm so sorry. I just can't get there. The roads are terrible and—'

'Yeah, yeah,' Faith cut her off. 'You're never here, Mum, and now everyone's going to be laughing at me.'

'Can't Aurora help you?' Maya suggested.

'Really, Mum. You want my little sister to help me because you suck and are never here? No, she *can't* help me. She'll make it worse. Next you'll be telling me Amy or Zidan can do it or, worse still, Dad, who, by the way is in a bad mood. Again!'

'Tell your Mother why,' she heard him say in the background.

'SHUT UP!' Faith roared at him.

'Faith, don't talk to your Dad like that,' Maya pleaded, feeling her anger grow. 'I know you're frustrated but it isn't his fault.'

'No, you're right,' she retorted. 'It's YOURS.'

The phone went dead and Maya had to assume that Faith had cut her off. She sat for a minute staring into nothing, feeling waves of guilt and hurt.

Useless, her critic said to her inside her head. Not a good Mum, not good at your job. What use are you actually? You suck at everything. You don't even deserve the nice car. You're a fraud.

'STOP IT!' she shouted out loud, before realising what she was doing.

'Stop what?' Freya enquired from the living room, oblivious to the events that had just transpired.

'It's Faith,' Maya replied miserably, dragging herself from the bedroom. 'She's really upset I'm not there.'

'Well, you can't do everything,' Freya chided. 'She should be grateful she lives in a nice farmhouse near a good school that you pay for. And she has a bloody pony!'

'It not that simple, Freya. I should be there. I'm her Mum,' Maya sighed.

'Well, doesn't she have a Dad there? Or is he being his charming self again?'

There was no love lost between Freya and Jacob. They were as different as two people could possibly be, and struggled to find common ground on anything.

'He should get a job, take the strain off you,' she announced whilst tipping crisps into a bowl.

'Okay, but who'll look after the children then? He can't get a job that pays like mine. We're too entrenched down this path to turn back now,' she huffed, feeling out of control and utterly dejected at the thought of her daughter's anger against her.

Maya flopped down on the sofa just as the doorbell rang. It was ironic really that Freya had always been the one who wanted children and Maya hadn't really been that interested. Now here she was, married with four, while Freya was childless and still on the desperate hunt for a partner.

Dee practically fell through the door in a huge fake fur coat, hugging Freya and almost detaching her neck in the process. She was exactly as Maya remembered her when she had met her briefly once before—loud and friendly with a kind smile and eyes that let you know her soul was alive and well inside her short, round body.

'Terrible traffic,' she announced, and shoved a bottle of bubbly in Freya's hands. 'Always a good night for bubbly,' she sang, as she turned and saw Maya.

'Hello lovely!' she exclaimed. 'Ah, you're feeling sad. What's up, chick?'

Gosh, Maya thought, rising for a hug. Most people can't read her that well, mistakenly thinking she's always okay—just one of those people that sails through life. Maybe this psychic stuff has a ring of truth to it, she mused. Maya was sceptical about it all. She'd seen and heard things that made her believe it was true, but then logic would kick in—how could it be? What proof did she really have?

Once the three of them had settled around the kitchen table with lighted candles, burning incense and flowing wine, Maya finally started to relax a little.

'Who's first?' Dee asked.

'You go,' Freya said to Maya. 'I want to see what comes up for you.'

'Okay, fine,' Maya agreed, taking a deep breath and, turning to Dee, asked, 'What do I need to do?'

'Relax and let go of expectation,' Dee replied, as she reached across and took Maya's hand.

Almost instantly, Maya felt tiny jolts, like low voltage shocks in her fingers. She quickly pulled her hand back.

'What's that?' she exclaimed.

'It's okay,' Dee reassured her, seeming to address someone behind her. Then she smiled, looked directly at Maya and said, 'You have a future in psychic abilities and spiritual work if you want it.' Then with a wink, she added, 'But your soul already knows that. You just don't let her out much to play.'

Maya was at a loss what to make of that, so she shifted in her chair and said nothing. Dee closed her eyes and concentrated, then picked up the cards in front of her and asked Maya to choose seven. As Maya leaned forward and reached for the first card, she became aware of a presence behind her, similar to the feeling she'd had on the motorway. Instinctively, she looked over her shoulder, as she'd done earlier.

'You can feel them!' Dee said excitedly.

'I feel *some*thing,' Maya admitted, unsure as to whether to tell Dee about the crash scene experience.

'Behind you is a lady with dark, greying hair and to her left a huge Angel. Maybe two Angels. I'm not sure, it's not so clear to me,' Dee said, then went on to explain, 'There's so much light, it's hard to tell.'

'My Granny,' Maya concluded. 'She's here?'

'She is. And she says that you used to love playing on her stair chair when you were younger.'

That's true, thought Maya.

'And that your favourite sweet was humbugs.' Dee laughed. 'Bit of an old man's sweet, isn't it?' she teased.

Maya rolled her eyes and Dee continued.

'I can see the old-fashioned sweet shop you went into with her.'

'Yes, it was huge and I loved it there, but I could never decide,' Maya reminisced.

Freya watched silently, topping up their wine glasses every now and again, seemingly fascinated by the memories of a time before she was born.

'She's telling me you're tired and worn down. She says she wants to show you it's her. She says you have a ring from your Grandad you want to give to your son Zidan. She says be careful—there's a sharp edge on the back that needs filing down. She also says that you should be careful he doesn't—'

'Run around with a lollipop in his mouth?' Maya finished.

'You can hear her?' Dee asked, sitting back in her chair with wide eyes.

'Well, I heard *that*!' Maya said, her tone giving away the shock of what had just happened. It had been a soft voice that seemed to come in from the right side of her head, but she had heard it nonetheless and it sent a shiver down her spine.

Dee paused, looking at Maya. 'As I said, you have great potential, but you push it down and deny it to yourself. Only you can work out why.' She paused. 'You have many responsibilities weighing heavily on you, always trying to please everyone and feeling you end up pleasing no one, always worrying about everyone but never really feeling like you hold space and time for anyone like you should.'

Maya felt a huge surge of emotion surface in her chest like a dam breaking. She tried to hold in a sob but it came out anyway and, thanks to her desperate attempt to keep it back, produced what sounded more like a fox mating-call.

'You feel trapped and alone,' Dee continued, reaching out for her hand. 'Yet you know,' her voice was steady and full of purpose now, 'that this can't be all there is to life. You have a lionheart but you suppress it for fear of consequence.'

Maya sagged her head forward. This was all true. She felt impossibly trapped—a huge weight of expectation and burden on her from morning until night. She felt like she was encaged in a prison, scared of something she could neither see nor hear, and conditioned by so many people and rules that had come before her. Since she could remember, she had felt she was different, like she had a vantage point few had, but none of the tools to unlock the ability to use it. It was like being handed a bottle of the finest wine with no corkscrew.

Tears trickled down her face as she nodded and, at this, Freya reached out and held her other hand as the two women did nothing but hold space for Maya while she cried.

When her tears had subsided somewhat, Dee continued turning over the cards in front of her.

'It'll come to a head,' she said earnestly. 'All of it. You won't be able to tolerate a fake world for much longer. They won't be able to keep you quiet—your moral compass is too strong. Your life will change over the next five years. Everything you think you know will be questioned, most of all by yourself. You have the strength and ability to navigate through it. And you are not alone.'

Maya felt the presence behind her grow, as if more people had joined the room.

'Are there more of my ancestors here now?' she enquired.

'Yes,' Dee confirmed, and proceeded to describe her grandfather, her aunt and two people in eighteenth century clothing she assumed must be connected to the family line.

'You long for love, for compassion and true depth to a relationship,' Dee said, looking at Maya for confirmation.

Maya nodded stiffly.

'You must first find that in yourself,' Dee said softly.

At this, fresh tears sprang from Maya's eyes.

'But I don't know how!' she sobbed.

Yes, you do, a voice answered loud and clear, but Dee's lips had not moved and Maya knew this was coming from something unseen, something full of gentle compassion that had entered the room a short time after the initial group Dee had described. Maya silently acknowledged the words, half hoping that maybe they were true, that maybe she could find a way through all of this.

'Thank you, Dee,' Maya sniffed. 'I appreciate your reading and I'm really shaken up at how accurate you are and what I can feel and hear myself.'

Dee smiled. 'Yes, I know. I remember the first time it happened to me,' she said. 'It takes a while to get used to.' And then, in a sudden mood switch, she exclaimed, 'Right then, too much bubbly! Where's the toilet, Freya?'

Maya sat quietly while Freya escorted Dee out the room, then returned to top up the bowl of crisps and retrieve a new bottle of wine from the fridge. Behind Maya, off to the left of the table, the two bright light-beings spoke in low voices, inaudible to any human in the room.

She's awakening, one said. *Stay with her and watch over her. She'll need our support in the days ahead.*

They seem to have a special interest in her, the other said, nodding to the dark silhouettes lurking at the other side of the room.

Mmm, his companion muttered. *We need her to come through this next stage of ascension with her talents intact and serving the greater good of the Creator and Mother Gaia as she once did.*

Agreed, the other replied, as the light-body who spoke first rose and passed through the ceiling into the night sky.

Later that night, as Maya lay in the makeshift sofa-bed in the lounge, she pondered the evening's events. Freya's reading had been about who she might meet, whether she would find a good job, you know, the 'human' stuff we all worry about. It occurred to Maya that maybe it wasn't about that, maybe it was about a bigger thing altogether, and these were just distractions and enjoyable activities along the way that the ego got attached to. She thought back to how she had heard the voice the same time as Dee did. It was like she now had proof of something she always knew but never admitted to herself. Or did she? Did she really know anything? Maybe it was just luck that she thought the same thing as Dee said. Mmm, a strange coincidence if that's the case, she mused.

As she lay there, she watched the dark shadows on the lounge curtains moving slightly. At first she barely acknowledged them, assuming it was coming from the hall nightlight, but as she focused more on the scene in front of her, she sat up and looked around at the hall light, the one that wasn't on. She gulped, feeling fear rise up her spine. What was that? It wasn't just the shadows, it was a feeling that someone was there. She shuddered and pulled the blanket closer. It took her a long time to fall asleep, even after the shadows seemed to have been chased away under the curtain into the night, and the room once again felt warm and cosy.

Maya woke up early to the yapping of the dogs and the rambling tones of Freya, who evidently didn't see fit to check if people were actually awake before starting to babble on about various topics.

'Are you awake?' she asked, poking her head around the door into the lounge.

'Now you ask,' Maya mumbled, placing the pillow back over her head. 'How long have you been talking?'

'About ten minutes,' she shrilled in a tone that practically only dogs could hear. 'Don't tell me I have to say it all again?' she exclaimed, stomping across the lounge floor and opening the curtains to allow the grey light from the street in. 'Are you staying *here* to do your calls or heading home?'

'Both,' Maya yawned.

'Right. Brilliant. 'Cause that makes sense,' Freya shrieked, throwing her hands in the air.

'I'll do the meeting with the boss and the team here, then drive an hour or so, stop for my second one, then get home for about five. Hopefully,' Maya patiently explained.

'Okay, okay. Right, well, let the puppies out for a wee before you go and give them cuddles and a treat. I'm going to work.'

Maya nodded, lying back down on the sofa-bed, and stared up at the ceiling. Another day, another dollar—is that the expression? she wondered. Her work phone was pinging away in the corner already and, just as she swung her legs over the side of the bed to find the floor beneath, her personal phone lit up. She looked at the screen—'Husband Mob' the display informed her.

'Morning!' she sang, trying to sound as jolly as possible. Jacob had requested of her to always sound happy when on the phone to him, since he didn't want to hear her 'whingeing'.

'Cheer me up,' he'd demand, because he had the kids all day and never any adult company.

'Nice night?' he snapped.

Oh boy, here we go, she thought. 'Jacob, it was late. I was tired. It made sense. I wasn't going to get back without falling asleep at the wheel anyway.'

'Whatever,' he sighed. 'Spending time with your sister instead of your family when you've been away all week already.'

'For work,' she reminded him, then added. 'And Freya's my family too.'

He huffed down the phone and before she could say anything else, he informed her he'd be texting her a shopping list of things to pick up. Then he hung up.

Great, Maya thought, tears welling up in her eyes. She felt the energy drain from her and sat down on the chair beside the sofa-bed. A familiar feeling of overwhelm crept over her body and tears pricked in her eyes.

'I can't do this any more,' she cried out to whoever was listening. 'I can't. I'm trying to please everyone and I'm pleasing no one. I'm so tired. Nobody understands, nobody cares. I just... I can't!'

She broke down into huge sobs that racked her body and she cradled her arms in her chest and rocked. The motion seemed to soothe her a little, but the tears kept coming. After what felt like a minute or so, but was probably nearer ten, she got to her feet, and carried on with her day, like she always did. This time, however, something had changed. There was, for the first time, a feeling that maybe life was about something bigger. She recalled the events of the previous night—the excitement of hearing the voices and the realisation that there was more to the world than what the eye could see. Somehow that helped to keep her going, because whether Jacob was with her or not, she was going to find her way to a better life.

What is that feeling? she pondered as she waited for the meeting to connect online. The strongest one, the one that gripped her heart? *Fear and guilt,* a voice offered from her right ear. For my children, she agreed, surprised at how easily she accepted the conversation. Maybe she was having it with herself anyway, she quipped. *There's so much for you to relearn,*

Maya, the voice said, *so much you've forgotten*. Okay, now I'm going mad, she thought, rubbing her eyes and focusing on the virtual meeting which was just beginning.

Three and a half hours later, Maya pressed the 'End' button on the screen in front of her. Her head hurt, her eyes were stinging, and she felt utterly drained of all energy. She felt like she'd been on a roller-coaster ride, but not of the good kind. The meeting had started fine, with some praise for the team, followed by lots of challenges and accusations, some of which team members tried to deflect from themselves and fling Maya's way. Then came the marketing spiel that made Maya feel angry without understanding why, and finally ended with her becoming highly agitated at the constant requests to focus on selling the latest drug to hospitals that most probably didn't even need them.

'You know,' the Marketing Manager had said, 'just work your magic.'

Right. Okay. This was a potent drug with a dangerous side effect, not sweets in a candy shop, she seethed under her breath, realising too late that her microphone was unmuted.

Tense silence had followed, but no one had said anything about her outburst. She shut the laptop lid firmly and stared at the flowers in the middle of the coffee table. I'm shit at everything. I'm a bad mother. I'm no good at work. I'm too emotional. And so it went on—negative thought after negative thought spilled from her mind, followed by images of crashing the car on the way home, or one of the kids having a choking fit and she wasn't there. She hung her head as she moved stiffly around the room, gathering her belongings, trapped in the dark energy vortex swirling around about and inside her head. *Yes,* they muttered. *Useless,* they hissed, trailing her to the car and consuming her thoughts as she drove north.

The Angel watched silently from afar, knowing that Maya herself must come to realise what was controlling her. *She* must be the one to set herself free. All he could do was be there to guide and support her. It was up to Maya when, and if, she asked the Demons to leave.

3

Maya swung the car onto the long track towards their rented farmhouse and turned into the parking space at the front of the building. The farmhouse stood proud and tall on the top of a hill with beautiful views over rolling fields. She noticed as she drove up that the daffodils were just starting to push through the mossy grass of the front lawn. Maya heard the chaos of screaming children and barking dogs as she opened the car door.

First out was Amy, Maya's and Jacob's youngest, full of fire and unafraid of the world. At five years old she still saw the fun in everything—even getting caught by her pants upside down on the trampoline failed to dim her light.

'Mummy!' she shouted, throwing herself at Maya.

'Hey, gorgeous,' Maya laughed, hugging her tight.

Sam barked repeatedly by the car door until she reached down and patted the top of his head, while Harris ran round the car peeing on the wheels like a true Jack Russell terrier.

The minute she stopped rubbing Sam's head, he started up again. A kind and loyal Golden Retriever, he had only one brain cell, and even working out how to enter an opened gate challenged him some days.

Zidan appeared from the bushes covered in mud.

'Hey Mum!' he yelled. 'I've made a mudpit. It's sooo cool. You should come see.'

'I will, I will,' she said. 'Just let me get a cup of tea first.'

She headed inside as Aurora zoomed past on her bicycle, dumping it by the back door and yelling something about showing Maya what book she'd like to read next. Maya pushed open the door that led through the hall into the kitchen, where Jacob was standing with a piece of wood in hand, staring at the table full of screws.

'Hi, I'm back,' Maya said.

'Yep,' he grunted. 'You are.'

'Right. No kiss or cuddle then?' Maya snapped, turning to the kettle.

'If you want a kiss or cuddle,' he said, looking up from fiddling with his screws, 'you can come over here and get one.'

'That's not how… Oh, never mind,' Maya sighed, flicking the switch on the kettle and dumping her bags at the other end of the table. 'Where's Faith?'

'Out somewhere with the ponies,' he replied. 'I lost it this morning with her,' he continued after a pause. 'We've got rats again. She just leaves the bin lids off and there's foodstuff everywhere. I cleaned up a quarter of a bag of horse food from the floor in the barn. She just doesn't care. She practically laughed at me when I challenged her about it. I can't deal with her any more,' he finished aggressively.

Maya sighed again, feeling the familiar overwhelm as,

outside, Zidan pushed his head against the kitchen window and shouted for her to see his mudpit again. She heard Aurora call her name from upstairs, as her work phone pinged its 15-minute warning for her next meeting. She grabbed two mugs and started pouring the tea, while shouting to Zidan she would come out in half an hour, purposely avoiding looking at his face and seeing his disappointment.

'Have you got time for a cup of tea with me?' Jacob enquired calmly, 'or do I need to book an appointment for that?'

Maya whirled round and bit back the anger rising in her throat.

'Jacob, it's a workday. I have to get on a call. Can we catch up properly this evening when we have more time?'

'Yep, maybe,' he shrugged and wandered out the room, leaving his tea on the kitchen table.

Maya splashed milk into the cups, knowing full well that by the time she'd finished work, spent time with the kids, seen to the animals and made supper—which no one seemed to want to do while she was away—Jacob would be snoring on the sofa and she would go to bed alone.

Once the last call of the day was done, Maya ventured outside to inspect Zidan's mudpit and den, trying not to get angry at the state of his clothes, the driveway and the trail of muddy footmarks all the way to the kitchen. She started back to the house as Faith came round the corner with the two ponies. Maya rushed over and grabbed one not a moment too soon, as Faith almost got sandwiched between them when they decided to move towards each other at the same time. Faith coughed and yelled at Shadow before sheepishly mumbling, 'Hello, Mum.'

Maya led Pilot into his stable and patted him softly. He was a stunning pony with a white blaze and jet-black mane and tail that stood out against his brown body. Pilot had been with them for three years now and had never put a foot wrong. She trusted him with all the children and the other animals, and was grateful for the snatched hugs she got and the occasional ride out. He had a calming presence that soothed her and, as she buried her head in his mane, she felt her shoulders sag a little as everything became a bit more bearable.

Maya and Faith made up the horses' feed and locked the chickens in the henhouse in silence. With a last look round to check everything was safe for the night, they made their way to the house.

'How was your disco?' Maya asked.

Faith stopped and turned to look at her.

'Awful,' she said. 'I looked fat. I hated what I wore. I wanted to go shopping the night before and get something more slimming, but Dad wouldn't let me. He's been so mean to me. I don't want to be here with him,' she choked out as she started to cry.

Maya felt the sick, guilty feeling wash over her once again, the one that always turned up when she thought she was letting the kids down for not being there.

'He hates me,' Faith continued.

'No, no, he doesn't,' Maya protested. 'You two are just so similar and Dad doesn't understand being a teenage girl and—'

'MUM,' Faith yelled, as she turned and stomped inside. 'Stop making excuses for him!'

Outside on her own, Maya looked up at the stars making their way out as the last of the day disappeared. She swallowed hard, feeling her lip tremble. How could she make this right? She knew it all felt wrong, but she seemed so trapped. There must be a way to live differently. She breathed slowly, thinking back to a book she'd recently read about living in the moment and how to call abundance in to her. She tried to follow the guidance in the book, but she couldn't do it—there was a block, something stopping her from creating a better life for herself.

Ugh, she sighed, making for the house and letting her thoughts switch to what she was going to prepare for dinner, since Jacob clearly had no intention of cooking anything.

Later that night, as Maya cleared up the dishes and walked past the door to the lounge, she heard the familiar sound of Jacob's snoring from the sofa. How does that man sleep so much? she muttered to herself, feeling frustration and injustice rise in her throat. They'd had many an argument about Maya's view of the marriage and how unbalanced it was—she ran around earning the money, then when she got home, she did everything there as well. Maya felt Jacob spent a good amount of time resting and simply floating around, while proclaiming that he was exhausted looking after the kids. I mean, yes, Jacob picked up the odd jobs part-time, but mainly he was here to keep the house and children safe and in order. They had agreed this approach shortly after they were married, in fact right after Maya had collected Faith from the nursery, only to discover that her nappy hadn't been changed and she was displaying some worrying bruises. Children should be cared for by one or both of their parents, Jacob had proclaimed, and Maya agreed. She was never comfortable dropping off her baby at what felt like the 'pound' for the day—they could never love and nurture her like parents could. In fact, in the beginning Jacob and Maya had seen eye-to-eye on many things about the modern world and how humans had got it completely wrong. But, over time, the realities of life had got in the way and now a big divide had formed between them.

She sighed and made her way upstairs, noting how her legs felt like lead. After tucking in the children and doing tummy rubs for Zidan for what felt like three hours, she sat in her bed, phone on her lap, mechanically scrolling through her social media feed.

Her eyes caught a post from a friend explaining how great the new childcare facility was compared to her previous one on London Road and Maya groaned and rolled her eyes. It always amazed her how people could convince themselves that Cage X was better than Cage Y. I mean, what the hell? Why not just get out of the cage? Yes, that's it, she mused. I feel like

I'm in a cage, but I'm not sure it's locked. I might be here of my own accord. As she thought about that, a book fell from the shelf beside her bed. Okay, I guess that's confirmation of that, she laughed, resuming her scrolling.

She stopped again at a post from one of the groups she'd recently joined called Spiritual Awakening. The words jumped out to her, typed boldly above a picture of a beautiful wolf head.

> An old grandfather was teaching his grandson about life: 'A fight is going on inside me,' he said to the boy. 'It's a terrible fight and it's between two wolves. One is evil—he is anger, envy, sorrow, regret, greed, arrogance, self-pity, guilt, resentment, inferiority, lies, false pride, superiority and ego.' He continued, 'The other is good—he is joy, peace, love, hope, serenity, humility, kindness, empathy, generosity, truth, compassion and faith. The same fight is going on inside you—and inside every other person, too.' The boy thought about it for a minute and then asked his grandfather, 'Which wolf will win?' The grandfather simply replied, 'The one you feed.'

Maya leaned her head back on the pillow and felt the words wash over her. Yes, she loved that and it really resonated, but there was something deeper still that this story misses, something just out of reach that she couldn't put her finger on. She typed a comment about how much she enjoyed the quote and how she felt such an affinity for wolves and then began to move off the post. But just as she was about to press the exit button a message dropped in from the author.

'Hi Maya, so pleased this resonated. Your energy feels like you're searching for some answers. Are you interested in a free confidential chat about the spiritual coaching I do?'

Maya paused. Is she? *Yes,* a soft voice came from above her right shoulder. Maya sat up. 'You know,' she said out loud to whoever was listening, 'most films show people reacting in terror when they hear voices.' She was deadpan but she didn't feel scared. It wasn't a loud voice, it was a whisper, like a part of herself that only got through every now and again. It was nothing like the description of crazy people who hear loud voices that drive them mad and they end up in the loony bin. No, this was subtle, almost part of her, she mused.

That's because it IS you—your higher self, your soul guiding you, the voice offered. Maya turned her head to the side. She could have sworn the room just became a little brighter and, with it, sensed a feeling of lightness or comfort. She turned back to her phone and typed her response before she had time to think about it.

'Sure, that would be great. I'm free tomorrow if you are.'

She settled down under the covers, smiling at the calm and comforting presence in the room, and drifted off to sleep.

At the foot of the bed the Angel watched quietly, considering the task at hand on the planet and how one by one the ancient ones were beginning to stir. Their souls were shining through, the veil was thinning, and the seeds of remembrance were beginning to sprout. They must be on their guard, for the enemy would be aware of every positive vibration that emerged, starving them of their much-needed fix of negative energy. *Keeping them in fear, small and hurt is your only weapon,* he whispered, *but each time you cut them down they grow back stronger.* He smiled, proud of the strength, courage and resilience the souls of planet Earth showed, for to volunteer to return to the polarity planet, with all its darkness and trickery, is not for the faint-hearted. Tal shifted slightly, feeling the darkness swirling above him. He was grateful he was one of the chosen ones to serve the light, and comfortable with any amount of darkness that tried to intimidate—it just reaffirmed to him this woman was a threat to them and therefore a spark of hope for the ascension plans of Mother Gaia.

Maya shut the front door behind her as she called the dogs for their morning walk. The children were already out playing and doing the morning routines of letting out chickens and arguing over which bit of oxygen was theirs to breathe. She opened the gate that led to the small wood behind the farmhouse and let the dogs run ahead. The path wove between the trees, and the snow which had been threatening to fall all morning began with earnest. Maya smiled and carried on deeper into the wood and up the winding path until she came to a small clearing at the top. From the shelter of the trees she could see the fields beyond and the grass disappearing rapidly under the blanket of white. She stilled her breath and closed her eyes, listening to the silence. It was beautiful. She wished she could stay here for an eternity in the quiet and beauty of Mother Nature.

She made her way to the centre of the clearing and sat down near a large pine tree. Closing her eyes she centred her breathing. Pretty soon she heard it, that now familiar sound, the soft whooshing of the trees, like a slow heartbeat. She felt the connected frequency of their roots, the soft melodies they used to speak to each other. She knew instinctively they could speak to other trees around the world like this, transmitting frequencies which received news of trees in pain being cut and burned or of others issuing their guidance from their huge form and others still, just starting on their long journey of growth, fighting for space in the centre of the forest. She could see images over the centuries of peoples coming and going under the same tall oak trees, places of shelter from the storm, of brutal hangings and torture, or of refuge during clearances and other such events. She thought back to the week at work, of the complete obliviousness people had about the fact that trees communicated like this beneath the ground, the same ground they frantically scurried around on. She mused on the fact that trees couldn't run away. They couldn't move locations—where they grew is where they died. It forced them to face the Demons, the Angels and everything in between, proudly and defiantly until the end. Perhaps we could learn a lot from trees, she thought. How easily Man dismissed them as furniture or nuisances in the way of progress, merely taking space that could be used to build more houses, more roads.

'MUM, MUM,' the shrill screaming of Amy cut through the quiet air as she bounced up the path with Harris and Sam in quick pursuit. 'There you are,' she smiled, flopping down next to her.

'What you doing, Mum?' she asked, peering up through the muddy blonde matted hair that was falling over her face.

'Just thinking, sweetheart,' Maya replied, offering Amy her hand as she stood up.

'Mum, come on. I want to show you my new hideout,' Amy shouted, letting go of her hand and running off in front of her on the path.

After time spent crawling under tree branches to a rather leaky, but admittedly cool, hideout made from branches and moss, the two walked hand in hand back to the house with the dogs fighting over a twig behind them.

Maya sliced some cheese and laid it on the bread in front of her. Children filed into the kitchen moaning about being hungry and, having anticipated this, she was busy making sandwiches.

'Mum,' Faith yelled from the front door, pony in hand, trying to stop it getting inside to investigate what may be edible. 'Richard's here for Dad.'

'Jacob,' Maya shouted down the hall, 'Richard's outside for you.'

Jacob grunted and walked past her to the door, returning a few minutes later to inform her he had been invited to a party at the shooting lodge and would be back later. Maya crossed to the window and watched him climb onto the quad behind Richard and disappear down the lane. Richard and Julie, their landlord and landlady—seemingly nice people, but Maya felt a different energy under the surface. Time would tell, she thought to herself, turning back to the kitchen counter.

Once lunch had been and gone, Maya sat down while the kids watched a film, and prepared for her call with the spiritual coach. She felt nervous, but at the same time like it was something she needed to do. She thought back to the events at Freya's house and what had happened. In truth, things like that had happened all her life, like the time she sensed there was a cow in the road and slowed the car to a crawl. As she turned the corner, there it was in the middle of the road, looking straight at her. I mean, what are the odds of that happening? She smiled at the memory and clicked on the link the lady had sent her.

'Hello!' exclaimed a bright, bubbly voice as a middle-aged lady with dark hair and warm brown eyes came into view. 'I'm Lesley. Pleased to meet you,' she said in an American accent. Californian, Maya guessed.

'Hi,' Maya said shyly. As they spoke more and talked about where they lived, their children, their history and so on, Maya had a feeling she already knew this lady. It was like an instant recognition. She voiced as much to Lesley when there was a natural break in the conversation.

'That's because you do, sweetheart,' she said. 'We are soul family; we've been together in past lives.'

Maya sat back, digesting what she was hearing. Past lives? Did she believe in past lives? She didn't know, but something about the conversation felt good, felt almost like relief. Maya continued to explain her current situation, how she'd been feeling there must be more, the challenges with Jacob and finally what had happened at her sister's with Dee.

Lesley sat back in her chair and smiled. 'You have a strong team of spiritual support with you, Maya. You are a wise old soul. You've just forgotten who you are. That's one of the things we'll do together—help you remember who you really are and why you're here.'

Lesley instructed Maya to close her eyes. 'Now take three deep breaths and listen to my voice.'

She continued to talk softly, asking Maya to recall a time they were together before. Suddenly pangs of fear and upset flowed through Maya and she felt tears prick at her eyes. The sensations grew as images flashed across her mind. A girl in Native American dress with a single brown feather in her hair, distraught, leaning over a taller girl who had fallen to the floor. The girl didn't look like Maya, but she nevertheless knew it was her. As she watched, she felt the horror of the situation and saw the fear reflected in the girls' eyes. She was trying desperately to work out how she could defend the two girls but it felt hopeless. She was crying, begging for the men standing around to leave them alone. One of the men was looking at the ground. Maya could feel his sadness—he knew he was doing wrong. He was dressed in a uniform, white with a red stripe, his eyes glazed with tears. The others laughed and mocked the girls, their eyes devoid of life; like hard steel reflecting off glass, they held no depth and their sneers and laughter seemed to drive others to keep kicking at the girls. The images shifted to her being dragged along a path looking back at the fallen girl on the ground—fear, hopelessness, despair, hurt, the emotions felt so raw. Maya couldn't contain a sob that escaped into the room.

'Do you see?' Lesley asked, clearly affected by the emotional energy. Maya explained the scene before her, struggling with her emotions and taking deep calming breaths to try to gain control. Lesley nodded solemnly. 'The Trail of Tears,' she said.

'The Trail of What?' Maya asked, confused.

'What you saw were Native Americans on the Trail of Tears, a mass clearance from the lands to another place the American government had decreed they should be settled to. The government wanted their lands,' she went on, 'stole it from them. Many died on the journey to the new settlements. Did you see yourself there?'

'I think so,' Maya replied. 'The girl I saw, she felt like me. And the older girl—,' Maya paused and welled up again.

'Was me,' Lesley finished. 'One of our lives together. I died,' Lesley confirmed. 'They shot me.'

'Oh, I felt so hopeless,' Maya sniffed miserably.

'Yes,' Lesley said. 'They wanted you to feel powerless, helpless, not in control. And you carry those memories still buried deep in your subconscious as dense energy because then you are easily controllable, but I can help you release and move past them.'

Lesley went on to describe how, over lifetimes, our energy had been depleted through hardship, war and evil deeds to the point where we have been made small, convinced that we are insignificant and without power.

'We've forgotten who we really are and have been conditioned to believe we can't do anything about it. You have given your power away, Maya,' she said. 'Now it's time you took it back.'

Maya looked up and felt the truth of it. 'Yes, that's it!' she said.

She didn't know how she knew, or even what exactly she knew at this point, but she agreed that she was not the one in control of her life. She had allowed something else to take the control panel from her.

'Lesley, I have such a fear of death,' Maya admitted. 'I think it's because I have children and I want to protect them,' she choked out, tears spilling down her face.

'The harder we hold on, the more likely it is to come,' Lesley warned.

Maya knew this, she had seen it before in others, like her uncle who feared cancer so much that she believes he brought his lung cancer into being. Nevertheless, she just couldn't let go of the fear.

'Tell me, Maya, what is it that scares you about death? Answer from your heart, not your fears,' she added.

Maya settled herself in the chair and took several deep breaths again. She felt the fear and anxiety surge forward, but as she pushed through it, she sensed a stronger feeling coming up. This one was different, like it came from a deeper, calmer part of her.

'The feeling is frustration, because I don't want to fail again,' she stated clearly. She checked herself. 'What does that even mean?' she pondered out loud.

'We'll find out,' assured Lesley, smiling.

After agreeing the terms and times of their next session, Maya signed off, feeling like she had made an important step forward in her future and a step back to a past she knew but couldn't quite recall yet.

Later that evening, as Maya was sorting through the socks and pants in the dried laundry pile after putting the kids to bed, a banging door alerted her to Jacob's return. Stepping into the kitchen, she found him attempting to turn the switch on the kettle.

'Hello. Good time?' she enquired.

He swung round, wobbling drunkenly with a grimace on his face. 'Oh yes, great time,' he slurred.

Maya knew instantly that no, he had *not* enjoyed himself and, worse yet, was about to go off on a rant to tell her exactly why.

'What happened?' she asked, sitting down at the table.

'You know what?' Jacob bellowed. 'I'm sick of people looking down on me because I don't have a posh job or I'm not a rich farmer. They made me feel like I was worthless because I don't hold money as the most valuable thing.'

'Hang on, slow down,' Maya said with an outstretched hand that he batted away.

'I don't want your pity, Maya. I'm done. I'm done with this

world and snotty landlords. Here's me doing a vegetable patch outside, my blood, sweat and tears that he'll just take back for his son. Not *mine*, *his*. It's all pointless. *You* don't value me, the kids take the piss out of me. I've had enough!' he thundered.

Maya backed away, hoping he would calm down before he woke the kids up.

'You, you think you're so perfect. Well, you can do it all, can't you? I'm out of here,' Jacob snarled and, with that, he turned and retrieved a bag from behind the door. Stumbling over to the kitchen unit, he pulled out a few tins, rammed them into the bag and staggered towards the door. Maya's eyes widened and a small smile started to spread across her face, despite what was going on. Jacob was leaving forever with four tins and no coat in freezing temperatures.

'Jacob, it's eleven p.m. and snowing. Don't be ridiculous,' she exclaimed as he swung open the front door. 'I'm so sick of this.' She followed him down the hall to the door. 'You don't appreciate anything you have, always think someone is being mean,' she said, her tone dripping with condemnation. 'Why don't you just leave if it's that bad?' Maya was seething, her frustration with him boiling to the surface.

He turned and, before she could acknowledge what was happening, picked up the stuffed ornament he had bought her last Christmas and threw it against the wall, causing the frame to snap and the contents to fly out all over the floor.

'JACOB!' she shouted, fear and anger overtaking rational thought. 'You absolute prat, just fuck off!'

As she turned, she caught sight of Faith standing in the kitchen watching the events.

'See?' she shouted. 'He's an idiot!'

'Faith, please stay out of this.'

Behind her, Amy had heard the commotion and was crying in the hallway. Maya turned back round to Jacob who was still ranting about how she was an awful wife and that everything they had was fake and how she only cared about her job and the ponies and not him.

'Oh, for God's sake, Jacob. Stop being a needy child,' she growled.

He stopped and stared at her and in that moment, she caught the sadness in his eyes, the desperate crying out for help. She softened, wanting to reach out, but then the voice in her head kicked in. No, don't be nice. Jacob's way of asking for help is by bringing you down and insulting you and that's not right, it said. You and the children deserve better, the voice challenged.

Maya turned, pushing Faith and Amy back through the door to the stairway.

'Go to bed,' she said to the now all four children standing on the stairs in various degrees of upset.

'Mum,' Zidan cried, 'are you and Daddy going to split up?'

'I don't know,' she answered honestly, sinking down and sitting on the steps.

'Mum, you can't!' Zidan sobbed. 'It's not Daddy's fault. He's sad, Mum. He's lonely,' he cried.

'Really?' Maya snapped. 'And I suppose I just have the best life, right? I'm fine. I'm just living it up in smelly hotel rooms stressed to high heaven!' she shouted.

No. No, this is not right, she thought. I shouldn't say this in front of the kids, but she couldn't help it. Something inside her was lighting a fire, urging her on to spill more vile things about Jacob, things that would show the kids how good a mother she was, what she had to put up with. The darkness gripped at her heart and she felt trapped and angry. How dare he treat her like this?

She yelled at the kids, 'GET TO BED, NOW!' and stomped off to her room, slamming the door and hiding under the covers, trying to block the world out. Her thoughts raced round her head. You should have left him ages ago. He's a danger. He's useless. You're weak, just like the other women in your family. You only care about what people will say.

'No. No,' Maya sobbed, shaking her head. 'That's not it. That's not why I stay.' But in truth she couldn't work out why she did.

She fell asleep and woke a short time later to a quiet house. Tiptoeing out of her room, she found all the kids asleep together in Zidan's room and Jacob wrapped in a blanket in the lounge, swollen-faced from crying. Relieved that at least everyone was safe, she locked the front door and went back to bed, trying to chase away the hopeless feeling and find a way forward, because if there was one thing that was now blatantly clear, it was that things couldn't stay like this. She hated her job, her boss hated her, her marriage was falling apart, her kids were unhappy. There was nothing left for her except change. She just hoped she could find the right way through this without too much hurt.

Maya was up first. She put the ponies out into the field, then turned her attention to the chickens, feeding them and letting them out of the hut. She smiled, watching as they ran around the yard flapping their wings, before turning and heading inside to start breakfast. She was thankful it wasn't a workday as her head felt woolly, her eyes were sore from crying and her heart was heavy. Jacob was sitting at the table in the kitchen when she came in. She ignored him as she walked around the table. In truth, she didn't know what to say and she would probably regret anything that came out, so she stayed quiet and went about pouring the oats into the pan and crossing to the sink to add water. When she turned around to set it back on the stove, Jacob had stood up and was looking at her. He looked terrible, black rings around swollen eyes that betrayed a lost, frantic look.

'I'm sorry, Maya,' he said quietly.

'Sorry's not enough this time,' she snapped.

'Just hear me out, please,' he sighed, sitting down again. 'Don't do what you normally do and talk over me. Just let me tell you stuff.'

Maya huffed, but acknowledged internally that his accusation was true. Despite her ego flaring and wanting to react, she accepted she did indeed find it hard to listen without getting angry. She sat down in silence and waited for him to talk.

'When you come home, you take over. And you parent

the children differently to me. You walk all over what I've achieved through the week and it just feels pointless,' he started to explain.

'You want me to bring in money but at the same time you're never here. How can I look after the kids *and* go out to work? You think the kids want ponies and fun, when in truth they just want their Mum here more. We all do. Even when you *are* here, you're thinking about work or you're exhausted by it and recovering. What's the point? What's the point in having this house and land if you're never here to enjoy it with us? You say that I leave everything to you when you get home but the way I see it,' he continued, 'you come home and stamp on everything I'm doing and sympathise with Faith, which allows her to think her behaviour is okay and I'm just a bad guy. I'm lonely and I'm tired and last night when Richard and his mates made me feel like nothing it was, well, it was the last straw,' he finished.

Maya had opened and shut her mouth several times during the speech, wanting to butt in and defend herself or react to things he said, but she managed to stop herself. Now as she sat and digested what he'd said, she started to understand that maybe from his viewpoint some of these things held true.

'So I'm resenting you for me having to work and be away all the time, and feeling like you don't do enough with the kids and the house. And you're feeling down and upset and it's hard for you to get out of that rut because you can't see an end to it and really no one is winning?' she summarised.

'Kind of,' he said. 'I know you think you're giving the kids opportunities, but you're also teaching them to be spoilt.'

'I am not!' she shouted.

'Yes, Maya, you are. You're putting their perceived needs based on what you had as a kid ahead of our marriage and the reality of the situation we are in. An example,' he laboured on, 'is Faith with the ponies. The way she looks after them, she doesn't even really appreciate them.'

They sat looking at each other a few moments longer. Maya broke the silence.

'I'm sorry Richard made you feel like that, Jacob,' she said, reaching out and catching his hand as he fidgeted with it on the table. 'I know things need to change, but do we want to make those changes together?' she sighed, dropping his hand.

'I do,' he said quickly, looking up at her. 'I don't want to watch you work to pay someone else's bills while we grow further apart, though.'

Maya suddenly had an idea. 'Do you remember the conversation about buying a holiday home up on the islands?' she said.

'Yes,' he answered, rubbing his head. 'What about it?'

'I think we should do it. I think you should go up and have a look at some of the houses. They're still quite cheap. We could get a mortgage and we'd have somewhere that isn't anyone's else's to lord over us. We could retire there,' she finished, feeling lighter in her heart already.

'Okay,' he shrugged, 'but right now I need to sleep. I feel like I'm going to die.'

'You don't look much off death,' she said, a hint of a smile playing on her lips.

After Jacob had gone back to bed and she had taken care of

the hole in Aurora's jumper and the rip in Faith's jodhpurs and read Smelly Pig to Zidan and Amy, Maya cast her thoughts back to their earlier conversation. She didn't know if she and Jacob would stay together or not, but she felt it was the first honest conversation they'd had in a while. She also felt a growing excitement about the idea of buying a house in the northern islands. She had always felt right when she moved north and, let's face it, she'd spent her life moving north—from the South to Yorkshire, then up to Scotland, every move had made her feel like she was getting nearer to her home. Scotland had always evoked strong emotions for her, deep feelings that were bigger than just a place on a map. It was part of her identity in more than just ancestral blood. Maya didn't know why, but she felt the answers she was seeking would be found by continuing to move north.

4

Jacob turned his head into the wind and stretched his arms above his head. The ferry was just pulling out of the mainland dock and the view was beautiful. From his viewpoint on the outside deck, he could see the contours of the rolling hills past the port as the sun rose above the headland. That was worth getting up at three a.m. for he smiled, as he headed back into the main hull of the boat in search of coffee.

He sat down with his cappuccino and shortbread at one of the tables at the back of the boat. He was really looking forward to the next few days. Jacob loved travelling; he thrived on new experiences and new places and there hadn't been much of that in the last ten years. It felt like he had been caught in a seemingly endless line of cooking, nappies and washing up, probably in that order, he chuckled. When he had suggested to Maya they let nature take its course he hadn't expected four to take their course in fairly quick succession and with very different personalities and challenges, but still he was grateful for his family.

He turned his thoughts to Maya. She worked hard, he

would give her that, and she was driven and talented when it came to business and leadership. However, he mused, she really didn't get this 'life' thing. She had been sucked into working and earning money, thinking that would bring happiness. Jacob thought back to when they were expecting Faith and he'd suggested they buy some land and live in a caravan. Maya had shut the idea down straight away; they couldn't possibly bring up a baby in a caravan in a muddy field. Maya had a huge dollop of conditioning about what was and was not possible by her well-to-do parents and, while he understood they'd just been trying to do the best for their children, and Maya now for hers, it really did mean she was trapped in her own cage with the door open and earmuffs on when it came to Jacob trying to show her another way. He had long wondered what she got up to on business trips. It's not that he didn't trust her, it was just that she spent so much time away from the family and seemed so distant at times when she returned, that he felt she had a different life.

Jacob's thoughts were interrupted by a man ushering clumsily past his table, causing his cappuccino to wobble and spilling some of its contents.

'Idiot,' he mumbled. 'Not even an apology?' he enquired out loud.

Jacob had little patience for most people and, for the large part, thought humanity had lost the plot. The man turned around.

'What?' he enquired with an irritant tone.

'You spilt my coffee,' Jacob answered, staring directly at him.

'Oh, right. Okay,' he said. 'Well, not *much* of it,' he added, looking down at the cup.

'That's not really the point, is it?' Jacob answered, the glare deepening, making the man look away. Uncomfortable with the intensity of his stare, and aware that Jacob was not the type to back down, he shuffled off.

Jacob could feel the adrenaline pulsing in his ears as he turned his attention back to his coffee. He mused how quick he always was to ensure people were put in their place and respect him. It was a good trait, he decided. Kept his family safe, he confirmed to himself.

Behind him an Angel sat in the rafters of the boat between the ceiling and the deck above, watching the scene. *No*, he muttered quietly, *that's your ego and you need to learn to move it aside if you're going to be the support your family needs in the times ahead.*

The Angel shook his head, observing the dark, dense energy swirling around Jacob's base and heart chakra energy centres. Jacob was a strong, old soul and was able to see past the 3D matrix Maya was currently held prisoner in and was slowly starting to crawl her way out of. But Jacob carried a lot of karma and negative energy from his previous battles on Earth. *Could he find the spiritual strength to clear enough to hear and see through the veil of anger?* he pondered.

The dark shadow hanging above him to his right sniggered at this last thought. *Ah, dreaming of the balanced divine human again, I see*, it sneered. *Satan is all but victorious of his dominion on this Earth, and most humans don't even think he exists!* he exclaimed in glee. *You should try your luck somewhere else,* he said, bursting into a loud demonic cackle that alerted a rat to his dense dark energy, causing it to scurry away from the spot the Demon occupied.

I have no need to lower myself to interact with your energy, Demon. Be gone, the Angel answered, following Jacob as he made his way outside for a smoke. *Save your energy for the real fight,* he whispered to Jacob, but alas his advice remained unheard.

Two hours later the boat docked alongside numerous fishing vessels and the doors dropped to let the passengers off. Jacob mounted his motorcycle and made the spontaneous decision to take a short ride round the island before checking into the hotel Maya had booked him into. As he left the small port town and headed out, he could see the rise of the mountains in the distance. He rode past several lochs, marvelling at the feel of his bike hugging the corners before he turned his full atten-tion to the scenery, and the true beauty of the island hit him. He followed the winding road south over the mountains and back down into the valleys where the terrain became rocky, almost moonscape—big grey rocks jutting out across the land, intermingled with patches of heather. The road banked right and then as it straightened out the most beautiful beach came into view. It must have been about two miles long by a mile wide and, from the uphill advantage he had on the road he could see all of it.

Jacob pulled into a lay-by, cut the engine and stared at the expanse of aquamarine ocean that met the yellow sands. He felt a lump form in his throat.

This place, it feels... well, it feels like home, he said to himself. The grasses had just started to grow and, among them, emerging buds were scattered in the swaying foliage. Unlike on the mainland, where huge tractors and toxic fertilizers can easily destroy their efforts, these grasses were alive with tiny flowers.

Jacob dismounted and bent down to take a closer look at the side of the field next to the lay-by. There was every colour you could think of—yellow, red, purple and, dotted through-out, the iconic Scottish thistle had started to push through the soil. He pulled off his helmet and wiped his eyes. Maya and the kids are going to love it here, he thought. Let's hope I can find the right house.

✦

Several hours later Jacob walked out of Tesco's with a pastry and a packet of biscuits. Crossing over to his bike, he leaned on it as he munched into his purchases. Having seen the prices in his hotel, he'd settled on a Tesco dinner. He was initially taken aback to find a large supermarket chain on a small

Scottish island, but then he considered the global takeover by corporations and questioned why he was even surprised.

As he people-watched, he saw a small, elderly lady coming out of the store. She was struggling with a large bag and stopped several times to rest on her way across the road. The cars went round her, people hurried past and he watched a group of worshippers come out of the nearby church and walk the other way, either not noticing the old lady or deciding they were too busy to help. Jacob placed the half-eaten pastry on his bike seat and rushed over to help. The lady looked up in surprise as he grabbed her bag, clearly unsure as to whether Jacob was trying to steal it or to help.

'Where can I carry this to for you?' he asked.

She paused, getting her breath and then pointed to a block of flats a little down the road.

'I'm down there,' she answered.

'Very well, let's get you home.'

They walked in silence and Jacob noticed the lady dipped her head as she walked. When they approached the door, she pulled out the key and put it in the lock and then turned to Jacob.

'Thank you, young man,' she said with a sincerity in her eyes that also glistened with tears.

'You're very welcome, although I'm not sure about the 'young',' he laughed smiling down at her. 'You take care of yourself now,' he added, before turning and jogging back up the street to his bike.

As he got closer, he laughed to himself as he saw the remnants of the pastry being fought over by three large seagulls.

'Ah, well. I could do with losing weight,' he scoffed.

Later that night, as Jacob lay in bed, he reflected over the events with the old lady. The world had seemingly gone mad at an alarming rate, and this was just another example of it. In Tesco's, he had seen people donating to charity boxes. Outside, he had witnessed people coming out of the church where they proclaimed to follow God's word. Yet the charity staring them in the face in real time they ignored and left to struggle. It seemed that as long as people ticked a few boxes and were good and faithful servants of God, they could do whatever they wanted the rest of the time.

Jacob thought about the last time he had been in a church; it had not felt as it used to as a child. He had observed quietly, at the coffee and mince pie gathering afterwards, the gossip and judgement of their conversations and came out wondering who they were really worshipping. More alarmingly, he could see clearly that, had he brought this up with the members of the congregation, they wouldn't have had a clue what he was talking about and would have insistently defended themselves as servants of God and good Christians. People had become blind to the true nature of things, he thought as he drifted off to sleep.

✳

Across the water, Maya tossed and turned in her bed. Her dream was vivid and she had almost woken up twice, but each time it pulled her back in. The woman in her dream had long dark hair, flowing in the wind as she picked flowers and root bark in a small, wooded clearing. In the background was a modest cottage. The woman turned towards it as she made her way through the trees, singing in a Celtic tongue as she went. Her long green cloak flowed behind her and she held an air of balance and peace, as though she were part of the forest and not a separate entity to it. She opened a wooden door and walked into a small kitchen with a large range. On the table were pots of liquids and herb concoctions. She placed the basket down and began sorting the collected items into the pots.

The dream shifted, seeming to jump forward in time. Three men riding black horses approached the cottage at a gallop, and as they reached the front overhang of the property, two of the men dismounted and ran at the door, the other circling on his horse to the back of the cottage. The woman knew they were coming, she had sensed it. She didn't struggle as they pushed and manhandled her out of the house and onto one of the horses, laying her across the saddle with her head hanging over the side, her wrists and ankles bound. She remained quiet, her eyes calm, as the men took her away.

The dream shifted again to a scene where the woman's long dark hair was wrapped in one of the men's hands. He was sneering and calling her a witch. She was led to a chair near a big pond and secured to it with thick rope. There were some other men around the pond dressed in black, and they watched silently as the chair was hung over the water using a thick rope. The lead henchman spoke but nothing came out that was audible, as if the woman with the dark hair didn't want to hear the filth coming out of his mouth. She was lowered into the water and a single tear tracked down her face, but still she didn't struggle or beg for it to stop. The chair disappeared under the surface and Maya's dream-self could see the water as the woman saw it—slightly murky with green strands of long grass and rocks jutting upwards. Once completely submerged, the woman screwed her eyes closed and then seemed to calm and open them again. As she focused, the pond filled with fish and frogs, water insects and tadpoles all surrounding her. The woman could feel a love coming from them and, as she slipped from this world, she felt their support and nothing of the pain and fear of drowning.

Maya awoke with a start, tears streaming down her face.

'Mum,' Faith yelled, bursting in the room and stopping when she saw the state of Maya.

'Mum, what's wrong? You woke me up.'

'Mummy,' Aurora ran in and grabbed her arm. 'You were screaming in your sleep and babbling something about 'Not again.' I'm scared,' she said, her eyes wide.

'It's okay,' Maya said, taking deep breaths and trying to calm the fear and rage that was coursing through her. 'It was just a bad dream. Go back to bed.'

'Mum, are you sure you're okay?' Faith asked, sitting on the bed as Aurora climbed in the other side.

'I'm sleeping with you,' Aurora announced. 'You scared me!'

'Faith, go and check on Amy and Zidan for me and get back to bed. I promise I'm fine.'

'Okay, if you're sure,' Faith answered, shivering against the cold and stepping out of the room.

Aurora lay on the opposite side of the bed, staring at her.

'Mum, are you sure everything's okay? Do you think you were missing Dad?'

'Yes,' Maya smiled. 'I'm sure it's something like that. Get yourself some sleep.'

Aurora settled against the pillow and closed her eyes and Maya lay down on her back. That was too real, she thought. That was me, I just know that was me. Perhaps it was another past life vision but it came as a dream, she mused.

Thirty minutes later, Aurora was snoring soundly beside Maya. Urgh, she sighed, I'm not going to get back to sleep at this rate. She wiggled out of bed, careful not to wake her daughter, and wrapped her robe around her against the cold of the night. Once she had checked on the other three children, she tiptoed downstairs and tried to coax a flame out of the dying embers of the log burner in the lounge. As the flames leapt to life again, she moved across the room to light an incense stick and a candle and threw a cushion in front of the fire before sitting on it cross-legged. She closed her eyes and sank into a meditation pose.

At first it wasn't any different to all the other times she had tried to meditate. Her mind whooshed by with a barrage of thoughts and everything felt frantic but, as she continued to breathe deeply, gradually she felt her mind still and a quiet take over her. She felt heavier on the floor, almost like a weight was pulling her down. Don't think, she told herself, just let it flow.

A few more minutes passed by and Maya was aware of the sounds of the fire crackling, but it felt strangely far away. She let her thoughts drift back to the dream.

'I know you,' she said to the woman in the dream out loud.

You do know her, a voice came in from her right side. She stilled. It felt the same energy as the last time she had heard it. Breathing through the temptation to tell herself she was losing it again, she asked, 'Who are you? What's your name?'

After a short pause she heard the name Tal clearly in her mind. *I know this seems strange, Maya, but what is happening here is nothing different than telepathy communication, which by the way humans can do but have forgotten,* he chuckled as he finished the sentence. *Aren't there lots of things being confirmed in your scientific community, like the ability of the placebo to heal and sound frequencies changing brain waves, that would have seemed impossible twenty Earth years ago?*

She nodded and then felt compelled to discuss the dream.

'The woman in the dream,' she said. 'I, I felt like I knew her.'

She paused as the energy of confirmation washed over her.

'Okay,' she carried on. 'I felt I knew all her thoughts, her feelings. She was sad and disappointed. She kept saying to herself, when will they learn? I don't understand,' she finished. 'What does that mean?'

Well, Tal spoke softly, *some of that you need to figure out yourself, Maya, but indeed what you picked up is true.*

'Was she actually me?' Maya asked. Her head started to hurt as she finished the question. She found the energy had shifted and she couldn't hear her new friend any more. She tried for a few more minutes and then heard him say, *This is a gift. You are only just remembering. We won't be able to talk for long at first. Be kind to yourself.*

She sighed and considered what he had said. While she was frustrated that they couldn't communicate for longer, she was feeling much more grounded and happier that, no, she was not going mad and that what she knew and felt was real. She felt like a piece of her had returned, now she was accepting of this information.

'There's so much I don't know,' she voiced out loud, but at the same time it feels so familiar, she added to herself. Her head felt heavy and her eyes were stinging. She stood up stiffly and went back upstairs to bed.

✳

She woke up late. Luckily she had time off work while Jacob was away, and the children were not at school, but as she sat up she realised she felt horrendous. She lay back down and pulled the covers over her. Aurora was already up and she could hear the children banging about downstairs.

'Mum,' Zidan shouted from the bottom of the stairs.

Maya didn't even feel like she could respond. Her throat was dry and she was shivering. She heard the banging footsteps getting closer and Zidan appeared round the bedroom door.

'Mum!' he exclaimed as she sat up to look at him. 'Faith ate all the Weetabix! I don't have any breakfast. I'm hungry,' he protested.

'There's some more in the pantry,' she reassured him, before groaning and lying back down.

'Mum, are you okay?' he enquired, his brow creasing with worry.

'I'm fine,' she said. 'I've just got a bit of a bug and need to rest. Can you ask Aurora to bring me a cup of tea, please?'

'Okay,' he smiled, running off down the stairs.

'Don't you do it, Zidan, you're too small,' she called after him, knowing he always wanted to please in his clumsy little way.

Twenty minutes later, Aurora appeared with half a cup of tea and Maya tried not to think about the other half which was probably by now sloshed all over the stair carpet. She drank the tea while trying to keep the covers as close to her body as possible, feeling herself sweating and shaking. She put the cup down after a few gulps and reached into her bedside drawer to find the thermometer. Turning it on and sticking it under her tongue, she mentally reeled off all the reasons why she didn't have time to be ill. The thermometer beeped and she took it out, looking at the screen in front of her.

'Oh,' she said, sitting up shocked. The gauge read 36.8.

Mmh, that's normal, she thought, surprised at the result, still shivering and pulling the blanket up again. She closed her eyes and tried to put into words how she was feeling. It was like she had full-blown 'flu but without half the symptoms.

It's spiritual 'flu, Tal offered through her jumble of thoughts.

You're releasing toxins of the spirit, dense energy held in what the modern physician would call Junk DNA, and some locked in the chakra centres stopping them from functioning correctly.

He went on to explain that her body needed to release this so that she could tune into the true nature of her essence through chakras and energetic life force.

Rest, he finished in her mind. Maya nestled her head into the pillow, feeling she had no other option anyway.

'Mum,' Faith hollered from her bedroom. 'Did you know it was a full moon last night?'

Mmm, makes sense, she sighed, rolling her eyes and drifting off to sleep.

✳

Jacob pulled his helmet off and made his way down to the beach he had stumbled across on his explorations of the island. He followed the grass paths and sand dunes and finally stepped down onto the flat sands. It was breathtakingly beautiful. There was no other way to describe it. He kicked off his shoes, peeling his socks off and stuffing them in his shoes before dumping them at a large rock and making his way towards the sea. The aquamarine water lapped gently on the sand, the wind having died down somewhat since the previous night. He sat for a while, watching the birds diving into the calm sea and squabbling over the fish that the lucky ones had caught, before walking around the headland to take a closer look at the remains of an iron house sat on the edge of the sand dunes.

This place felt familiar, like a land he had lived on long ago. He could breathe here—the lump normally wedged in his stomach that felt like low anxiety was barely present. This land reaches the soul, he thought, stretching out his arms and breathing deeply. It would do Maya the world of good.

The first few houses had been unsuitable. In fact two of them had been barely standing but, ever the optimist, he had a good feeling about the one he was viewing today. He smiled and turned back towards the place he left his shoes. As he walked towards the rock where they were nestling in the ground beneath, he saw that two Highland cows had made their way down to the beach from the moorland above and were currently watching him curiously. He froze in place. Cows. Jacob was fearful of few things in life, but cows were one of the things he did admit to being terrified of. It's okay, he told himself, it's just a couple of cows. With HORNS, his head hissed at him, VERY BIG HORNS. He started for the dunes again, quickening his steps and, as he did, the cows started moving towards him, the one behind breaking into a trot to catch up with the larger black cow at the front. Jacob broke into a run, feeling conflicted between being genuinely scared and calling himself a sissy. He grabbed his shoes and scurried up the sandbanks, imagining himself meeting his fate on the end of one of the long horns sticking out of each side of the black beast's head. God, Maya will kill me if I get taken out by a cow, he cursed, pulling on his helmet and roaring off on his bike without a backward look.

As the bike climbed the road away from the beach, Jacob allowed himself a quick glance back and felt himself blush as he realised the cows were still on the beach where he had left them and perhaps he had overreacted to the situation just a tad. Good job no one had seen—the cows won't talk, he frowned, hoping there was no one hiding behind the rocks with a camera.

✦

'MUM!' Faith yelled, jerking Maya from her sleep. The shadows were long against the wall of her bedroom, as she realised she must have slept for most of the day and it was now late afternoon. Feeling a little better and hoping the two older girls had fed their siblings something other than sweets, she dragged herself downstairs, clicked the kettle on and sat down at the kitchen table rubbing her head.

'Mum!' Faith shouted again, now a lot nearer and clearly on the phone to someone.

'Mum,' she said a third time as she stood at the door of the kitchen.

'Yes,' Maya replied, becoming slowly frustrated by the fact the kids had to use her name repeatedly while she quietly waited for them to continue.

'It's Dad,' she said, handing the phone over.

Maya lifted the receiver to her ear and was surprised at how heavy it felt.

'Maya,' Jacob drawled down the phone, his voice heavy with intent. 'I've found it.'

5

Maya sat down at the small desk in front of her and moved her work notebook to the side. She leaned down and took out of her bag the beautiful new journal with the Tree of Life on the front she'd gifted herself earlier that day. The last few weeks had been somewhat easier at work, mainly due to the fact that she was out in the field with several of her sales team members, offering her much needed relief from the politics of the office. Right now she was in Ireland, which she enjoyed, as the healthcare system was quite different from that in the UK. Maya always liked learning about the different ways countries delivered healthcare, although recently they seemed to have more in common than differences. It was almost like a global grab was sweeping through the healthcare industry, similar to MacDonald's in the food branch.

Today they'd been in a small hospital in Sligo visiting a Dr White, whose views on modern medicine were surprisingly refreshing. Dr White had detailed in depth how he felt the pharmaceutical industry was trying to take over the world, seemingly able to cure every single disease known to man and leaving no room at all for traditional medicine or a stellar mindset. While Maya agreed with everything he was saying, she felt she couldn't voice her thoughts too much, given she'd been sitting next to one of her sales reps. Nevertheless, her heart had filled with hope that there were others like her who recognised that the balance between pharmaceutical medicine and traditional, ancient medicine had gone completely out of kilter to the point of simply becoming the pursuit of more and more profit. How does anyone try to stop this out-of-control juggernaut? she wondered.

She turned her attention back to her upcoming meeting with Lesley. She'd been really looking forward to another session. The screen flickered to life and she clicked on the link, feeling excited for what was to come.

'Hey,' a voice came over from the screen, promptly followed by a face.

'How's it going?' Lesley asked, as Maya noted the lack of clothing and the suntan.

'Must be warm in San Diego at this time of year,' she chuckled.

'Yeah, well, it's colder than the summer but it's still around eighteen degrees here today,' Lesley answered.

Maya laughed. 'Well, that's got to be better than the seven degrees with rain that we're experiencing at the moment.'

Lesley smiled. 'So, how have you been?'

'I've been good,' Maya confirmed after a pause. 'I feel like, I feel like maybe there's more that I can do to change my current life. It's like a small crack in the door has opened and I want to discover more and test the waters. Yes, that's probably the best way to describe how I've been feeling. I've had some really strange symptoms and quite a few connections with an Angel Guide that really freaked me out at first but now I'm getting used to it. In fact, he feels like a sturdy companion. Sorry, I'm waffling—,' she finished abruptly.

'That's great!' Lesley exclaimed. 'A bit of spiritual 'flu is nothing to worry about as you develop your skills. It's likely dense energy is being released.'

Sounds familiar, Maya thought dryly.

'I was thinking about you the other day when I was doing a session for a couple of women on awakening the Divine Feminine. I know you're going to be so powerful when we awaken the Divine Feminine within you.'

'Um, okay,' Maya responded with trepidation.

'Let's begin, gorgeous girl. So, take a nice deep breath and tell me what you know about energy.'

'Well, I don't have enough of it most of the time,' Maya joked.

'There's a reason for that,' Lesley responded. 'Do you understand anything about the word Empath?'

'I've heard it before,' Maya said, thinking for a second. 'But no, I don't really understand what it means.'

'Okay, let's start from the top,' Lesley continued. 'An Empath is somebody that can feel other people's emotions and is very sensitive to the energy in a place. With what you've described so far, you're definitely an Empath, Maya, and I feel that a lot of your energy has been taken from you. So let's get back to some basic energy principles. Your energy needs protecting and we need to call back all parts of yourself which you've given away voluntarily or involuntarily. The energetic cords that are attached to that must be cut.'

'Oh, okay, I guess that makes sense,' Maya replied, somewhat bewildered.

Lesley proceeded to run through twenty minutes of further explanation on how Maya can protect her energy, cut negative cords tied to other people, and recognise when the emotions that she's feeling are not hers. Those she should send back to the giver with love.

'I'm sure you have plenty of time to practise this, from what you've described of your dealings in the office,' Lesley chuckled. 'Now, let's do a meditation together. Perhaps we can call in the guide you got to know recently, and any others that want to support us?'

Maya took a deep breath and imagined her feet growing roots down into the Earth. She thought of the trees that stand proud behind her house and imagined joining her roots with theirs. Lesley began talking her through a guided meditation, starting with walking through the forest but after a couple of minutes Maya no longer heard Lesley's voice. In its place there was a flow of visions and pictures coming through her head. First, of a young boy running while being stabbed in the back by someone behind him—strange, as her right shoulder blade, where the knife was entering, had been plaguing her with stiffness and pain recently.

Next was a man playing with a wolf in the Canadian mountains. He seemed at home there, almost like he was part of the pack. The vision moved again to a young man who presumably fell overboard from a ship and was calling for help.

Lastly, it centred on a young woman with long brown hair, not dissimilar to the woman she'd seen in her dream, but she knew this person was different in some way. Maya watched as the woman walked through a small village and out onto the moorland. She seemed distraught. She followed a track down to the fishing dock, the scarf wrapped around her head and neck blowing in the wind, her skirts covered in mud. She hid behind a wall as another woman joined her and they seemed to have a conversation.

The next vision took Maya to a small house where a young boy rushed up to greet the woman as she entered the door, clutching at her skirts and overjoyed to see her. A man sat by the fire stirring gruel in a pot. They seemed like the perfect happy family, but Maya could feel the fear in the young woman's heart. She tried to follow the vision more to see why the woman was so scared. She struggled to keep it in her mind but it cut off and she came back to the sound of Lesley's voice.

'So,' Lesley said, as she finished. 'How was that?'

'I saw so much, I don't really know what any of it means,' Maya said. 'It feels like it was me but it wasn't. It was different people but it really felt like they were part of me.'

'Maybe they were,' mused Lesley. 'Sounds like Spirit wants to show you your past lives. This seems a really important step in your spiritual journey. Perhaps there are many things in your past lives that need to heal, or at least clear, and that's more pressing than your life at the moment. It may be that the key to opening up and improving your current life is that you are able to let go of the karma and heal from the past.'

Maya sat back on the chair, letting out a breath she didn't know she was holding.

'Yeah, I think you're probably right.'

'Okay, my lovely, your homework is to work on all the points of energy we talked about and to really start to understand where your energy is going and how to protect and defend it. Keep asking to be shown more from your past lives and what needs to come up for healing.'

Maya said her goodbyes and closed the computer lid. She stayed in her chair for a long while, staring into the mirror in front of her. There's clearly much more to this world than she'd thought, and she wondered if she needed to unlearn most of what she'd been told and relearn it with her own truth. She spun a pen in her hand as she contemplated what other untruths she might have been conditioned to believe in. She already saw that the pharmaceutical industry and the miracle of medicines wasn't quite what she'd signed up to. She'd started to see that the declaration that there was no spirit world, that there was nothing beyond the grave and that God didn't exist was also a fabrication, however she didn't fully resonate with the Church, either—there seemed to be a lot wrong there. However, she coached herself, you know enough to realise that what you thought you knew was diluted truth at best. It's like Chinese whispers—the more and more it's told, the further you stray from the absolute truth that you started with. Is this what's happening in the world today? Are we basing some of our most momentous decisions and platforms for further development in life on a badly-formed Chinese whisper? What about the children? What about what they're taught in school? How much has that been diluted from the absolute truth? Maya pondered on these and other thoughts, as she completed her work reports and got ready for bed.

✳

The following morning Maya arose early and spent half an hour in the gym, trying to arouse her body into enthusiasm for working without stiffness. She went down to the hotel breakfast room and, after perusing what was on offer, settled on scrambled egg on toast with tea. A short while later, Charlie appeared, storming across the room with his usual swagger. He slumped into the chair opposite Maya and dumped his bag on the floor.

'Morning, Boss,' he said, turning and signalling to the waitress. 'Can I get a black coffee please? You want anything?'

'No, thank you,' Maya answered between mouthfuls of egg. 'I'm done. So, Charlie, what's on the agenda today?'

'Well,' he answered, spooning a small stack of sugar into his coffee. 'We're heading up to Belfast to see Dr Dreyer and after that we'll get you on your flight home.'

'Sounds like a plan,' Maya mumbled through her teacup. 'Let's go through your pre-call objectives and what you prepared for today before we leave. Much more comfortable than doing it in the car.'

'Sure,' Charlie agreed.

She pulled up the form on her iPad—the never-ending

document with thirty-two checkboxes to fill in, assessing Charlie's performance in his calls yesterday and whether he was well prepared for his calls today. After the revelations she'd had last night, it occurred to Maya this morning that there was little room for Charlie's true personality to shine through while talking to the doctors. The checklist demanded that he would open the conversation in a certain way, that he would cover what someone higher up in the company deemed key points of the products and that he would close in his most persuasive way. It's all just manipulation training really, Maya thought. If people were really passionate about selling these products, and the products really were the miracle they're claimed to be, then it would come through naturally. Reps would make sure they knew the information that mattered for the condition and would help the clinician make an informed choice. That's not what this is. This is just a 101 on persuasion and manipulation, put into a really, really long form.

Maya sighed and switched the iPad off.

'You know what, Charlie? Let's have an honest conversation about how you think things are going and where I can help you.'

Charlie looked at Maya for a moment and then leaned forward in his chair before speaking.

'You see, that's what we love about you, Maya. You're a real leader, not a manager. I know you don't like the tickboxes any more than I do.' He smiled. 'I'd love that conversation,' he said.

Later that day Maya turned and waved goodbye to Charlie after he dropped her outside the airport. Stepping through the large doors, she was relieved to see that her flight was on time. She checked in her suitcase, cleared security and went off in search of a tea and a toilet. Once both had been accomplished, she settled down on a seat to wait for the gate to be called. She started people-watching and, as usual, passengers were scurrying around or on their phones, several were rushing to get their flights and, across from the seating area, she watched a group of smartly-dressed businessmen enjoying champagne, and a couple cuddling, presumably on their way to an exotic location. She scanned the seats in front of her. Most people were on their laptop or phone, a few sat staring into space or watching the large screen behind her.

Maya's attention was drawn to a middle-aged lady in a suit sitting a few rows in front of her. The lady looked to be in distress—Maya could see she was trying not to cry. She was hugging her laptop case as though it could provide her some comfort. After a few moments observing, Maya stood, walked over to the woman and stopped in front of her.

'Excuse me,' she said. 'I'm sorry, I didn't mean to intrude, but I noticed that you seem upset. Is there anything I can do to help?'

The lady blinked and looked up at her.

'Do I know you?' she asked.

'No,' replied Maya. It's almost as though the lady couldn't comprehend that a stranger would come over and ask her if she was okay.

'To be honest I'm having a tough time,' she sniffed.

'What's your name?' Maya enquired.

'Claire,' the lady replied.

'Well, Claire, I've got a few minutes before my flight. Do you mind if I sit down next to you?'

'No, it's all good. Please do,' Claire confirmed, moving her bag.

They sat in silence for a minute.

'I don't want to trouble you,' Claire started.

'It's no trouble,' Maya reassured her.

There was silence for a few moments before Claire launched into a speech.

'It's just I always thought I'd have lots of time, you know? Time after you've earned lots of money and then you've paid off your house, then you could retire a bit early. See the kids grow up a bit, maybe have the holidays I always dreamed of. I can't have it now because I'm always away with work, and I don't have the money. You know, I had all these visions in my head of how it would go and I've been working so hard, flying everywhere, trying to make commission every quarter to put towards paying off more of the mortgage so that day might come nearer. Well, last week I got the news I've got cancer.' Claire paused, looking at her feet.

'I'm really sorry to hear that,' Maya murmured quietly.

'I mean, it's just mad,' she said. 'I'm a really healthy person. I exercise, I eat well, I do everything I'm supposed to,' she explained, welling up. 'I just don't understand why me.'

Maya held her hand, which seemed to make the tears flow more.

'I mean, I'm going to beat it. I've already decided I'm going to beat it,' Claire sniffed.

'That's great. Positivity is really important. Clinical studies show how a positive mindset greatly increases the chance of success of getting rid of any disease,' Maya offered.

'Yeah, I know, I've read them. That's going to be me,' Claire said.

'That's good to know,' Maya smiled.

She looked up at the board and saw Flight 416 flashing.

'I've got to go but I wish you all the luck in the world and I really hope things turn around for you soon,' Maya said.

'Thank you,' Claire smiled, squeezing Maya's hand. 'I really appreciate your support.'

Maya nodded and turned and, as she did, she felt a knot in her stomach, which, thinking back to her recent conversation with Lesley, she wasn't sure was totally hers. She hurried away to catch her plane.

Sitting back and looking out at the clouds passing by the window, Maya stared, enjoying the scenery for a few minutes with little in her head. After a while a thought came to her. Actually, it felt like it had been put there and she wondered whether Tal was sitting over her shoulder, but when she enquired she couldn't get a straight answer. Never mind, she thought. It doesn't matter whether it's mine or his thought. She settled again on the trail that had come into her head and let it continue. While Claire probably *did* look after her exercise regime and her food intake, what she maybe didn't look after was her mind and soul. Perhaps she spent too long in a negative mindset, in a polluted environment or perhaps she didn't feel like she had purpose in her life. Maya supposed that these things could be just as detrimental to health as a bad diet and no exercise. Even if Claire *did* beat the cancer, if she didn't address these points, then the 'dis-ease' in her body would just return.

Maya shivered as confirmation ran down her spine. We humans, she thought, are so much more complex than 99.5% of the population realise. She sat back in her seat, closing her eyes. Above her, the dark shadows scurried among the plane chassis.

That's it, one of them muttered. *Let her think it doesn't matter where her thoughts come from. If we can get her vibration low enough we can feed her anything and she'll believe us. Many a so-called awakened one has fallen prey to that method, she'll be no different.*

Idiot! Those thoughts were of the light and will help raise her vibration, another argued.

Yes, for now, but in time she'll trust any voice and then we'll seed the lower thoughts, the ones that will trap her in self-doubt and fear. She won't hear the voices of the Angels, only of us.

Ah, excellent, a third Demon sniggered.

Be careful not to underestimate her, a loud voice boomed from the dark, making the little Demons scurry for cover. *She's an old soul. We cannot risk her reaching a higher vibration than we can command. You know the Universal Law—we can't vibrate higher than the Fourth Dimension. See that she does not, either,* it snarled, before bursting through the top of the plane and out into the clouds, gathering a storm in the direction it flew.

Yes, Master, they quivered, regrouping above seat 22A.

6

The plane touched down and Maya felt a sense of relief at being almost home. She was drained and tired but wanted to put on a happy, upbeat face for the kids that were waiting for her behind the airport screen. She took a deep breath, picked up her suitcase and made her way to the exit.

The doors opened and she heard the familiar squeal of Amy's 'Mummy!' from across the entrance hall. Amy ran over, throwing herself into Maya's arms, quickly followed by Zidan who was trailing a stuffed dinosaur behind him.

Jacob hung back with the two older girls and, as Maya smiled over at him, she noticed how exhausted he looked.

'Rough day?' she asked, reaching out to give him a hug as she approached them.

Faith was quick to grab her suitcase.

'What you got? What did you bring us? I'm starving. Please tell me you brought the Irish lollies with the strange man on.'

Maya laughed, ruffling her hair.

'Hasn't Dad fed you?' she exclaimed.

'No!' they all shouted back.

'Oh, okay,' Maya said, directing a questioning look at Jacob.

'I've been under the weather today. They've had some toast and fruit. They're being melodramatic, Maya,' Jacob huffed as he started to walk out towards the car.

'We really aren't,' Zidan moaned. 'You can see my ribs and everything, Mummy. Look!' He lifted his top, exposing his tummy to the cold night air.

'I think you'll survive,' Maya said, pulling him close and placing her arm around his shoulders.

'Come on, we'll get salty chips on the way home,' she added, secretly annoyed with Jacob for not doing what she considered a basic stay-at-home chore. How hard is it to feed kids anyway, even if you *are* feeling a bit rubbish? She shook off her annoyance, knowing it would only end in another argument, and focused instead on all the questions the kids were throwing at her at the same time.

'I know what you're thinking,' he said as she climbed into the front seat of the car, pushing aside papers and rubbish.

'Do you?' she grumbled, sighing.

'Yes,' he snapped. 'Maya, it does them good to have basic food, and not so much of it, from time to time. It helps them value food for what it *should* be, rather than the obesity-generating garbage modern society would have you believe it's there for.'

Maya struggled with her thoughts. On the one hand she agreed with Jacob; she knew only too well of the consequences of allowing kids to eat at will, associate food with emotions and have whatever they want—they inevitably grow up overweight and unhappy. But the other voice in her head was nagging her to be angry about the children practically starving. Why couldn't he just have cooked them wholesome food? Why can't he do his part? She's been out working all week. The voice got louder and louder until it was encompassing all her thoughts. She gritted her teeth and, as she did, she heard a soft voice whisper. It was so quiet she could barely grasp it and she mentally tried to remain calm while she reached for it.

Ask your ego to step aside. There, she absolutely heard it this time. It felt like Tal.

But it's not fair, she replied to him in her head.

What is fair? he asked. *Perhaps you need to ask yourself what is truly fair and what you've been conditioned to believe is fair. Your thoughts are of negative vibration designed to bring anger and chaos. Breathe deeply*, he commanded.

Maya took a sidewards look at Jacob and noted the dark circles on his eyes again. For the first time, she felt compassion seeping into her thoughts. She expected a lot from him, assumed he could move at her pace, compared his work to that of hers. But we're all different, and sitting in a hotel room wasn't the same as putting up with screaming, arguing children. She knew one thing—fighting wasn't the way forward. It just took them round in circles. So many times she was going to leave and so many times an invisible chord kept her there.

She couldn't explain it, but she knew there was a reason they were together.

When they had first met, her father clearly didn't approve and Jacob had done some pretty crazy things in the first month's dating, including throwing chips at her sister during a heated debate on whether Freya thought she was the centre of everything because Jacob clearly thought she did. Maya smiled. The chip incitement was pretty funny on reflection.

'What are you smiling at?' Jacob enquired, looking over. Maya softened her face and reached out to touch his hand on the gearstick.

'I was just reminiscing about when you threw chips at my sister. What a waste! They were good chips, you know,' she said in mock annoyance.

Jacob smirked at her, taking his eyes back to the road ahead. They had driven this road a hundred times and were approaching the section that had several tight corners and bends. Maya looked out the window at the fields whooshing by and then turned her attention to the cars coming the other way, wondering if she might pass her friend Katy as she was driving to work. She hadn't seen Katy in ages and she made a mental note to text her when she got home.

As Jacob took the second bend before their turning, Maya sensed a sudden dread. She checked his position on the road, noting he was still in his lane, but as she looked up she saw a large white van coming the other way in the middle of the road. A split second was all the time they had as they were positioned for a head-on collision at the sharpest point of the corner. Maya had no time, no time to check the kids had belts on, no time to even stretch her hand out across the middle between her and Jacob to try desperately to stop the impact sending them forwards. She knew Jacob had no time to react, despite him being an advanced driver and very sharp behind the wheel. She only had time to process the fact that there was no way they were not going to crash.

Suddenly it was over, and they were free of the white van and on a clear road coming out of the bend. Jacob was gasping for breath and it brought her back fully into the present. The kids, unaware of anything, carried on their rambles in the back, talking about some social media influencer that Faith was saying was old and Aurora was insisting was their age. Maya felt the lack of blood in her face, her heart was hammering wildly in her chest and she looked over to Jacob, who was indicating to pull over in the lay-by.

He stopped the car and turned off the engine. They sat in silence, trying to process what had just happened, before Faith piped up from the back, enquiring in her usual bossy voice, 'What's going on? Has Dad powered down?'

Neither of them answered.

'Mum, just reboot him. We need to get chips. I'm seriously starving,' she whined.

'What just happened?' Jacob gasped, turning wide-eyed to Maya. 'We were going to crash. There was no way we weren't going to crash,' he stammered.

'I know, I know,' she responded. 'I saw it. I don't know. One second the car was head on, the next... It's like the wheels had changed direction, but there was no time at all in between, no room for that to happen.'

Jacob took a deep breath.

'Well, maybe it's time to start believing in Angels,' he said, raising his eyebrows. 'That was mental.'

'Dad, hurry up. The chippy will close,' Aurora urged from the back.

'Always thinking about your stomach,' Faith snapped. 'You had a sandwich earlier. I didn't have anything,' she grumbled, giving her sister a shove on the shoulder.

'Girls!' Maya interrupted, as Jacob re-started the car and pulled out onto the road again.

'Seriously strange,' he whispered, shaking his head.

Above the trees Tal closed his eyes and telepathically spoke with his brothers from afar.

That was too close, he reflected. *We need to keep nearby. She's clearly a target—once they've awoken to their true self, they can protect themselves and their kids, but for now we must be vigilant. The Demons are everywhere. Their Master must be worried about these ones awakening and the impact it can have on this planet.*

I know, Brother, the response came instantly. *Be careful yourself. Satan's world is full of deception and trickery and it doesn't just stay in the Third Dimension. You also must be on your guard.*

Tal nodded, feeling the love shared by the band of Brothers supporting the inhabitants of Earth at this time. The love and courage they showed never failed to reignite the power of light within his soul. He gathered himself and took off after the car again.

7

Maya stared at the motorway in front of her, trying to keep her eyes open. It was nine p.m. on a Sunday night and she was heading south on her way to a week of work in the office, including three days of company conference hosted in a large, nearby hotel. She felt like she had slipped into robotic mode; the numb weird feeling of 'Just do it' helped her pack her things, kiss Jacob and the kids goodbye and turn the car south. More than once or twice she had the overwhelming urge to turn around and just go home and exist. To stroke Pilot, feel the softness in his coat and the horsey smell of his mane she loved so much. To watch the crazy ducks dance across the yard and the geese fly overhead. To sit in the trees and watch the world outside from the sanctuary of the woods. Just to be, just to have space to be her, the real her, not the woman who feels like she's drowning every day, like someone has her head in a lock, ducking it in and out of the water while she takes quick breaths between the onslaught.

The crazy thing is she can't work out who is responsible for making her feel like this. She brought most of it on herself,

87

didn't she? I mean, look, she argued with herself, you're the one still driving south, aren't you? To a job you mostly don't agree with, right? Yes, but it's nice, isn't it? the other part of her whispered. The hotel's posh and the food's prepared for you, and everyone thinks you're so cool, having a good job and a nice BMW.

That bloody word. 'Nice,' she huffed to herself. What does that even mean? It's 'nice', is it? 'Define nice,' she challenged herself. Urgh, she growled, flicking on the CD player and turning up the bouncy sound of Imagine Dragons.

The phone cut in during a particularly dramatic part of *Mouth of the River* that had Maya singing at the top of her voice.

'Oh my God, Freya!' she shrieked at her sister. 'Why do you always call during my favourite song?'

'Maya,' Freya replied, deadpan. 'You say *every* song is your favourite song. How can that be possible?'

'Well, no, okay, yes, that's probably true. What's new with you?'

'Oh my God,' Freya answered with a heightened tone. 'You'll never guess what happened at the yard today.'

Maya sat back, relaxing a little in the seat after turning the volume down on a far too loud Freya, and waited for the latest updates in the traumatic life of her sister. She smiled as she listened. While Freya often drove her mad, ringing to ask her advice then promptly doing the exact opposite, she enjoyed listening to her and it certainly made the five-hour journey go a little quicker. When Freya finally paused for breath, Maya relayed the near car accident to her. Freya listened quietly—so quietly in fact that Maya thought the phone had disconnected. Freya was never quiet for more than ten seconds and Maya had been speaking for at least a minute.

'That's mental,' Freya said at last. 'It sounds like a Guardian Angel.'

'Yeah, I know,' Maya agreed.

They spoke a little longer and then Maya hung up. She continued questioning in her head why she had to do x, y and z, when suddenly she felt as though she wasn't alone. A presence had joined her in the back seat. Maya looked in the rear-view mirror but couldn't see anything. She reached out with her mind and got a soothing response that felt half familiar.

'Tal, is that you?' she wondered out loud.

Yes, confirmation came back immediately. *Maya, how many words in the human dictionary do you think are overused?* he asked, throwing her off somewhat.

What a strange question, she mused. Mind you, this is a strange connection and a strange conversation, so whatever...

She mentally shrugged in her head. Erm, come again? she threw the thought back to him.

The word 'nice'—you were contemplating it earlier, correct?

'Well, yes,' Maya confirmed, trying not to think about whether Tal had also been listening in on her and Jacob having sex last night, or what else he may just happen to hear and see. If Angels see, that is.

It's all the same to us up here, he laughed. *We don't see earthly acts as separate. Sex is the same as smiling to us in terms of its need to be private.*

Okay, weird, she thought, trying to come back to the topic they were discussing.

What do you really mean by the words 'nice', or 'happy', or 'safe'? he pressed on. *How many untruths have you told yourself through these words? Words are spells, Maya. The world can easily trick you into believing something is 'nice' when indeed it may be the complete inversion to that.*

Maya sank into her car seat pondering his advice. She wasn't fully sure she understood but something was resonating for her. For example, she thought, last week I said that new Lady Gaga song was nice, but actually on closer inspection, and while watching it over Faith's shoulder on her phone, it was demonic, full of satanic symbols, far too much flesh exposed and, in fact, the song lyrics weren't really in line with what I believe or want to listen to. But the tune is catchy and Lady Gaga has a good voice, so I suppose I would have put it in the bucket of 'nice'.

Right! Exactly! Tal confirmed. *How much have you done this all your life with everything?*

Maya thought about this for a while, briefly side-tracked by a very slow Audi in front, which she had to manoeuvre around. She chose to travel at this time on a Sunday night to avoid the mad Monday morning rush on the M1 motorway but there was always one out to get her and tonight it was an old lady in an Audi. She suddenly had a realisation that felt like ice crawling down her back. But if I really let myself think about that deeply, then you could expand and apply it to *everything* I think I know or have ever been taught.

Exactly! Tal's voice replied again, sounding like it was getting further away, and then he was gone, and Maya couldn't feel his presence in the back seat any more. She felt slightly sick knowing that she was being challenged to start looking in some places in her mind she really didn't want to look. She glanced down at the beeping phone on the dashboard to see that one of her nurses had called in sick for the week.

'Don't fancy conference, then?' she scoffed out loud, followed by a quiet acknowledgment that she didn't really fancy it either.

Maya was still chewing over the thoughts around what she tells herself versus the truth of the matter as she swung the car into the hotel car park. She couldn't find a space near the door so had to opt for somewhere at the bottom end. She hated the dark, more so when it was a creepy hotel car park late at night. She quickly gathered her things and walked briskly towards the entrance. Crossing the lobby, she waved at a few familiar faces, regular visitors to the hotel with whom she had shared conversations at breakfast or in the gym, and headed to check-in.

Maya never really unpacked anything properly—she just flung things around the room across chairs and tables, opting in the main for non-iron work clothes. She sat at the desk for a while, checking over the speech she had prepared for the conference and what she needed to cover in tomorrow's office meetings, which were to be a mixture of pre-conference planning and budget meetings and reviews with her managers, before closing her laptop and climbing into the bed. She put a few customary drops of lavender on her pillow and settled down to sleep.

She awoke startled a few hours later with her heart pounding. Somewhere between her sleep and awake state she was aware of the sensation of being held down. She registered the utter panic in her mind. Why couldn't she move? Her heart was beating out of her chest and a sickly feel was crawling in her stomach. What's happening?

Then she heard it—a voice, distraught in its tone. It sounded like a middle-aged woman. She was screaming, 'Where is she? Where is she? You took her!'

Maya still couldn't move, although the weight felt lighter, like maybe she could push off the presence if she could only work out how. I don't know, she answered in her mind.

'You took her! You did! Where is she?' the woman persisted. Between her vicious outbursts, she racked into huge sobs and Maya could feel her hurt and despair.

Tell her to follow the light. Tell her to ask me for help, another voice reached out, pushing the words at Maya from the other side of her consciousness.

Maya was aware of tears tracking down her cheeks as she felt the agony of the woman. She could feel it in her own heart.

Tell her, Maya, the voice insisted.

Okay, okay. She reached out to the woman.

'Shh, it's okay. Go with him. Go to the light.'

'NO! NO!' the woman wailed. 'No, you're trying to trick me.'

I'm not. I'm not, Maya cried in her head. Her eyes were streaming with tears and her fingers felt rigid. I'm not. Please, she's there. Your daughter is there, Maya pleaded with the woman.

Suddenly she felt a shift of energy. The woman seemed to be getting more distant and Maya's hands raised high off the mattress, free of their invisible restraints. She sat up, gasping. Now fully awake with her eyes open, she continued sobbing for a few minutes, trying to make sense of what had just unfolded.

How did I know the woman was looking for her daughter? she asked herself once she was a little calmer.

'What the hell just happened?' she asked out loud, feeling like she was losing her mind. She was a ghost. I'm sure of it, Maya fretted. Where's my phone?

She quickly started grappling by the side of the bed while turning the reading light on. Having located her phone, she searched the internet for the site on which the hotel was built. Scrolling through the results, she came across several articles about the location. An asylum! she breathed out loud, where inmates in the fifteenth century were often tried for witchcraft and taken in the night.

Maya collapsed back on the headboard. The woman was looking for her daughter. Even after passing, she was still searching for her and she thought I had taken her. She must have been accused of witchcraft and taken for burning. Maya shuddered, welling up again and trying to calm the searing pain in her chest. This room must have been the last place she'd seen her alive.

Feeling hot and feverish, Maya lay down again, trying to slow her breathing. Eventually she felt calm enough to release her taut muscles, but not anywhere near a state of calm to sleep again that night.

✦

The next morning, she showered and dressed, stopping by the front desk on her way out to work.

'Can I help you?' a young blonde lady asked, sounding far chirpier than her face said she was.

'I'd like to move rooms to the other side of the hotel,' Maya said. 'Have you had any strange complaints?' she asked. 'About that room, I mean,' she clarified when the girl looked confused.

'Err, no Madam. Was there a problem with your room? It's in the older part of the building, but it was all refurbished recently,' she said, seemingly feeling offended at the idea that Maya didn't like the room.

'No, no, it's not that,' Maya responded quickly. 'It's just, well, I'm pretty sure it's haunted,' she blurted out, looking down embarrassed at the quizzical look the girl was now giving her.

'Not heard that before,' the girl said, leaning down to authorise another key in the machine. 'Here's Room 120 on the other side of the building. Hopefully that will be to your liking,' she said with a strained smile. 'I'll have your things moved for you.'

'That's great,' Maya said, smiling meekly. 'They're packed on the bed.'

She turned and walked out of the lobby to the car park, aware that there was now one more person on the planet who thought she was stark raving mad.

✦

'Ah, the wanderer returns!' Ben exclaimed, one hand outstretched towards her as she crossed the room to her desk.

'Why are you in my chair?' Maya grumbled, dumping her things on her work station.

'I was wondering,' Ben said, leaning down under her desk and producing one of the pair of high heels that were stored under there, 'just who you were planning on trying to kill with these?' He lifted an eyebrow and smirked at her.

'You, most likely,' Maya rebuffed, 'if you don't get out of my chair.'

Ben hopped out lightly, plonking his rear on the chair at the next desk, alerting her to the fact that Natalie was late yet again. Maya flopped down on her seat.

'Yuck, it's still warm from your big hairy butt,' she grimaced.

'Nice,' Ben mocked fake hurt. 'Anyway, Madam Maya, I need your report to put into my team's marketing chart. You know, the one you were supposed to send to Catherine last week?'

'Right. Yes. Okay,' Maya said slowly. 'I'm still chasing the contractors for the data.'

'Maya, you have to get hold of them,' Ben growled. 'Seriously, what do we pay them for?'

'I know, I know,' Maya responded. 'But Ben, they're short-staffed and under-supported. Their management takes on projects, seeing the pound signs without a clue how they're actually going to resource them and when it goes wrong, they shout at our people delivering the projects and then those people get fed up and quit! This just leaves us in a stickier position than before. All this while we're fighting to keep the service afloat and safe,' Maya continued. 'Meanwhile, un-abated Anna is flouncing around the Halls of Power at Global bragging about how we're the only country to offer such a comprehensive patient safety service. It makes me sick,' Maya finished, anger boiling up in her veins.

'Take it easy, it's only Monday morning,' Ben laughed. 'Just do it first, please. For me,' he said, walking backwards to his desk, his hands in mock prayer position.

'Fine,' Maya conceded, swinging her legs under her desk and opening her computer.

'Tea, Boss?'

'Sure,' Maya responded, smiling. Rajendra—the one in her team with the IT skills, practically unflappable, liked by Anna and he said yes to everything.

Maya skimmed through the papers on her desk. Stopping at last week's news in the Pharma Times, she read the article entitled '*MHRA gives go-ahead to off-label medicine use in MS*' and rolled her eyes. So if a medical rep says things that are considered inaccurate they can be sacked and fined, yet national bodies can make decisions without a full review of risks and without ensuring biases don't interfere with decision making.

'I just don't get it,' she mumbled, shaking her head.

'What don't you get?' Rajendra enquired.

'The world,' Maya summarised, taking the tea from him while trying not to spill it on her laptop.

Maya fell into silence working at her computer. She managed to get a few things ticked off her list and her items collated for the next meeting that she guessed Anna would ask about. She turned and saw people starting to make their way over to the meeting room. Scooping up her belongings, and an over-ripe banana lying on her desk, she hurried over. Anna was already seated at the head of the large table, tapping away on her computer, and a few other members of the leadership team looked up and nodded at her, clearly already on their best behaviour.

Maya helped herself to the tea laid out at the side of the room, reaching for and then deciding against a sweet fruity biscuit. She was wired enough without adding sugar to the mix. She took a seat opposite Ben, who was frowning at his computer and frantically typing what Maya presumed were the last bits of the Marketing Leadership Plan he was about to present. The last few people filed in and closed the door behind them. Maya became aware that her breaths were short and quick. She felt a heightened level of anxiety before they'd even started. Why did she feel like this? she pondered.

Because you're picking up on everyone else's anxiety as well as your own, Tal supplied into her consciousness. *Try calling in protection and visualising a shield around you,* he continued.

Maya took a deep breath and started to visualize a circle of light around herself. At first, she really struggled but after a few seconds she started to see it.

You need to practise it regularly for you to get better at it. It works like a mirror bouncing back negative energies from where they came and helping you not to absorb general low energy.

'Maya,' Anna cut into her discussion with Tal.

'Yes,' Maya responded slowly.

'I think you should go first. Let's have your statistics for the blood service for the month.'

Maya dutifully stood up and went to present by the screen. She talked through the latest figures, appointments done, appointments missed, and then went on to summarise the key issues and positive events that had happened in the last month. Anna set her jaw as Maya finished, looking like she was bubbling with anger, barely containing it in her face. Everyone seemed to be holding their breath as Anna fiddled with her pen and began to speak.

'Maya, I fail to understand why we have ten missed appointments. As you know, if patients don't get their bloods taken on time then the doctors could miss a potential problem and that could lead to serious consequences for the patients' health.'

'Yes, I understand the risk,' Maya responded. 'But we have

multiple challenges and, given those, I actually think this is a good performance for the team.'

Anna shifted in her chair and opened her mouth to shout her down, but Maya was ready this time and was tired of feeling intimidated by Anna's responses.

'Anna, we are working this project on a shoestring compared to what's being asked. We have over one hundred and twenty nurses on the ground and we pay them less than any competitor through our third party. The ultimate responsibility lies with the doctor to make the call on bloods, and we always try to build in a week's leeway to ensure they don't go over, even if the appointment is missed because, for example, the nurse doesn't show for work. In comparison, we have ninety-eight missed appointments because the patient wasn't home, despite sending three reminders. I know we sell this service as part of the product and tell doctors they can rely on us to make sure the bloods are back at the hospital and all they have to do is look at them, but in reality we shouldn't be doing that. It goes against the code and it is not a true and accurate statement of our capabilities. It's not always within our control. They must be comfortable prescribing a potentially dangerous drug, and also be accountable for the aftercare. After all, the doctors are the ultimate people responsible.'

Maya finished, took a deep breath and waited for a response. If looks could kill, everyone in that room would be dead. Anna seemed to be unable to form words for a few seconds. It was true nobody pushed against her, and Maya had just flung a lot at her publicly, but truth is truth and, Maya justified to herself, Anna needed to think of something other than her ego and the pound signs. The seconds ticked past.

'I am well aware of the patient safety concerns, thank you, Maya,' she said through veiled lips. 'I want that miss rate cut to half next month and the opinion you just shared does not go out of this room. I certainly don't want the reps demotivated. We need to push harder to reach our targets in the next few months.'

Maya crossed over to her chair and sat down, avoiding the various looks of her colleagues that were a mixture of awe and 'I can't believe you just said that', to the young and impressionable marketing girls who spent most of the time trying to crawl up Anna's arse and now looked like they wanted to kill Maya to defend their mistress.

When the drug was first launched, Maya generally saw the potential to help people and, despite the side effect risk, for those that had a poor prognosis outcome and could end up in a wheelchair in a few years, she felt a genuine ray of hope to slow the progress and give them a good chance of enjoying an active life. Yet a few years later they were pushing more and more into groups where the prognosis was unknown and the side effects were. It was becoming ever more difficult for Maya to stay silent as she watched reps try to convince doctors to use the drug early on patients as a prophylactic treatment. Some of these patients' diseases may not have progressed at all for years, yet they were being treated with a medication that could rob them of their chance to have a child. The scales of risk versus benefit had tipped towards the pursuit of money and no one seemed to care but her. Those doctors that had a wait-and-see approach were labelled resistant, and elaborate PR plans were conducted to try to change their minds.

Maya's mind came back to the present as the marketing duo were starting their plan. They talked through a glossy leaflet, bragging again at how the statistics had been manipulated, while in the next breath ensuring that everyone knew they were following the rules, which just showed that the rules had plenty of loopholes.

'Maya,' Christina turned to her with a high, fake voice. 'We thought you could help us get access to this Dublin account on the back of the nurses we have in there,' she stated, pointing a well-manicured finger to an account name halfway down the list on the screen.

'We're a post-prescription service, Christina,' Maya responded. 'We can't be promotional, you know this. And they're already using the drug in patients that are at severe risk of rapid progression.'

'Yes, I know,' Christina said. 'But it's not promotional. I'm not asking you to *sell* the drug—just help us get access to the nurses. I think if we show them some of the stories in our marketing brochure and ask them how they would feel if they could stop a young woman ending up in a wheelchair, it would emotionally motivate them and they would nag the doctors.'

I think the words are 'manipulate' and 'guilt-trip', Maya thought darkly. She could feel Anna watching her intently and, for the first time, she realised that this woman would remove her from her team in a heartbeat if she could find a reason.

'I'll see what I can do. I'll speak to the team,' Maya mumbled.

'Thanks!' Christina fake smiled and turned back to carry on her presentation.

✦

Later that day Anna stopped by her desk, standing with her hands on her hips until Maya had finished her conversation and hung up the phone.

'Maya, I hope you haven't forgotten about Elijah's leaving do tonight? Since you're actually in the office we booked you a space. Good team-building opportunity, don't you think?'

The energy that accompanied those statements was loaded with venom and Maya could easily translate them into 'You're never here' (even though that wasn't true and Maya was having to miss her kids growing up to be somewhere else for the company every week) and 'I know you hate evening activities and in particular you mentioned you really don't want to come to a black-out dinner, so I'm going to make sure you come and hopefully give me more reason to try to fire you.'

Maya looked at Anna for a second, wondering how one woman can be so blinded by who she thinks she is (her bio claims she's a caring, driven, compassionate leader, for heaven's sake!) versus the beast that stood before her.

Ego, Tal offered as an answer. *She's consumed by her ego and she doesn't even know it.*

'Okay, I'll see you there,' Maya smiled, which was enough to get Anna to move on to her next victim.

Maya gathered her things from her desk and stood up. She felt exhausted and not at all like going out tonight but Elijah was a good guy. The team's Medical Director but also a practising doctor, he had given her plenty of health advice and the two had struck up a friendship over the year and a half she had worked with him. He had a practical approach and had helped her work out areas of her role that she didn't really understand relating to process and red tape, for which she never had any support from Anna. Maya was not the best at bureaucracy and detail—she viewed most of it as being pointless and hypocritical, preferring to look through the lenses of, Will it hurt anyone? What's the risk? If the risk is low, why spend hours ticking boxes? Her real passions lay in leadership coaching and finding creative ways to deliver patient care, something that almost seemed frowned upon these days. She reflected as she made her way to the car that she was sorry to see Elijah go and dreaded to think, with Anna in the recruiting panel, who might come in to replace him.

'Hey,' Ben hollered from behind her as she walked across the car park. Maya turned and looked at him.

'Don't,' she said flatly. 'Just don't say it.'

'What?' Ben feigned innocence. 'Like I was going to say anything about whether you were trying to work up the Annaster earlier and have you got a deathwish to be moved into another role? Nope, nothing like that,' he grinned. 'Look,' he said, his tone growing serious. 'I know you care, Maya, but sometimes you just care too much. You're going to land yourself in hot water. Just play the game.'

'It's not a game, Ben,' she responded, tears suddenly

pricking in the back of her eyes. 'It's people's lives. It's the need for responsible medicine and I just don't see us helping to facilitate that any more.'

'Oh, come on, Maya, it's not that bad.'

It is, she thought as she bade him farewell and climbed into her car. It's slippery and hidden and it's hard to put a finger on, but honestly, she thought, it *is* that bad. Her stomach twisted at the racing thoughts going through her head.

Earlier that year at another conference, she had watched a presentation on the 'flu injection for children. The focus of the session was on a distraught young woman who had lost her three-year-old child to 'flu. The story told to the audience, which was clearly meant to tug at the heart strings and make the reps double down on selling the 'flu jabs to the National Health Service, had Maya in tears. However, she later found herself in conversation with the bereaved mother, who had shared with Maya that she had met several people who had told her some of the vaccines caused autism and that she believed the risks were not always presented accurately. Despite losing a child, this woman could still see that there must be a risk/benefit to every drug and was open to understanding more about all opinions. That's exactly how Maya felt now about the drug she was working on and wished people could see she isn't against its use, only the relentless pushing of it for profit, with no regard to the risk/benefit conversation. She had discussed this with one of her colleagues at the time, but they quickly dismissed the woman's friends, citing 'conspiracy crap'. At the end of the day, most of her colleagues around her were happy to believe everything they were told and to come to work just for the pay cheque, as she did. How can she judge them when she still lives in that world?

✦

The restaurant looked shabby from the outside, with a grey concrete front and a small sign. A billboard at the side promised an amazing experience. The group shuffled through the front door, waiting to be led to their table. As they stood, making light conversation about weather, children and curtains, the waiter came out to welcome them and explain what happened with a dining-in-the-dark experience.

Maya suddenly started to realise with a sense of dread that they were in fact going to sit in the pitch black and eat. This could be a problem, she muttered to herself, groaning inwardly. Maya never slept in darkness—she'd always had a nightlight on since she was a small child, despite Jacob's objections. She started to feel anxiety rise in her chest. I can't do this, she thought to herself. But if I don't then Anna has another reason to hate me—and worse, she would see another weakness. She stood rigid while the waiter continued describing this apparently delightful experience.

Tal, Maya whispered in her head, but nothing; she couldn't feel any presence there. Maya had noticed that when she was in the city it was harder to connect than when she was out in the country, but right now, she felt abandoned and alone worrying how she was going to get through the next ninety minutes of her life.

Elijah lent forward and whispered quietly to her.

'Are you okay?'

'I don't like the dark,' Maya whispered back, tears pricking at her eyes.

'It'll be okay,' Elijah whispered back, taking her hand and squeezing it. 'Sit next to me. I'll look after you.'

Maya felt tears threatening to spill over at his kindness. She nodded back, not trusting herself to speak. The group started down the corridor to the main dining hall, with Maya reluctantly trailing at the rear. The waiter pulled back the curtain and ushered the group through, closing it behind him.

'Please hold the shoulder of the person in front of you,' he announced, and Maya placed a shaky hand on Elijah's shoulder as they moved forward. Her chest felt tight and she had a dawning realisation she was in danger of reliving the panic attacks she'd suffered in her teenage years. She stopped, frozen on the spot, fighting to control her breathing. Elijah turned to her, putting an arm around her shoulder.

'Maya, slow your breathing. Take nice, deep breaths. Small, quick breaths will only worsen the anxiety.'

By now most of the group were seated and she could hear whispering, with her name threaded through the conversation. Elijah led her over to a chair and helped her sit.

'Close your eyes,' he commanded. Maya continued in her attempts to get a hold on her breathing and to fight the urge to bolt for the exit, knowing she'd probably trip over half the restaurant in the process. She became aware of a soft material moving over her face.

'What are you doing?' she said in panic, bolting upright.

'Shh, it's okay, it's okay. I'm putting a cloth round your eyes. It'll help, trust me.'

Maya sat still, allowing Elijah to tie the napkin around her head and over her eyes. When he finished, he took hold of her hand.

'Now,' he proclaimed, dropping their joined hands on her thigh. 'Tell me about your kids. What's going on with them?'

Elijah kept Maya talking through two courses of mediocre tasting food, of which she was unable to eat much. They discussed the kids, her horse, and some of Elijah's childhood and current life. Maya almost forgot she was sitting with her eyes closed and a napkin wrapped round her head, as Elijah shared with her some of the traumas from his past. He had huge amounts of money, passed down through his family, but she realised they came with an emotional cost. Events that had happened in his life because of that wealth were huge burdens for him. It had caused all manner of self-doubt and under-confidence, and yet he was sitting here, comforting and looking after her. In fact, she mused, he always tried to take care of everyone around him and she realised with sadness that she was really going to miss him. Anna, of course, was always moaning about him, citing he was useless, which really translated to 'He won't do what I want him to do.'

Eventually Anna announced it was time to go. Maya had never felt such a sense of relief.

'Okay, I'm going to take off the blindfold, Maya, and we're

going to walk to the exit,' Elijah announced calmly. Maya nodded mutely and followed his lead out of the restaurant. As the door to the lit corridor opened, Maya realised her mascara was probably all over the place and tried to wipe under her eyes, excusing herself to the ladies' bathroom nearby. She shut the cubicle behind her and sat down with her head between her knees for a while trying to orientate herself. After a minute or two had passed, and she'd witnessed the hustle and bustle of her colleagues coming in to pee and leaving again, she stood up and walked over to the basins. Anna was washing her hands and, on seeing Maya, she looked up at her face.

'Gosh,' she exclaimed. 'You look very pale. I heard you didn't enjoy the dark. Are you okay?'

'I'm fine,' Maya responded, washing her hands in the adjacent basin.

'Okay, well, that's good,' Anna smirked, floating out of the toilet on her long, lean legs.

Maya rolled her eyes and sighed. I need to get to bed, she realised, suddenly feeling very tired. She emerged from the toilets to find Elijah waiting for her.

'How are you feeling?' he enquired, genuine concern on his face and in his voice.

'I'm okay,' Maya said. 'Thank you so much for your help. I really appreciate it.' She smiled at him.

'You know, Maya,' he continued. 'Being afraid of the dark is often just a symptom of claustrophobia.'

'Really?' Maya answered, surprised. 'That's so weird because when I fly I get quite anxious and I've never been able to go into small caves. At school, when we did potholing, I couldn't bring myself to do it. I had to sit it out.'

'You suffer from claustrophobia,' he confirmed. 'You did great tonight. You proved to yourself that you can overcome the fear.'

'So I'm not just a scaredy-cat girl then, like everyone's probably thinking,' she sighed, starting to walk down the corridor to the exit.

'No, Maya, you're not a scaredy-cat girl,' he laughed, opening the door for her.

The next morning, she left the hotel early and drove across town to the location of the three-day conference. The driveway up to the large complex was long and sweeping and she could see marquees being erected in the far field—no doubt for the 'team activity' later today, she thought, rolling her eyes.

She pulled up in the car park, found a space and read through her notes for her presentation later that day. Okay, I think I'm good to go, she thought, turning the last page of the scribbled notes over and stuffing them in her handbag. As she jumped out the car and smoothed down her dress, the General Manager pulled up alongside her. He nodded in her direction and Maya reached for her suitcase, slowly getting her things together, as she'd received the unsaid message that he wanted to talk to her.

Peter was a quiet man and Maya found him interesting; he seemed to play the fine line between genuinely caring for his staff and doing his Master's bidding quite well, or that's how it seemed from the outside. He smiled as he approached.

'Maya,' he exclaimed. 'How are you? It's been a while since I've seen you.'

'I'm good,' Maya said, but found herself at a loss to add anything else to the statement.

'I hear many patients are taking up the offer of having their bloods taken at home and the hospitals are grateful for the service. How are your new staff getting on?' he enquired.

'Really good. Really keen,' Maya responded. 'It's nice to have a full team and share the load more. I think Charlie was about to buckle with the workload,' she added, feeling giving him a mention was the right thing to do, as he worked such long hours without complaint.

'I was speaking to the CEO of the company you use for the nurses yesterday,' he said, stopping at the front door of the hotel. 'She felt that things were going well. I was surprised to hear that, given Anna's report to me the other day.'

'There have been some issues,' Maya admitted. 'However, I think it's right to allow Sarah the chance to right these things without escalating it. I feel sometimes we can be too quick to change, too quick to pull in top management and it destroys relationships. We don't really have another viable option for the delivery of this service. We need to keep the relationship on an even keel.'

'That's true,' Peter said, looking up from his phone. 'However, we also need to deliver the service without hiccup—a difficult balance,' he concluded.

As he uttered these words, Maya caught a flash of something across her mind. She clearly heard the words: *And you aren't in the right place on this planet—you should be playing a different game.* She blinked rapidly trying to understand what had just happened.

'Maya?' he said, staring at her. 'Are you okay?'

'Yes, yes, fine, thanks. Just tired.'

'At the start of conference? That's not a good sign,' he chuckled, opening the door for her.

Maya smiled and stepped forward, still trying to make sense of what had happened. His eyes indicated they acknowledged what she had just heard, and it had indeed come from him, but she knew if she said anything he wouldn't have a clue what she was talking about and would probably label her more emotional than he had already allocated to her.

What just happened? she pondered again as she checked in and went to drop her bags in her room, which was thankfully ready early.

Once she'd located the room down an array of winding corridors, she sat down on the comfy bed. She breathed deeply and closed her eyes.

Tal, she enquired. Are you there?

At first, she felt just a strange kind of static, but after a minute or so she sensed the familiar presence. She recounted to him what she had seen and heard in her mind but, as she did so, she felt another energy come in from her right shoulder.

It felt colder and immediately told her that Peter thought she was pretty useless and that she should prepare herself for a new role. Tal looked across to the scratching Demon alighting on the table across the room, wanting nothing more than to flick it out of the planetary atmosphere and back to its demonic lair, but he held strong, knowing that this was part of something Maya had to learn about the unseen energies of this realm.

Maya shuddered, bringing Tal's attention back to her. He watched quietly as she seemed to dismiss the other energy she was feeling and focus her attention back to him.

You heard his thoughts but they were not of his ego, Tal explained. *They were of his Higher Self. The ego is concerned with the 3D world, Maya—your title, your job, how you're performing based on the box you're supposed to fit into. But the Higher Self— that's more concerned with achieving what you really came to Earth to do and to assist and support that development. Peter's Higher Self is here to help you. You need to remember that in the weeks ahead,* he finished.

Maya nodded. The message had come over clearly. She paused, remembering a book she had read a few months ago. She felt she needed to clarify something.

'But to intrude and overhear his thoughts—is that not invading his personal space and not considered good spiritual etiquette?' she said out loud. 'I mean, I'd be horrified if people could hear *my* thoughts and listened in without seeking consent.'

That's true, Tal confirmed. *But that message was clearly meant for you to hear.*

Maya nodded, rolling her shoulders and trying to release the tension she felt there.

With spiritual gifts come the responsibility to use them correctly and in a way that serves the collective consciousness. Many times this has not happened—think black witches, Tal said, showing her the stereotypical view of a bad witch casting spells over a big pot.

You've been told these tales are myths, but don't be so sure they aren't real. The thing is, the Fallen Ones, they must tell you some truths or the Law of Karma will prevent them making the progress they want to make, to further their agenda on this planet of free will.

'Free will!' Maya snorted. 'Really? I don't feel like I have free will here. Believe me, I would not be here at stupid work if I had free will to do anything!'

Tal paused, choosing to ignore this comment. He could see from her vibrational energy that any wisdom shared about this wouldn't be integrated by her right now. She wasn't ready.

Within all things are truths and lies woven together, he quietly offered.

Maya tried to grasp the lesson Tal was clearly trying to help her with, but her mind was struggling to process his words. She grabbed a pad of paper and a pen laid out on the desk in front of the bed and scribbled a few key words down, hoping to come back to it later and give it further thought. Taking a glance at her phone in her bag she realised that the opening session was due to start in five minutes.

She hurried out the door, applying lip gloss as she went.

She moved quickly down the hall to the lift and soon found herself in a large room filled with people. Maya was struck by a huge sense of impostor syndrome as she sat down next to one of her team. She just felt like she didn't belong there. The problem was she didn't know where she *did* belong and she was in so deep with regards to the salary and expectations, not only of her family but the expectations she had of herself, that she felt there was no way out either. Maya desperately wanted to have a house and some land and to enjoy days gardening and caring for animals but couldn't see how she could ever get enough money to do this. A familiar feeling of frustration started to rise in her. It was like an internal fight but she couldn't work out who she was fighting and what for. She felt tears threaten as she thought about her children at home with Jacob again while she was here. She never had enough time for them, or enough time to build a meaningful relationship with the man she loved.

She sighed, leaning back on her chair. It was all just snatched pieces of something that had the potential to be so much more. She fidgeted in her seat, suddenly aware her tights were itchy and uncomfortable and she would give anything to be in her pyjamas or jodhpurs or joggers, anything but a restrictive business dress and stockings.

'Hey,' Paul smiled, sitting down next to her. 'How's tricks?'

Paul used to report to Maya and the two still had a good relationship. Paul could talk about company car choices for hours and deliberate over various models for days before making a decision. Yet every car she'd signed off for him, to her it looked exactly the same.

'I'm good,' she smiled. 'What about you? How are the boys?' she enquired.

'Loud and growing,' he sighed, turning his head to the front as the lights began to fade and the music started up.

Maya sat and listened to various presentations about the achievements of the company and certain individuals over the next few hours. She mused that a lot of the people given recognition seemed to have achieved their successes on the backs of other people, or had done things that five other colleagues she could name had also done, and then spent an equal amount of time worried she was just jealous and it was her ego speaking to her.

The day finally wrapped up and she scurried upstairs with everyone else to get changed for dinner in the twenty minutes they were given. She showered, dressed quickly and grabbed her phone to ring home.

'Hey, Mum,' Faith bellowed, sounding reasonably cheerful. 'Guess what?'

'No idea,' Maya answered. 'What?'

'I rode Pilot today. He was crazy. He tried to dump me.'

Great, Maya thought. Teaching my horse bad habits. But she simply responded with an, 'Oh, okay, but you didn't actually fall off, right?'

'Nah, it was fine,' Faith said, chewing mouthfuls of something. 'Here's Dad.'

'Hi, love,' Maya started.

'Hi,' Jacob sighed. He sounded tired and flat.

Maya took a deep inward breath, suppressing the urge to lash out. Here she was working away, making the money in a job she didn't really like while he was at home. Why couldn't he at least be a little chirpy? She steadied herself.

'You sound down. What's up?'

'Kids, Maya. Kids arguing with me, with each other. The house is a mess and I'm sick of tidying it.'

'Well, just take it easy. Have a movie night,' she suggested.

'Whatever,' he responded curtly.

'Right,' Maya snapped. 'I've got to go.'

'Of course you do,' Jacob replied hotly.

Maya stabbed at the hang up button, feeling the anger boiling within her. Furious and frustrated, she applied the rest of her makeup and headed downstairs, seething with thoughts of how selfish and lazy Jacob could be sometimes.

Jacob let the phone fall on the sofa and lay back, rubbing his hands through his hair.

'Dad,' Zidan shrieked from somewhere behind him. 'Faith hit me and told me to crawl in a hole and die.'

'Brilliant,' Jacob muttered, staring at the ceiling. 'What's the point?' he groaned. Where were they going with all of this?

He felt a rising sense of despair. Maya is always away while he's trapped at home, expected to be this great house-husband, supposed to feel grateful for her paying for their big country home which always needed cleaning when he would have, as he'd explained to Maya years ago, been happy in a wooden cabin. He was fighting to steer the older two away from twenty-four hour mobile phones but it felt like a losing battle. Maya came in and out of their lives. He never really felt a genuine connection with her any more. Even when she *was* at home, she was thinking about work and recently she seemed more and more distant. When she rings she only has a few minutes, always wanting to rattle through pleasantries and then dash off to whatever dinner she was going to.

'Dad,' Aurora shouted, standing with her hands on her hips at the lounge door. She threw her hands up in the air when he turned to look at her. 'What's for dinner? We're starving.'

'Go put some beans and toast on,' he muttered, rubbing the front of his head.

'Dad, seriously! I want some proper food.'

'Well, grate cheese on it, then!' he exploded. 'Just go away and leave me alone,' he growled, throwing the cushion at the door as she slammed it.

He was being a shit Dad in that moment, he knew it, but he just had a sense of hopelessness tonight. And, besides, they only told Maya the bad things that happened while she was away. They won't tell her about the homemade lasagne and marshmallows on the fire last night or the great dog walk they had three days ago where he spun them around and made a tepee for them out of sticks or how he ran Faith to her friend's yesterday. No, none of that. They'll just say they were starved and had to make their own dinner all week. He had in recent days considered whether he should try to get a full-time job again instead of picking up odd jobs, but the truth was they all seemed pointless. Most jobs were what he would describe as fake, or gigs that are paid far too little for hard manual labour. He didn't agree with most of the way society was going and didn't want to be part of the digital revolution and red tape tickbox jobs. Most of the time he felt like he'd stumbled onto the wrong planet. How did he really make a meaningful difference for his family? But then if he *did* get a full-time job, he couldn't trust the system to look after his children. He was deeply concerned about some of the topics the schools were teaching the kids and often felt they came home mildly brainwashed rather than being encouraged to make up their own minds about things.

He turned over, squashing his face into the side of the sofa. I mean, Maya feels he uses her sometimes because he smokes and he spends money on work tools but really, she spends far more on bloody horses that she isn't here to care for most of the time. He debated how many burgers he could make out of the four-legged money munchers before reluctantly peeling himself off the sofa to see if Aurora had burnt the kitchen down yet.

Perhaps, he mused later while tucking the two youngest in after reading them their bedtime stories, when they went away next week they could talk about some of this. He sighed as he figured it would be the same outcome as always. Maya would start talking over him and then he would get flustered and wouldn't be able think straight and before long it would descend into a screaming match. The island was too beautiful for that, he thought, smiling, as he recalled the stunning beaches and aquamarine water. No, the arguments would have to wait, he concluded.

8

Maya sank back into her chair as the awards and recognition speeches finished and the night's entertainment began. The company seemed to have spared no expense on acrobats and dancers, claiming that we, the employees, had earned a night of celebration. She felt woozy from the wine that Heather had kept pouring into her glass, and the familiar feeling of comfortableness washed over her. Surely it wasn't so bad—fine wine, nice food, a good wage and a decent car—maybe all this stuff that had happened since that night at her sister's had just been in her head.

The music changed and she looked around as people got up from their chairs and moved to different tables to socialise.

'Hey,' Tyler popped up behind her, putting his hand on her shoulder. She turned and looked at him. 'You want a drink from the bar?'

Tyler had been in a team with her a few years ago and now worked in the business management department. He was well thought of by the powers that be and seemed to harbour a soft spot for Maya.

'Sure, why not?' she said, smiling as she rose from her seat. 'Vodka and Diet Coke, please.'

'Okay, I'll be right back.' He gestured for her to wait and swung around in the direction of the bar.

Maya continued to watch the dancing until Anna appeared next to her.

'Hi, Maya,' she offered, after staring at her for a few seconds.

'Hi,' Maya answered.

'You having a good night?'

'Not bad,' Maya responded, wary of Anna's intentions.

'I got some feedback from your team as part of your mid-year review. It was very positive.'

'You seem surprised,' Maya bit back, brazened by the alcohol.

'No, not at all,' Anna answered, softy fiddling with the small red clutch bag in her hand. 'I know your team think a lot of you, Maya. I've always admired your ability to get them to rally behind you,' she confessed. 'I started my management career at a difficult point in my life. I found it hard to relate to people during my divorce with my alcoholic ex,' Anna supplied, in a rare moment of vulnerability.

Maya looked at her, watching something distant cross her face that Maya would have placed as past trauma and a cry for help, but before she could respond, Anna took a deep breath and continued.

'The thing is, that's not how you get ahead. It's great being an inspiration to people and all, but you aren't going to make it up another level to where I'm at with that attitude.'

Maya stood speechless.

'Attitude,' she was finally able to say, while blinking rapidly and watching the vulnerable woman in front of her disappear, the mask covering her face once again and a darker, more aggressive look drawing over her features.

'There's a lot of fine paperwork detail needed in this job also, Maya,' she carried on, before stopping abruptly as the looming figure of Tyler approached with two drinks in his hands.

Maya watched as Anna turned and elbowed her way into a nearby group that was talking to Peter.

'What did she mean by that last comment?' she wondered out loud.

'What?' Tyler said, now standing in front of her looking confused.

'Oh, nothing. It's just Anna throwing her weight around again.'

'Yeah, well,' he said, passing Maya her drink and clinking the glasses. 'She's floating on the good sales results at the moment. I was in Belfast last week—seems they're handing the drug out like candy there. I didn't realise there were that many severe patients over there.'

'Mmm,' Maya mumbled, taking a sip of her drink. 'I think Dr Fraser uses it for moderate and light diagnosis as well, which I don't think is a good idea,' she griped, suspecting the doctor clearly hadn't fully considered the risk/benefit ratio.

'Yeah,' Tyler answered, sipping his drink. 'But he speaks for us, like, all the time. It's like he's on our payroll!'

'I know,' Maya rolled her eyes. 'He sure is lining his pockets.'

Then, becoming irritated with this line of conversation, she smiled and changed tack.

'What's new with you, anyway? I haven't seen you for a while. How's the new role in Business Management?'

'Yeah, it's cool,' Tyler said, resting his arm on the ledge next to her. 'Things still aren't great at home but hey, what can you do?' he shrugged.

'Still not getting on with your wife?' Maya enquired.

'Let's sit down,' Tyler answered, putting his hand on the small of her back and guiding her past an inquisitive Ben to the tables in the far corner of the room.

Maya sat and listened as he described the deterioration of his marriage and, in fairness, could relate to some of the things he relayed to her. The room had quietened after the performances had finished and some people had already made their exit. Tyler seemed to have moved closer to her and his arm was now touching hers. Maya started to feel uncomfortable and rubbed her head, leaning back in the chair. She wasn't sure she liked where this was going. Sure, Tyler was attractive, and loaded, which would solve quite a few of her financial problems, but a deeper part of her, even through the alcohol, knew it wasn't right.

'Come on,' Tyler whispered next to her ear, snapping her out of her thoughts. 'Let me walk you to your room. You look a little drunk,' he finished, chuckling.

Maya stood up, wobbling and grabbing a bottle of still water from the centre of the table, knowing with certainty she would need it later. Tyler guided her down the corridor and into the lift, pausing to ask her what floor she was on.

'Oh, me too,' he answered brightly when she told him. 'Fancy that!'

As the lift door closed, he stared at Maya with a questioning look in his eyes. I could, Maya thought to herself. I mean, he's gorgeous and he wants me and I could. But even as the words formed in her head, she knew she couldn't and didn't want to. He moved closer and as his leg touched hers the doors opened and a couple of colleagues got in, clutching bottles of wine, clearly headed to someone's room for an after-party.

Tyler sprang back and stood facing the group, making polite conversation. It was just long enough for Maya to come to her senses and realise she definitely didn't want what he was suggesting and she was going to have to say something. Sure, it might feel good for a few hours but on a deeper level she knew it would take her off path, whatever path that was. It would be wrong. It wouldn't solve anything, it would just create more problems and it wasn't right. She didn't want to break Jacob's trust—despite all their issues, something unspoken bound them together that would be broken if she ever cheated on him.

The doors opened again and everyone exited the lift. The room party group turned left and Maya took a right towards her room, with Tyler trailing after her.

'This is me,' she said turning by her door. 'Thanks for seeing me here. I do feel very woozy. I'm such a lightweight,' she rambled, hoping he would get the message.

Tyler stood looking at her.

'Shall I come in?' he asked after a pause. 'I could make

you some coffee. Help sober you up?' he laughed raising an eyebrow.

'No. No, it's okay. I have a really bad headache coming on.' Which isn't a lie, Maya thought grimly as a pulsing started to pound at the sides of her forehead.

'Okay,' he said, stepping back and looking dejected. 'I guess I'll see you tomorrow, then,' he said over his shoulder coldly, as he turned to carry on walking down the corridor.

Maya had the distinct feeling he was seething about the waste of time that had been and that he should have chosen another girl to chat up tonight, one that wouldn't lead him on and then drop him.

I didn't do that, Maya thought, putting her key to the door and entering her room. *But you did*, the voice came back in her head. *Now you've pissed him off.*

Oh, go away! Maya screamed into her head, flopping face first onto the bed and groaning.

She woke several hours later and made her way to the bath-room, feeling like she was aboard a ship in a storm. She knew she was in that horrible mid-way place of feeling awful but not quite awful enough to hurl her guts up. She brushed her teeth, drank some of the water she'd thankfully brought up with her and lay back down looking at her phone. Six a.m. Great. She had to get up in an hour and pretend she was fresh and bright for the day's meetings.

The alarm went off at seven and she dragged herself out of the bed, robotically going about preparing for the day. She couldn't face breakfast, choosing instead to grab the packet of biscuits on the tea tray and scoff them down as she headed out the door and down to the meeting room.

Shit, she thought as she got in the lift. She didn't ring Jacob back last night and now she didn't have time. She'd have to ring him on the road tonight. Maya felt a huge guilt crawl across her. God, I should have realised quicker where Tyler was trying to take things last night.

Urgh, she groaned inwardly. I'm just a bad person all round.

She caught sight of herself in the mirror—her makeup done, her hair twisted into a pleat in the middle of her head, a black top and dark blue pencil skirt with black heels and skin-coloured tights. She looked the part but she felt like an impostor. She couldn't look herself in the eyes and she certainly didn't want to see what was really going on behind them. The truth was, though, she already knew; sadness, a sense of being utterly lost, not knowing who she was, holding on to something that didn't feel real but that she couldn't let go of. Fear, guilt, misalignment—it would all be there and today she couldn't deal with that. She just needed to get through the day in one piece.

She exited the lift and entered the meeting room. Many of the team were already there, clutching coffee mugs in their hands, some looking bright and breezy—the early-to-bed water drinkers, Maya guessed—while others varied from looking rough to being ten seconds away from throwing up.

Maya found a table at the back and sat down, pulling out her speech notes and going over them one last time. She heard Anna's voice getting nearer and looked up to see her weaving her way through the tables and chairs with a tall, suited, dark haired man in tow.

'Ah, Maya. Morning!' Anna sang. 'I wanted to introduce you to our new Medical Director. He will be replacing Elijah.'

'Hi.' Maya offered her hand to the already outstretched one but pulled back after a brief shake. The man's energy felt yucky and she had a strong urge to escape through the nearest door, but she forced herself to stay put with a fake smile plastered on her face.

'We're so lucky to have Gary join us. He's still a practising GP as well,' Anna continued.

Great, another one, Maya grumbled to herself.

Gary had opened his mouth and started to reel off a list of his accomplishments and achievements. Like I asked, thought Maya, feeling his ego swirling around her aggressively.

'I'm sure you'll get to work with Gary a lot soon, Maya. He's going to take a look at all the contracting and compliance aspects of our services.'

'Right,' Maya said slowly. 'Is there a problem?'

'Well, we'll see, won't we?' Anna shot back. 'I just feel it's a vulnerable area of yours and your team's and, like you said yourself, you don't have a background in compliance so I'm sure Gary's expertise will come in handy. He's much more thorough than our last Medical Director,' she added, looking across at Gary who gave her a smug grimace.

'Oh, here comes Ben. Let me introduce you to him,' Anna said, grabbing Gary's arm abruptly and dragging him off.

Heather came up behind Maya as she watched them leave. 'I don't like him already,' she mumbled. 'He'll be her little bitch doing her bidding to get to the top.'

Heather, always a good judge of character, Maya thought. She turned and looked at her colleague, offering a tight-lipped smile but saying nothing.

'Ten minutes to starting,' the presenter announced. 'Grab a coffee and use the toilets now if you need to. We'll be starting with an update from Maya on our post-prescription services.'

Maya felt a rising fear and panic in her chest, threatening to interfere with her breathing. What's wrong with me? she thought. I love presenting. Why do I feel like this?

Maya quickly left the room and made her way to the toilets. Once the cubicle door was shut behind her, she burst into tears and sank down to sit on the toilet lid. I can't do this. I can't do this, she repeated to herself. I'm losing it. Oh my God, what am I going to do? She grasped her head in her hands, desperately trying to get control of her breathing. It's all messed up. It's all messed up! she wailed to herself in her head.

Maya stared at the floor. Come on, come on, get back into your robotic place. Just do it. Somehow, she couldn't find it, like the programme was disrupted and no matter how much she tried to flick the reset button, it wasn't working. Her wiring had changed. She'd felt it start after her encounter with

Gary and Anna, like they had ignited it. Their energy was horrible; it made her feel so small and useless.

She calmed her breathing, remembering what Lesley had taught her about grounding and seeing deep roots coming out of her feet into the Earth. As she visualized this she felt calmer, felt the familiar presence and a soft pressure on her shoulder.

It'll be okay. It'll be okay, a firm, kind voice reached into her head.

Okay, okay, Maya sniffed. I want to believe that, she sobbed to the voice, screwing her eyes up and praying for help. I can't fall apart. I can't. I have too much responsibility.

She scooped up the bag that she had chucked on the floor by the toilet and exited the cubicle, proceeding to try to fix her face in the mirror in the remaining minutes she had left.

She came back into the room just as the doors were closing.

'There she is,' Anna pointed, talking to the crew who were running the stage set. 'Where have you been? Come on, you're up,' she chided. 'You didn't rehearse either. Oh yes, I forget,' she carried on, clearly assuming Maya was listening to her, despite not looking at her once. 'You like to be natural and authentic. I, however, think it's much better to practise. It gives a more professional, polished look,' she announced, now turning to look at Maya with a growing triumph on her face as she noticed Maya was clearly upset about something.

Maya pushed past Anna and up onto the stage. Something took over her—a fierce need to stand her ground against something unseen. She started flicking through her slides and bringing to life the emotional aspects of the disease and how her team had helped to support patients in these areas. She wove passion into her figures and painted a picture of something she was proud to be part of and—that was true—she *was* proud to be part of a team that delivered value to patients and healthcare professionals and didn't just charge exorbitant prices and give nothing back.

As she finished and introduced the next speaker, the crowd applauded loudly and Maya felt in that moment some genuine appreciation for what she did. She took her seat and Lucy leaned over and hugged her from behind.

'Great job, Boss. That was awesome! You made us sound like the Super Nurse Team and I know our Irish colleagues will be so grateful that you flew the flag for all their work too.'

Maya patted her arm and sat back in her chair, trying to still the queasiness in her stomach. Yeah, she definitely had a hangover.

✳

The presentations flowed on and eventually it was time to leave. Maya stood up stiffly and went about saying her good-byes and thank you's to the team before grabbing her suitcase and heading out to the car. As she crossed the reception hall, she caught sight of Tyler who, on seeing her, turned his back and continued his conversation with Anna and another member of senior management. Maya sighed to herself. Great. Another person who has influence on Anna and who now dislikes me. What, I'm basically not worth speaking to or acknowledging now because I wouldn't sleep with him? What a dickhead, she confirmed to herself, unlocking her car and throwing her bags in.

✦

Maya turned the car north and felt the familiar relief. North. It was like where her soul was headed, whereas south was the direction her ego wanted to go. Where did that come from? she mused, swerving around an indecisive car that clearly didn't know whether to head north, south, east or west. Do cars have egos too? she chuckled.

As Maya headed up the motorway she slipped further and further into a black hole of emotions—guilt from last night, fear as to what Anna was up to and a complete feeling of overwhelm sitting like lead in her body. As she grappled with her emotions, she looked at the central reservation that sped by. I could just swerve into that now, she thought, looking down at the odometer which read eighty-five miles per hour. Geesh, was she really going that fast? These BMWs were deceptive with speed.

She could, she refocused on her previous thoughts, and it would all just stop. I mean, let's face it, Jacob would get a big payout if I died at work. He and the kids would be okay.

Tears threatened behind her eyes and above her a dark

swirl of Demons feasted on what remained of her energy, feeding even more negative thoughts of blame and self-doubt to her as she drove. The Angels above looked on, unable to touch her, waiting patiently until she brought herself out of the negativity she was entangled in and came back to an energy field that could allow them once again to reach her.

Maya pulled the car into the drive. It was a little after eleven p.m. and the house was quiet and dark. She only had tomorrow to pack and organise everything before their trip to the island.

Maya sighed, noticing Jacob had messaged her earlier complaining that Faith had left horse food everywhere and the rats had got in. His text finished with a sarcastic note about how nice of her it was to ring. She banged her head off the steering wheel, deciding the only thing she could do right now was crawl into bed.

She made her way through the house and paused at the living room door. The television was on and Jacob was asleep, sprawled out on the sofa. She decided to leave him, having one lingering glance at how peaceful he looked, before going up to bed and pulling the covers over her head, hoping the world would be a better place for her when she woke up.

Maya opened her eyes to the sound and smell of a steaming mug of tea being gently placed on her bedside table. She saw Jacob turn quietly and walk round to his side of the bed.

'Yeah,' she said, pulling her hair out of her eyes and sitting up.

He said nothing, just stared out of the window, watching the sheep grazing in the field outside.

'You okay?' Maya asked. 'Thanks for the tea,' she added, scooping up the mug and cradling it in her hands.

'Mummy!' Amy shrieked, as she raced into the bedroom and jumped up onto the bed, narrowly missing the mug.

Maya quickly set it down again, managing to save most of the contents from spilling over the bedsheets, and wrapped her arms around her youngest.

'Hey, Baby,' she soothed, smelling Amy's hair and kissing her face. 'How have you been?'

'I'm good,' Amy smiled, looking up at Maya through messy curls. 'I'm packed. I'm all packed!'

'Already?' Maya exclaimed. 'Wow, you *are* organised. Well, you can help me, then, can't you?'

'Mum, Dad says we can only have one bag each. That's not much room, you know. Isn't that right, Dad?' Amy said, tugging on his sleeve as he continued to stare out of the window.

'That's right, pumpkin,' Jacob nodded, ruffling her hair.

'I'm going to get some breakfast. I'm really hungry, Mummy. And then we're going to pack for you, okay?'

'Okay,' Maya said, watching Amy jump down from the bed and scuttle out of the room.

'She's lively,' Maya commented, looking back at Jacob.

'Always,' Jacob confirmed. 'Yesterday she talked for ten minutes about the holes in my socks. Like, a whole ten minutes! I didn't know whether to laugh or cry.'

Maya chuckled, returning her attention to her mug of tea and sipping it slowly.

'So what needs doing?' she asked Jacob.

'Lots,' he replied. 'The animals need cleaning out, you need to sort the stables and the feed room and have a word with Faith. She's not looking after those horses right and I said when you got them, Maya, I don't do horses. I don't want to be involved. Tanya's coming over at three so we can show her what needs doing with the dogs and cats while we're away so, yeah, a lot to do.'

'Okay,' Maya replied, pulling the duvet off her legs, but really wanting to pull it back over her head. 'I'll get dressed.'

Jacob left the room and could be heard a short while later trying to get Zidan out of his pit. Maya sighed as she dressed, staring out the window and wishing she could just find the time to sit and watch the world go by. But, she mused to herself, even if she found the time she wouldn't be able to relax enough to enjoy it.

Oh bugger, she thought, swinging round to pick up her phone from her bedside table. She had a call with Lesley at ten. Great. That's not going to go down well with Jacob.

'Maya,' he yelled from the hall. 'I'm going out to get fags and milk. You need anything?'

'No, take your time,' she answered, thanking the divine intervention that meant, by her calculations, he would be back just as the call would finish.

✦

'Hey,' Lesley waved as the picture loaded on the computer. 'How's my gorgeous Scottish girl?'

Maya smiled, which just made her worry she was going to burst into tears before she even started talking. Maya chose instead to explain quite factually what had happened at conference and, in particular, how the interaction with Anna and Gary had gone. Then she listened patiently as Lesley explained the basics of energy.

'You see, Maya,' Lesley began, pushing the chair back from her desk, 'there's so much we don't see that happens when we interact with each other. People take energy from other people when they are negative themselves or narcissistic in nature. Highly egoistic people can send harsh, negative energy to you, which you then absorb and, in turn, they can steal your more positive energy, leaving you feeling depleted. It sounds like you're becoming more aware of all of this, but what you now need to learn is how to protect your energy.

'You see, Maya,' she carried on, after pausing to sip her tea, 'you're an Empath and that can be a curse when you don't understand it. Empaths feel others' emotions and often mistake it as their own. They're very vulnerable to psychic attack and can have their energy stolen easily. However, once you learn how to protect and use your gift correctly it becomes a powerful tool. I'm going to teach you how to do that.

'Firstly, what Gary and Anna did was send you their demonic negative energy and you absorbed it. Next time, I want you to form a shield so it bounces back to them. Imagine this shield surrounding you every morning, protecting you, sending negative energy back to where it came from. Ask yourself, when your emotions suddenly change, is this my energy or is this someone else's? When you feel your child's pain or discomfort, understand it is there and that you don't have to fix it, just coach them through it. It's theirs to experience and learn from.'

'Okay, okay, I think I understand,' Maya nodded, suddenly feeling more positive and hopeful.

'And Maya, remember—fear and guilt are negative emotions. Be kind to yourself. Understand that there are those on this planet that know they can manipulate the human race through the negative energies of fear and guilt. We all make mistakes; it's what we learn and how we act next time that counts. Be kind—in every moment you're doing everything you can at that time.'

'Okay,' Maya nodded, although she knew she wasn't at a point to believe that about herself, maybe not yet anyway. She could do better a lot of the time, like the night with Tyler. She shouldn't have let it get to the point where he thought he had a chance. She took a deep breath and relayed her thoughts to Lesley.

'Yes, but you also could have gone to bed with him, Maya, and you didn't. You did the right thing, so learn from your mistakes but love yourself and praise yourself also.'

'Okay, but that feels very alien to me,' Maya admitted. 'I mean, growing up, if I did something wrong my parents would go on about it for days.'

'Yes, but that's a story you no longer need to define yourself by,' Lesley stated softly. 'We must break the negative conditioning from our parents if we want to be free of our negative circles of thought.'

'Yeah, that makes sense,' Maya concluded.

Lesley set her a few exercises and then warned her she may feel a little ill as she released some of the unhelpful belief systems her body was holding onto. Maya acknowledged this, not really understanding what she meant by it, and then hung up just as the tyres of Jacob's car were heard crunching on the gravel outside. That was good timing, she thought, heading downstairs to greet him.

Later that day Maya mentally checked off her to do list, which Jacob kept adding to, and concluded she wasn't doing badly at all. As she folded away the clean kitchen towels, she was alerted to Tanya's arrival by barking dogs, and shoved the rest of the laundry into the washing machine before heading out to greet her.

'Hey,' she waved, as Tanya climbed out of her truck and descended into frantic dogs and kids.

Maya showed her the food store for each animal, as Jacob trailed behind them, smoking and adding his input as they went.

'Don't go in with the horse,' Jacob warned Tanya. 'That one—I swear it's out to get me,' he pointed, deadpan, to Shadow, who seemed to understand what Jacob was saying and, snorting, turned her tail on him.

'No, she isn't, Jacob!' Maya shrieked. 'Ignore him,' she reassured Tanya. 'He just wants to turn them into burgers. Do you fancy a coffee?'

'Sure. Time for quick one before I help gather in the sheep,' Tanya said, encouraging the crowing cockerel in front of her to move out of the way.

Once inside and coffees made, the two ladies sat down in the kitchen. Maya rested her elbow on the table, suddenly feeling very drained.

'Are you okay?' Tanya asked, looking up from the list of instructions Maya had handed her.

'I just feel a bit off,' Maya groaned, taking a deep breath and closing her eyes.

'I don't know how you do it,' Tanya retorted, blowing the top of her coffee to cool it. 'I really don't know how you do it. You're doing too much, being a Mum, running Aurora to ice skating, Faith to pony club, working full time, all these animals. When do you get time to rest?'

'I don't,' Maya said. 'I can't remember the last time I did nothing for the day. It was probably before I had Faith. It's just been non-stop for fourteen years. I didn't even really get time off for maternity, in all honesty, always worrying about money.'

'Maya,' Tanya sighed, taking her hand, 'You'll burn yourself out. Please try to relax while you're on holiday.'

'I will,' Maya assured her, showing her to the door and thanking her for holding the fort while they were away.

＊

Maya finished the essential jobs, fed the kids and was collapsed in bed by the time Jacob came in from fixing the chicken run.

'Hey,' he said, slipping under the covers and drawing her close to him. 'You're in bed early.'

'Yeah, not feeling so hot,' Maya groaned, pulling the covers higher over her shoulders and resting one hand on top of the arm that he had snaked round her waist.

'Of course you're not,' he said, half-joking, half-serious. 'You're always ill when you're at home, but you never seem to be ill when you're at work.'

'Oh, come on, Jacob, that's not fair!'

Truthfully, she didn't have the energy to argue about anything right now. Jacob sensed this and rested his head on top of hers, drawing circles on her back.

'Fancy some, you know, that thing we did and the four children appeared?' he said with a smirk in his voice.

'Maybe later,' Maya mumbled, half asleep.

Jacob rolled on his back and looked at the ceiling. Here she was, back from work and exhausted again. They got all of her, that workplace—her energy, her time, her passion and they, her family, had to scramble around with whatever shreds were left. It was like a never-ending trap pulling her further and further away from him and the kids, yet she didn't seem able to see it. He swallowed the frustration rising in his throat and turned his thoughts to planning the route to the ferry terminal in the morning.

'Come on!' Jacob shouted out the window of the packed Land Rover. 'We really need to go. Zidan, how long does it take you to poo, for God's sake?'

'Oh, yuck!' Faith groaned, screwing up her nose so that all her freckles became one big freckle. 'That's gross, Dad.'

'What, pooing? No it's not. It's perfectly natural. I mean, even you, an angry teenager, poos.'

'DAD!' both Faith and Aurora shouted in unison. 'Shut up!'

'Get off me, Faith!' Amy protested from a squashed position in the back seat. 'You can't have all the room.'

'Move your great big donkey and you'll *have* more room,' Faith shoved back at her.

'It's not a donkey. It's a horse called Charlie,' Amy glared at her, while flinging the teddy by its head and swinging it across the back seat.

'Ouch!' Zidan shrieked as he was hit by said teddy while climbing into the car. 'My eye! I can't see!'

'Oh, shut up before you shit yourself again,' Faith grumbled.

'FAITH!' Maya fumed, spinning around from the front seat to look at her. 'Don't say that to your brother!'

'Whatever,' Faith responded, jamming her earphones in and closing her eyes.

'Where the hell are we going anyway?' Aurora piped up. 'I hate being in the car.'

'Right!' Jacob roared. 'Shut up, sit down, put your seatbelts on and let's go.'

Silence fell over the car as Jacob released the handbrake, pulled out of the drive and accelerated down the road to the junction below.

✳

As they got nearer and nearer the ferry terminal, Maya felt worse and worse, to the point where, half an hour before the port, she ordered Jacob to pull over so that she could be sick. She sat in the heather by the side of the road, head in hands for five minutes, but nothing came. It felt like her body had been poisoned and she desperately needed to rid herself of the toxins. She thought back to what Lesley had said to her and groaned, holding her head tightly and clutching her stomach with the other hand.

It needs to come out, Tal reassured her, his presence appearing at her side. *All those toxic emotions and trapped negative energies. It all needs to clear so you can hear your true essence.*

True essence, Maya laughed. I feel like I'm dying, bloody true essence. Oh, beam me up, Scotty, she growled, picking herself up and making her way back to the car.

'Come on, Mum,' the kids chorused. 'We're going to be late!'

'Okay, okay,' she whispered, getting in the car and pulling the door shut. The car followed the winding road along the hillside before descending down towards the port.

'Morning!' a short, fat man shouted against the wind as Jacob wound down his window and handed him the tickets. 'Lane Three, please,' he said, gesturing to the right area of the port side.

Jacob drove into the waiting line, cut the engine and leaned back in his seat. He closed his eyes. The kids were arguing over who was going to eat the last of the creamy biscuits and Maya had a sudden urge to vomit.

'Shit,' she mumbled, opening the door of the car and stumbling outside.

'What!' Jacob shouted sitting upright from his position of blissful half-asleep, half-awake mode.

'Oh God,' Maya whined as she clutched her stomach and started to throw up, trying to aim the contents down a nearby drain. In the background she was vaguely aware of laughing and giggling as she gasped between retches and struggled for breath. Eventually it subsided and her shaky legs took her back to the car.

'Oh my God, Mum, that was hilarious!' Faith roared, as Maya stumbled back into the car and curled up in a ball, pulling her coat over her head.

'You sounded like a dying turkey,' Jacob choked between snorts. The whole car was laughing.

'Leave me alone, you horrible people,' Maya cried, debating whether she was going to be sick again.

The laughter and discussion about exactly what type of distressed animal she most resembled continued as she slipped in and out of a restless sleep, and she barely registered that they'd driven onto the car deck of the ferry.

'Maya,' Jacob nudged her. 'We have to go up on deck. You can't stay in the car. Come on.'

He helped her up the stairs to the main deck and deposited her in a seating area, where she quickly lay back down again, oblivious to what was going on around her.

'Mummy,' Amy shook her. 'Are you okay?'

'Mmm,' Maya groaned. 'I'm okay, Baby,' she said, patting the young girl's head. 'Go with Daddy. Mummy needs to rest,' she slurred.

She awoke a short time later, still feeling very rough but a little more together. She looked around and saw that Jacob had left a cup of tea on the table in front of her that had now gone cold. She sat up as he came round the corner with the kids.

'Hi, Mum,' Zidan said, throwing himself down next to her. 'Are you feeling better? We're nearly there. Look out the window. It's sooo cool!'

Jacob stood back, holding an empty can of beer.

'Starting early, I see,' Maya said dryly.

'Yeah, well, I thought we might have had a drink together and admire the scenery, but you're clearly too busy dying.'

Maya rolled her eyes and pushed herself up from her lying position just as the attendant announced it was time for car passengers to return to their vehicles.

She didn't remember anything about the drive to the holiday cottage and had only a vague memory of Jacob helping her up the stairs to the bedroom. The next time she opened her eyes it was morning and Jacob was not next to her in the bed.

9

The first sounds Maya became aware of were the lapping of the sea followed by the squawk of seabirds. She sat up, feeling like she had lost twenty pounds and her body had turned to jelly and been moulded back together.

Pushing the covers back, she followed the sounds to a small window and looked outside. The sun was just rising above the horizon. Below her, a small track bordered the house and, across from that, a narrow path, lined with small flowers and heather, led down to a bay with a red and white boat moored just offshore. The birds swept over the bay, alighting from the cliff faces at each side. Further out, the endless ocean was visible on the horizon. The atmosphere was calm and quiet and Maya felt her body sag, almost in surrender to the invisible arms holding her weak form.

She sat down on the chair next to the window and stared at the beauty of the scene in front of her. Silent tears tracked down her face as she felt for the first time in years a sense of peace.

Jacob appeared a little further down the lane coming back

from somewhere with the two youngest kids. He stopped to talk to someone and Maya strained to hear the conversation. An elderly woman was asking him how he was settling in and telling him she hoped his wife was feeling better. He nodded and passed through the gate into the front garden, leaving Amy and Zidan playing by the water's edge.

Soon enough she heard the thud on the stairs and Jacob appeared beside her. He knelt down, wiping one of the tears away from her cheek.

'It's beautiful,' Maya whispered. 'Thank you for bringing me here.'

He smiled, looking at her, and for the first time in as long as she could remember, she saw the reason why she had married him. She saw the spark that had made him unique, that had attracted her to him when all the others had seemed so dull and normal. She reached out for his hand, not having the words but grateful for the moment they were sharing.

It lasted about two minutes before Faith came into the bedroom, mumbling about the place being boring with nothing to do already and they both laughed and rolled their eyes at her.

'Come on, let's get some pancakes made,' Jacob suggested, pulling Maya to her feet.

✦

After breakfast was done and the dishes tidied away, they headed out to explore the local scenery.

'Dad, where are we going?… Wow, look at those rocks! They look like they're from the moon!' Zidan shouted, sitting up in his seat as the car made its way south to pick up the track Jacob had found when he'd first arrived.

'That's so cool. I want to climb them,' Zidan said, sitting back in his chair and grabbing one of the biscuits Faith was handing out from the back seat.

The car followed the winding road as it curved left and right and finally turned a corner to expose the huge expanse of beach and aquamarine sea.

'Wow!' Maya exclaimed, coming round from her half dozing state. 'That's absolutely beautiful.'

She leaned forward to get a better view. 'It's like something from a painting. It doesn't look real.'

'Well,' said Jacob, chuckling. 'Let's go spend some time down there, just to check.'

Maya smiled and nodded and a few minutes later Jacob parked up in a lay-by and the family made their way down the grassy track to an area that opened onto the beach.

As soon as Maya's feet hit the sand, she had a huge urge to take off her shoes and socks, despite the cold, and she left them on a bank of sand near the track. She felt the golden grains between her toes and she took a deep breath, raising her hands to the sky. The children were long gone, ripping clothes off and jumping in and out of the gently lapping waves, squealing at how cold the water was. Jacob had found himself a large rock to watch from and sat motionless, staring at the children, clearly lost in his own thoughts.

Maya remembered the exercise that Lesley had taught her

but that she hadn't been called to do yet, and grabbed a long stick of kelp root that lay on the beach. Carefully, she drew a spiral in the sand, big enough to enable her to walk between the lines. She started at the outer line of the spiral and walked slowly, following the path to the middle while thinking of everything she wanted to let go of.

Images flashed quickly through her mind, memories of being younger and of not feeling good enough, her Dad leaving for months on end again and again, fights with Jacob, feelings of anger and hurt at the words said. Images of leaving her children to drive to work, the memory of hearing that a young woman's death had been caused by a drug she'd sold, the conversations about hushing the incident up. Memories of being told what she should be or think or do. And then an image of a woman in a long dress walking in heather.

She gritted her teeth as she reached the middle and had an overwhelming feeling that she'd touched only the tip of the iceberg of what really needed to come out.

Okay, now, what had Lesley said? Oh yes, walk back the way you came, calling in and visualising everything you want. She started walking and then stopped—what *did* she want? Nothing came. It was a void. All she could think of is what she *didn't* want, what she wanted to run away from or let go of, but she didn't know what she *did* want. Why not? Because she didn't think anything was possible, she guessed. She'd become so programmed about what she could and couldn't have—society had told her exactly what she would and wouldn't achieve in the box that life had carved out for her.

She felt huge anger and frustration. How could she bring in abundance if she didn't even know what it looked like? I mean, it's a simple question. What did she want, apart from lots of money? Did she even want that? As soon as she thought it, she realised she didn't. She knew plenty of rich people that were totally miserable, and she'd had more than one chance to marry a rich man, but she knew she'd have had to close her eyes ten seconds before each kiss for lack of attraction. She snorted to herself. If she wanted money, she wouldn't have married Jacob. Yet she thought back to when he proposed—she'd had no doubt it was the right thing to do.

She sighed, stomping out of the circle as Jacob wandered over. She clearly needed to give this more thought.

'Hey, what are you doing?' he enquired, shoving her gently.

'Trying to sort my head out,' she responded, kicking the sand with her toes.

'Okay, well, it might take a bit more than some drawings in the sand. What *is* that, anyway?'

Maya explained the process to him and, to her surprise, Jacob walked to the edge of the circle and quietly followed her instructions. As he exited the circle, Maya noted how calm he seemed. Jacob was a tale of two men. He had times of anger and aggression like a raging bull, but equally he had times of complete calmness and peace, like a still pond on a summer's day. Maya could never find the peace to be that calm, or the energy to be that angry. She lived in a whirl of chaos somewhere between those two states. She needed control, control of herself, but how to get it? Well, she was still learning. She really felt that stopping other people's energies affecting her was the best start, and that was what she had agreed to work on the most in her last session with Lesley.

Together, Jacob and Maya extracted a blue-looking Zidan and Amy from the sea, gathered up the moaning teenagers laid on the sand dunes, and headed back to the car. They drove to another equally breathtaking spot and sat drinking tea while the kids kicked off their shoes and played at the edge of the Atlantic Ocean. They rolled among the tiny flowers of the Hebridean machair and picked out their favourite Highland cow from the herds on the heather covered hills.

As the sun set, they cooked fresh crab and potatoes and sat by the light of the fire while the kids played Monopoly in the next room. Few words were said but there was a silent acknowledgement that something was shifting, both for their relationship and for them as individuals, and Maya felt for the first time that maybe there *are* options in the future that don't involve life the way it currently is.

Later, as she curled up to Jacob's sleeping form, she felt the light touch of hope pass over them and she snuggled in further, smiling at the feeling that perhaps things would turn out okay.

✳

'Right, did you listen to everything I just said?' Jacob asked, hands on hips, staring at Faith in the kitchen of the holiday cottage.

Faith was stirring hot chocolate, splashing most of it over the sides of the cup, while smudging the cup into the chocolate granules that had spilled all over the counter when she had spooned them in earlier in the process.

'Yeah, yeah, Dad. Don't beat the siblings. I've got it,' she rolled her eyes, stomping into the lounge with her drink and flopping down in the chair.

'Okay, we'll be back in a few hours. Please behave, kids,' he reiterated to the rest of them as he left the house with Maya in tow.

'I've got to say,' she piped up as she jumped into the passenger seat of the car. 'I'm a little apprehensive to see the house you've bought without me having viewed it. What if I don't like it?' she grimaced, looking at Jacob who was starting up the car.

He stopped and turned his head to face her. 'You *will* like it, Maya. Don't worry.'

Okay, she thought, settling down in her seat.

After thirty minutes of driving, Jacob announced that they were nearly there. Maya sat up and rubbed her eyes as they crossed over a small bridge and climbed a hill on a single-track road.

As they rounded the corner, a beige bungalow with a slate roof came into view. It sat behind a clump of fir trees on a peninsula and behind it, the great expanse of the Atlantic Ocean, partly shielded by the rocks and hills in the sea loch, opened out into the vastness of water.

The house felt familiar, like she'd already been there, like it had been sitting waiting for her to come back. Tears pricked in her eyes as Jacob turned the car down the lane and pulled up in front of it.

The façade of the house had unique, island stone built into its structure, decorating a square shape around the door. A thick stone pillar ran up the side of the chimney. It was different, exceptional but not posh, nor in any way showing off. It was perfectly her.

Maya looked at Jacob, her eyes full of tears.

'Yeah,' he agreed. 'I did that first time I saw it too.'

She smiled, wiping her eyes and got out of the car.

Two middle-aged ladies greeted them at the door, explaining it had been their mother's house before she died and they couldn't afford the upkeep and live with their families on the mainland at the same time.

Maya smiled as they showed her round the house. It needed work but somehow it didn't matter—neither the gold bathroom suite nor the 1970s kitchen could change the feeling of the house, the energy there. It held her, but made her feel very vulnerable at the same time.

The lounge boasted a huge window at one end, giving a beautiful view of the opening of the tidal loch to the ocean and the grassy hills beyond.

'Perfect,' she breathed.

Maya wasn't exactly sure what it was perfect for, but it was. Jacob followed the two women around, silently watching Maya's expression. He felt the same calming energy. It could heal them, given the opportunity. He just hoped Maya would let go and give it a chance to help her. Eventually Maya and

Jacob took their leave and climbed back into the car, waving goodbye.

Travelling back, the two talked about mundane topics such as how to finance the deposit and what they would need, but it didn't dampen Maya's mood. In the afternoon, she spent time with the children, reading books with Amy and playing ball with Zidan. As night fell, she cooked cupcakes in the kitchen with Aurora and, for the first time in what seemed like an age, spent time listening to what she had been up to at school and which media celebrity's book she was currently reading.

Faith kept to herself in the lounge. Maya supposed she spent more time with Faith than with the other children, mainly because she was always running her around with her pony. After cleaning up the dishes, she went and sat down next to Faith and listened to her talk about a saddle she had seen for Shadow online. They fell into a conversation about pony club and they concluded that it wasn't as fun as it used to be. It had become too competitive, too militant and often the people there were quite cruel to their animals in order to get them to do what they wanted them to.

Faith shared her frustration at how most of the kids acted towards their ponies, and how she simply wanted to spend time with her horse. It all felt like a lot of pressure, it seemed. However, when Maya suggested she stop going, Faith immediately turned defensive and started trying to justify why she should still go. Maya watched as Faith battled in her mind between her ego, and what people would think if she stopped going, and her real self, who didn't resonate with it in the first place. She knew in her heart that a more natural horsemanship was the right way to go. Maya made a mental note to work through *all* of her family's lives, sorting out what they were doing simply because they *felt* they should and their ego was telling them to, and what really brought true satisfaction and had meaning and purpose.

✦

On the day before they were due to leave, Maya woke early to the sun streaming through the window. It took a second to remember where she was, but the sounds of gulls quickly brought her back into the present. As she sat up, she noticed Jacob sitting by the window. On seeing her rise, he turned round and smiled.

'You know, I'm going to miss the sound of those gulls and the view out the window.'

Maya agreed silently. In fact, she never wanted to leave.

'You made it upstairs, then,' she chuckled. 'I swear you could sleep anywhere, Jacob. You were half on, half off that tiny sofa downstairs, snoring away when I walked past.'

'Why didn't you wake me?' he grumbled.

'Yeah, right,' Maya laughed, kicking off the covers and swinging her legs out of bed. 'We both know what a delight you are when you're woken up. No thanks. I didn't want to ruin my night,' she finished over her shoulder while padding to the door.

Jacob watched her leave, then turned back to the view out

the window. Yeah, that was fair, he thought. I *am* a grumpy sod in the morning.

'So where to today?' Aurora asked as they sat and ate cereal and toast.

'Today,' Jacob announced through mouthfuls of toast, 'I want to head to one of the beaches in the south. It's supposed to be really nice, according to the old gentlemen I met last time I was here.'

'Great.' Faith rolled her eyes, flicking crumbs across the table. 'So some old git said there's a nice beach and that's the most exciting thing forecast for today,' she groaned, flopping her head into her arms on the table.

'Oh, come on, Faith,' Maya chided. 'It'll be good for you. Try to stop being a grumpy teenager for a minute and feel the beautiful energy around you. You might even have an epiphany!'

'Right, Mum. Whatever,' she sighed, playing with her skull-covered bracelet.

Half an hour later they had piled into the car, with a bag containing biscuits, sausage rolls and a flask of tea, and headed towards the chosen destination for the day.

The beach was accessed by a gate and a path through grassy fields. Maya's arms began to ache with the weight of the picnic, which she had somehow managed to get the job of carrying, along with Amy's coat that she had flung at her before she ran off shrieking at the seagulls.

As she rounded the corner of the grassy dunes, she stopped and put the bag and coat down. The beach stretched out before her both left and right for about a mile. It wasn't as wide as some of the other beaches they had visited, but the sand was a rich, coarse beige that seemed to pull her into it while she stood there. As she looked to her left, she noticed the beach finished at the bottom of a mountain in the distance, and Maya immediately noticed it had a peaceful energy that radiated out from the grassy slopes.

She left the bag and coat and walked towards the water's edge, feeling a great wave of emotion pass through her. Before she knew it, she had dropped to her knees, all strength seemingly vanishing from her legs. Her head hit the sand as her hands pushed deeper into the grainy particles of shells and stone. She stared at them, looking at the array of colours in a handful of the sand she was grasping. A huge feeling of relief and letting go passed through her again and huge sobs started to be released from her. She cried ugly and loud for what felt like an age. She cried for all the times she felt trapped, felt worthless. She mourned the times she needed a hug and got harsh words instead, the times she wanted to reach out and make amends, but her ego wouldn't let her. She howled for the injustice of working all hours and missing the precious moments of her children's first words and steps, for the world as a whole and how wrong the system that had been built in it felt to her. She cried for it all and, as she did, the negative energy held inside started to dislodge and flow down to the sand to be transmuted. She felt for the first time in her life, instead of trapping more dense emotions in her body, that she had started the process of releasing all the deep, murky stuff she had held buried inside.

Eventually she felt as if she'd calmed herself enough to come back into her surroundings, and raised her head to see Jacob and the children scattered around her, staring at her. No one seemed to know what to do.

Zidan was the first to move when Maya sat back on her heels and turned her face to the sky. He came over gingerly and put his hand on Maya's shoulder.

'What's wrong, Mum?' he asked, his voice full of concern.

'I'm okay. I just needed a cry,' she said, looking at him and pulling him in for a hug.

'You're tired, Mum,' he said.

Never a truer word, she thought. That's exactly what she was—worn down, under-confident, chronically tired, full of toxins and crying out for help. For the first time ever on that beach, Maya decided she was going to put herself first for a while. She needed that—she always put other people first, even if it didn't work out and even when she ended up making the situation worse, which was actually quite a lot of the time, she mused, though her intent was always good and she only ever wanted to fix things.

She heard Lesley's voice in her head: Fill your own cup first, she had told Maya forcefully. Let your children learn the lessons they came to learn. You need to discern when you need to step in and when not to, instead of rushing in all the time to fix things.

She took deep breaths, holding Zidan close. Jacob continued walking on ahead, away from them both. Maya sensed he was struggling with his own emotions and suppressed the urge to call out to him. Jacob liked his space to work things through before talking, and she needed to respect that more, she reminded herself.

✳

Above the beach, Tal swirled, watching the scene unfold. *She can feel us here. We can help her here,* he announced to his companion. *This is the right place for her to heal and remember who she is.*

Tal's companion nodded, looking thoughtfully over the family below. *Can they all make the shift in energy?* he wondered out loud.

If Maya and Jacob can get there, Tal responded, *if they can heal themselves and grasp what really matters and what's really happened in the past, then they open the gates for the children to follow. It's up to them and they have free will, but I'm positive Maya will reconnect to her soul. She just needs some more time. The next few weeks will be decisive for her.*

Yes, his companion agreed. *I've seen the energies ahead. She needs to let go of her ego—it's got a pretty big hold. So much negative energy trapped from this life and past lives.*

I know, Tal cut in, *but she showed us in her childhood what she's capable of fighting through. She's got what it takes. Jacob too— he's constantly pushing her to let go, and their connection is old, like their souls. They'll get there.*

Tal smiled, banking right to head out over the ocean and spread light across a seabed scarred by deep sea trawlers ripping up the sediment.

A few miles away in the rafters of an old church, a group of Demons huddled together discussing yesterday's mass.

It's brilliant, one cackled. *There's a growing number who think they're worshipping God but instead are worshipping Satan and all negative energies. Judgement, so much judgement at service yesterday, and so many donations to the council's latest moneyspinner. The more we can corrupt and confuse, the more we can achieve here, in this place where God's rule is slipping and they're becoming more and more our slaves.*

Our Master is the Great Deceiver! another one declared, while starting to push his way to the centre of the circle.

But these humans are so far in, they're executing his plan without any further deception needed, the first one agreed. *They crave to be told what to do and how to do it. Give them money and instructions and they'll do anything!*

Not all of them, interrupted a small Demon who had been sitting in the shadows and now moved closer to the centre of the group. *There are still the rebels, the souls that, no matter how much we have beaten them down over the centuries, how much we manipulated them to believe they were doing bad witchcraft and burned them at their stakes by their own hands, they still come back, they grow back like seeds. We haven't won yet. We need to keep going. Light pierces darkness in places around the world still and the girl Maya and her husband, and people like her, have the potential to disrupt all the darkness we have sown here. Now, get out there and stir up some fear and guilt!* he roared, becoming agitated with the blank looks on the faces of his fellow Brothers of Darkness.

They scattered out of the rooftops, sweeping out across the land, squabbling and shrieking as they went.

*

Jacob reached the end of the beach and sat down on one of the rocks that jutted out from the dunes. How could they afford to do the things he felt they clearly should be doing? Things like living off the land, homeschooling their children? Ever since he was a kid he mistrusted authority. It's like he knew intuitively that corruption is rife everywhere and that the truth of life was being hidden. Humans, he mused, so caught up in the hamster wheel activities of work, marriage, pension, status, job title. It took them away from seeing through the illusion that none of that really mattered.

Was he just paranoid? Was he lazy? Did the weed smoking of his youth cause him to be like this? No. No, it started before that. There is a lot hidden in this world. Someone or something is pulling the strings and he didn't want to dance to their tune. He wanted to be free and he wanted to be free with Maya. She's so stuck in her family's tradition of horses. I mean, the connection Maya has with horses is wonderful but it's tainted with the older family energy of its expectation as a competitive sport and being viewed as being posh because you have a horse. It's the same as her conditioning that they needed to earn a good wage and send the kids to good schools. Basically, repeat the same tragic stories of their ancestors' slave-to-a-system-they-can't-see. They spent Maya's increasing wage on more and more things—bigger houses to rent, more animals. When does it stop? When is enough, enough?

He sighed, playing with the small stones at his feet. There is a way to do this, he told himself determinedly. Maybe he should go to work, let Maya have time off. She can't even see the wood for the trees at the moment. She's going to hit the deck soon, then she'll be no use to herself, let alone anyone else. She comes home and always allows Faith to get away with things he has said no to. It's like they're rowing in different directions and, Lord knows, bringing up four kids is hard enough without adding that to it.

He sighed again, getting up and assuring himself that one day the answer would come. He looked over to Maya and silently prayed it would come soon. It feels like she's getting further and further away every time she comes back from that hellhole down south.

'Hurry up, Aurora, we're going to miss the ferry! Why does she take so long to get dressed?' Jacob demanded of Maya, as she piled tinfoil-wrapped cake into her bag.

'It's her long hair,' Maya snapped, defending Aurora.

'Right, yeah, that's what she's doing,' he rolled his eyes exasperated, holding Aurora's hairbrush up for Maya to see.

'I'll go and get her,' Maya huffed, throwing her handbag in Jacob's direction.

Maya stomped towards the room the elder girls were sharing as Aurora came out the door, dragging her coat and bag behind her.

'I'm here, I'm here,' she grumbled, pushing past Maya.

Maya stood in the hallway, now silent as the kids made their way to the car, and closed her eyes. I don't want to leave. I don't want to have to go on holiday to take a break from my life, she thought. I want to have a life I don't need to take a break from. She sighed and thought of the house that would soon be theirs, instantly feeling lighter. Turning on her heel, she silently thanked the cottage for its hospitality, and made her way out the door to travel home.

10

'Brilliant!' Maya exclaimed, dramatically slamming her hand on the steering wheel, as the traffic in both lanes of the M42 motorway slowed to a stop.

'Already late and a boss that's looking for a reason to fire me. This isn't good,' she groaned to anyone that could hear, which, if you didn't include Whaley the killer whale staring at her from on top of the dashboard, was absolutely nobody.

Maya tapped the wheel rhythmically, feeling highly frustrated. It was as if she couldn't catch a single break when it came to work at the moment. She reflected on the previous day as she sat waiting for the traffic to move. It had started well—she had been on a field visit with Merran, visiting a large hospital in the north-east, where the management and staff were open to all types of treatments for chronic neurological diseases, and she had really enjoyed the chat with the consultant and nurses.

She had then called in at her sister's, where she had experienced an interesting evening, finding she could read her sister's cards with amazing accuracy and point out things that had happened which Freya hadn't revealed to anyone before. It was almost a relief to see proof that she wasn't going mad, and she did indeed have a gift to see and hear and feel beyond the veil, as Tal affectionately referred to it.

Her thoughts caught on Tal and the discussion she'd had with him while lying in her bed trying to doze off. He had said there were a great many things that she still didn't understand and that she had only accessed a few memories of a small portion of her past lives. Maya had wondered what that meant.

Generally, she was struggling more and more with the 3D world of eat-sleep-work-repeat, and then dipping into something that offered far more, something that made her feel like it was the land beyond the prison walls she was trapped in. There was something just out of reach she could not understand, could not grasp, that would set her free. She had tried the eagle meditation that Lesley had asked her to do after their last session, but every time she did, the eagle soared up into the air and headed out over the ocean in search of a new adventure, before circling and turning back to solid ground. It was like an invisible cord was there, even in visualisations.

Fear. The word came in clearly over her left shoulder. It wasn't Tal—the presence felt different, feminine in nature.

It's fear and guilt, the voice repeated.

'What am I ultimately scared of?' Maya mused out loud. 'I mean, yes, of death a bit, I suppose. But no, that's not it in the end.'

She sat breathing slowly as a wave of fear seemed to rise up from the bottom of her womb. It was almost suffocating.

'I'm scared I'll fail again!' She broke into a sob as she uttered these last words.

Maya felt tears stream down her face and blinked her way back to the present.

'What the hell was that?' she cried, jerking back in her seat as the car behind beeped twice, letting her know that the traffic was moving and she was in the way.

Maya wiped her eyes quickly and put the car into first gear, trying to shake the confusion. She would need to think about this later. Right now she had to pull herself together and get in the correct frame of mind for the meeting that she may never get to.

✦

Maya rushed up the stairs, reaching for her computer that was hanging out of her bag to save it from tumbling to the floor. Two minutes to go but she had made it. No idea how, she chided herself. You should have got up earlier, lazy cow, she followed on in her mind while swinging open the door, bashing it off the wall and thus announcing her hasty arrival to the whole office.

'Hey!' several of the team greeted her as she threw the contents of her arms on the desk and rushed over to fill her water bottle.

'Ah,' Ben shouted from across the room. 'Ever the organised and graceful lady we all expect to see.'

Maya threw him daggers with her eyes as she riffled through her handbag looking for her phone.

'Come on, let's go,' he beckoned, opening the door to the smaller office, where several of the leadership team were already sitting.

Maya scurried through, trying not to notice how calm and beautiful Anna and Natalie looked, with pristine clothes and makeup, a far cry from the sweaty mess Maya presented.

'Right,' Anna barked, standing up. 'Come on, let's get on with it.'

The first hour or two passed without much interest. In fact, Maya was struggling not to fall asleep. She felt her phone vibrate and glanced down to see an email flash up from the solicitor confirming the house purchase had now been finalised. It almost felt like it was happening to someone else, buying a house on a remote Scottish island. I mean, everyone sitting at this table right now would have thought she'd lost her mind. Maya thought about how she'd been on autopilot for the last few weeks, dealing with the paperwork for the purchase, as if it was something she knew she had to do but had no idea why.

She was jolted back to the present by Marketing bleating on about the latest campaign that twisted the truth on efficiency, spending twenty minutes justifying why it didn't really twist the truth but conformed to all the rules and regulations, even though no one had thought to ask what they were.

Then they handed over to Anna, who ran through the figures and attempted to lift team morale by literally saying everyone needs to lift their morale. She had finished off by announcing a new observational recommendation of reporting for anyone trying the drug they were promoting, which, in Maya's eyes didn't go nearly far enough, given it was highly likely it had already caused the death of one patient. She had challenged Anna on this and asked her whether it had been fed upwards but, as usual, was met with a seething glare and an answer any seasoned politician would have been proud of.

The group broke for coffee and Maya was relieved to get a chance to pee and find something to eat. She hadn't had breakfast and was now ready to start chewing at Ben's arm.

As the group began to take their seats again, Maya's eyes landed on the new Associate Medical Director who had replaced Elijah, shuffling papers at the end of the room.

Gary, she remembered, although she could already think of a few better names for him.

He rose and switched on the PowerPoint at the front computer and then brushed down his suit and stood like a Stormtrooper on duty, while everyone fell silent.

'Well,' he started. 'It's great to be able to talk to you as a group for the first time. I wanted to discuss the findings of a recent audit I've run as my first project as Medical Director. Obviously, I found quite a lot wanting in the predecessor's work,' he paused, seeing if anyone was willing to take the bait and blow up his ego further.

There were a few nods but no one spoke, so Gary continued, after throwing Anna a sideways glance that Maya felt as a prickle down her spine.

'So,' he said. 'The other department I found a lot of concerns in was yours, Maya.'

He stared directly at her.

'Oh?' Maya responded, feeling her hackles rise and gripping the chair to calm herself.

'Yes, I'll take you through them one by one, but we must see an improvement immediately. As the Medical Director, I have ultimate responsibility here and I don't want to be carted off to jail,' he finished, still staring at her.

Maya could see Ben out of the corner of her eye, willing her to behave herself.

'I would have thought,' Maya started, ignoring Ben's pleading looks and focusing again on the attack being made at her, 'that it would be a more team-friendly approach to have discussed this with me one-to-one before announcing your findings.'

'Oh, no,' he snarled back. 'I spoke to Anna about it and she said she was going to speak with you.'

Maya swirled her eyes to Anna who looked up from drawing doodles on her page.

'I was going to speak with you at our next one-to-one on Thursday,' she shrugged.

Maya sat back, actively trying to calm her racing thoughts and the urge to run out of the room. She knew for a fact that other department heads in the room wouldn't have agreed with the long list of utter rubbish that Gary had come up with, and that she was being singled out because she didn't fit with Anna's and his way forward for the department. Too challenging, too ethical and caring, she heard herself shriek inside her head.

Maya dropped her eyes and played with her notebook,

trying to get other people's attention off her as Gary started to reel off the names of her team members and their supposed offences, finishing with a few minor problems with the general literature and messages in the field.

The meeting finished just as Maya had calmed down enough to assure herself she was not going to spontaneously burst into tears. She lagged behind and then went over and sat down next to Gary, who had buried his head in his computer for the remainder of the meeting.

He looked up, startled, like she was approaching with a dagger in her hand. Maya chuckled inwardly.

They always are the biggest wimps, really, Tal whispered inside her mind.

'Gary,' Maya started. 'Perhaps you can share with me now what your issues with me and my team are. I'd like to understand it so we can start to think of remedies and additional training needs.'

'Okay,' he said slowly.

Maya sensed his suspicion that he was walking into a well laid out trap. Nah, that's just how *you* work, mate, she thought to herself.

He dipped his head, reading over his paperwork.

'Ah yes,' he said, lifting his head and proceeding to outline minor issues with layout, typos and references that Maya had not picked up, or that in his opinion could be considered a possible grey area.

Maya tried to quell the frustration growing in her. Most of what he had pulled out was nothing in comparison to the twists in truths and manipulation of statistics by other teams, which he apparently had no issue with. He had hit on Maya's weakness. Though she concurred she wasn't good with proof-reading long documents, it was so boring that she was fully aware she would have missed some errors made by her team.

They continued to discuss the points for several minutes, becoming a little animated at times, but Maya felt overall they were finding common ground on the way forward.

Just then, Anna abruptly threw herself down next to Maya and demanded to know what was going on.

'Erm, sorry?' Maya asked, looking over at Gary and seeing he was equally as puzzled by Anna's question. 'We're discussing what needs to be looked at in the audit and any training needs the team has,' Maya finished, looking at Gary for agreement.

He stared at Anna, but he seemed to have powered down for a nap and so said nothing.

'I won't tolerate this,' Anna snapped.

'Sorry? What?' Maya replied, feeling herself about to burst. 'Tolerate what?' she pressed, seeing Anna pulse her lips at her.

'You were arguing and causing an atmosphere in my meetings.'

'No, I wasn't,' Maya shot back.

'I agree, though,' Anna continued, ignoring Maya's comment and clearly not willing to discuss whether her statement was actually accurate, 'that we need to talk about your training needs, Maya.'

Gary, who seemed to have rebooted, jumped in and agreed, helpfully supplying an additional comment. Clearly feeling brave with his new backup, he continued ranting about how he could go to prison if Maya didn't take the approval of internal and external documents seriously, and how he had found a spelling mistake in one of the patient information leaflets published. He barely paused for breath before he continued to reel off the number of documents out of the yearly approval sign-off.

'Wait. Hang on,' Maya interrupted. 'That was before my time. I've been working to fix all that.'

But it fell on deaf ears. Anna sat back while Gary attacked her again, which finished with him asking her if she was in the right job.

Maya stood up, gathered her things and left without a further word. She'd been bullied before. She knew what it felt and looked like, and that was exactly what was happening now, while her boss sat and watched and, at times, joined in.

She walked down the stairs and out of the building, throwing her things into the car. Only when she had cleared the car park, did she let the tears fall and found somewhere nearby to cry and scream into the steering wheel.

You must go back, the voice nagged in her head. It'll be fine. You can't make this easy for them. If you disappear, it'll give them more reason to come down on you. It's not fair, though, they are targeting me!

STOP! Maya screamed in her head at her own thoughts. STOP! She felt the auto switch flick on, the one in her heart that could not cope with the reality of her life, that put her into zombie mode outwardly so she could continue. Even the switch felt broken somewhat today, though, like it could click off at any point and she would just lose it.

Okay, she breathed to herself. Go back, sit with the team, look at the points, but do it tomorrow. Just go to the hotel early tonight and start again in the morning. She sighed and leaned forward, restarting her engine and turning her car in the direction of the hotel.

✦

'Mummy, Mummy,' Amy shouted down the phone as Maya scrambled to lower the sound on the car audio before it burst her earphone.

'Hi, sweetie. What's up?' she asked.

'I saw an eagle today. It was sooo big. Daddy said it was going to eat my toes,' she giggled.

Maya's heart melted listening to her daughter recount her day and describe the eagle and the newborn lamb that had come over and tried to eat her hair through the fence while she'd been playing in the garden. She felt a huge hole in her heart. She was missing all of this, for what? She knew at least the kids had a safe roof over their heads and good food on the table, but could Maya carry on like this for the next fifteen years, pretending she was okay, pretending the job wasn't stealing her soul? She very much doubted it, and it scared her immensely.

Zidan was next on the phone to describe his latest mud invention and the horror of a lamb apparently being born out of a sheep's butt. Lastly, Jacob came on the line and chuckled as Maya suggested it was time he explained female anatomy to his son.

'Where are the big two?' Maya asked.

'They wanted to go to friends after school. I'm going to get them both at seven,' Jacob confirmed, yawning halfway through telling her.

Maya began to tell him about Gary, then stopped as she recognised the futility of spending this precious time talking about work. Jacob sensed the sadness in her anyway and told her it would be okay.

'It's all bollocks, Maya,' he said.

'What is?' Maya asked, confused.

'All of it. The fancy clothes, the pointless meetings. We can't cure cancer but we can find ninety drugs that slow it down. The 'work hard, be miserable, get old and die' mentality of this world. It's all upside down, inverted, not how it should be. We're trapped on a slave planet, but the crazy thing is we trapped ourselves.'

Maya could feel the truth behind Jacob's words, but she was fighting with the reality of it.

'Yeah, okay, I get it,' she sighed, feeling a huge wave of frustration and anger. 'But that's not realistic, Jacob. We still have to earn money and look after our children. We can't just shirk our responsibilities and run away.'

'Can't we?' he swiped back. 'That's the problem with you, Maya. You've already decided what you *have* to do. There's no room for the possibility of chance. What if we left it all and just see what happens?'

'We'll be poor and homeless, Jacob. I know you don't have to worry about the money but—'

'Maya,' he cut in. 'There will never be enough money. The system is designed that way to keep us enslaved.'

'Oh, whatever, Jacob. I've had a bad day. I really don't need this.'

Maya felt overwhelming anger towards Jacob and the conversation. Why couldn't he just be grateful? For a start, he isn't in her shoes—he's at home getting hugs every day from the kids. Why does he have to make her feel worse?

She said her curt goodbyes and headed for the gym in an attempt to release some of her emotions on the treadmill.

✳

Early next morning Maya rose and made her way into work, hoping to get a small office in the corner to speak individually with her team away from prying eyes. She spent the morning talking to each of them. There were mistakes, she concluded, as she stared at her notes while eating her lunch, but some of them were simply due to updated guidelines that Elijah had not shared with them. Probably because they're ridiculous, she bustled to herself.

For example, they could no longer refer to patients as 'patients' and instead had to call them 'individuals with disease symptoms'. But they couldn't have known that because they didn't get the updated Standard Operating Procedures to work from. Other, more simple things Maya had simply missed through rushing or because she didn't know otherwise.

Maya put her pen down and rubbed her forehead. At the end of the day, she told herself, she'd received no training for this role and Anna's predecessor had kept proudly declaring they were treading into the unknown with the formation of Maya's department and team. The whole thing probably needed four people to set up and Maya had done it pretty much single-handedly. Plus, she had also taken over the current patient programmes that hadn't been managed properly for years and had tried to work through the issues with them as well.

She stared out the window, thinking about how much she missed Elijah and what a jerk Gary had turned out to be. I'm a GP, he had declared to her the first day they had met, and Maya had felt like saying Elijah was a cardiologist and had half the ego you do, little man.

Mmm, Maya smirked, I wonder if he *is* a little man. Oh, that would cheer me up, she laughed to herself.

Ben abruptly banged on the door, pulling her out of her thoughts.

'Come in, loser,' she shouted.

He smiled as he shoved his head in the door.

'Busy?' he enquired.

'No, I just like to sit in offices all day doing nothing so I can be as useless as Gary has decided I am,' she answered politely, with a slip of sarcasm showing.

Ben rolled his eyes and plonked himself in the chair next to her.

'I come with more bad news,' he grimaced at her after a few seconds.

'Urgh. Of course you do, Grim Reaper. What is it now?'

'I overheard Gary talking to the GM.'

'GM?' Maya interrupted .

'The General Manager, Maya. God, you are useless with abbreviations. It's like you were born in my nan's era. Anyway, Gary was going on about how he'd started to sort you out, which coincidentally made me howl with laughter. Like anyone could actually sort you out!'

Maya deadpanned him. 'How funny. Please continue laughing.'

Ben took a deep breath and composed himself.

'Anyway, he also said something about the new Head of Medical overall starting next week who will be Gary's boss. Imran is his name. He's from another company I used to work at. The guy's an asshole, Maya, hungry for fortune and fame. Got the regulators in his pocket apparently, so for God's sake don't bring up the whole 'We handled the woman's death badly' thing again or he'll find a convenient thing you've done wrong, spin it into something big and get you shoved off somewhere. He's already made comments about the phlebotomy programme you run being defined as offering the wrong service.'

'Yes, I know, Ben, but we couldn't have defined it any other way because of the partner's legal terms. Anna told me to sign it off as is.'

'Yep, I know,' said Ben. 'But is she going to back you up when the shit hits the fan?'

'No,' Maya conceded.

'Then you can't win, despite your best efforts,' he replied, 'which, by the way, are considerably large. I wouldn't want your job.'

'Wow,' Maya said after a few seconds of Ben staring at her with a You-can-thank-me-later look in his eyes. 'And you're okay with everything you've just said and think we simply need to do as we're told and everything will be okay? Ben, it's all wrong! We have a slogan that says Every Patient Matters— sorry, every 'individual with disease' matters. I mean… Hey, wait! How come we can have it on a slogan and not in the literature?' Maya growled.

'Different operating procedures, probably,' Ben shrugged.

'Oh my God!' Maya gasped, raising her eyebrows to the ceiling. 'This is nuts! How can everyone be okay with this madness?'

'Well, because,' he said, looking at his watch, 'I'm off to Spain in three and a half hours for a week with my beloved. Fine wine, good food, awesome sex, not a thought of work for a whole week,' he grinned. 'Maybe you just need some sex, Maya.'

He winked as he stood to leave.

'I hope he goes soft,' Maya retorted, pointing at Ben's trousers and shooting him a look that says, Get out before I scream at you.

✳

The next morning Maya rose from her hotel bed and prepared to drive north. Despite wishing with all her heart she was going home, she was in fact en route to a northern airport to fly to Ireland for a two-day field visit, having already received an order of leprechaun lollies from the children. She thought about their energy earlier on the phone, so light and playful—when is it that it gets beaten from them and becomes dense and hard? she wondered to herself.

When was it for you? Tal enquired.

I guess it was when I became a teenager and when my Dad went away. Actually, no, it was before then.

'I don't know,' she replied, feeling confused and sensing the familiar feeling of emptiness in her chest.

It was when you were surrounded with dense energy all the time and were made to feel weird for being light and love and not wanting to conform to all these crazy Earth rules, Tal suggested in her mind.

Yes, that's it. Maya straightened her back in the driver's seat and turned the banging music down. That *is* it. We're born with lighter, happier energy, but then it got denser because that was what was around me.

She thought back to her childhood—her Mum always busy and stressed, her Dad most often not there and when he was, he was very serious, insisting on utmost cleanliness and order. There wasn't much room for fun.

So, I learned to be miserable to fit in with everyone else? she queried.

In a way, Tal confirmed. *It's more complex than that but yes, in effect.*

Being an Empath doesn't help either, I guess, she mused. I can feel everyone's energy and I didn't know as a child that's what it was. I assumed it was *my* energy, so I kept all of that negative stuff and it stored as dense energy inside me.

'Bloody hell!' she laughed. 'Where did that come from? Look at all my inner wisdom coming out today. Go me!' she exclaimed, feeling like something had shifted and a bit more of the mystery had unravelled.

A thought to leave you with, Tal offered. *Do birds charge each other to live in nests?*

Maya sat back in her seat, suddenly becoming aware of braking traffic ahead.

'Bloody hell,' she cursed out loud. 'No, they don't!'

And just like that Maya wanted to learn everything about the things on planet Earth that she did without thinking and now she felt needed challenging.

Further up the road Maya checked the time and, after calculating how long it would take to get to the airport, decided she had time for a toilet stop and a coffee. Maya always needed the toilet. It had started after the birth of Zidan. The doctors had told her it was just wear and tear from carrying big babies and offered her some medication, which she had refused. Now it was just something she managed but there had been a few near misses recently, she thought to herself, as she swung the car into an empty parking spot.

She grabbed her purse from her bag on the passenger seat

just as her phone started to ring. Cursing and debating if she would pee her pants if she answered the call, she flipped the phone over to see who it was. Scott, she acknowledged with surprise, given that this was the team member she was due to meet in Ireland tomorrow and had spoken to not an hour before.

Maya suspected there must be a problem with their plans and pressed the Answer button.

'Hey,' she said, leaning down to retrieve the card that had just fallen out of her purse and smarting at the sudden pressure on her bladder. 'Everything okay?'

'No, not really, Boss,' Scott answered brusquely, making Maya acutely aware that something was amiss. An outgoing Northern Irish fella, straight with his words and actions, Scott was nonetheless a calm, caring and honest type and generally not easily rattled.

'I've just had a call from our Medical Liaison Manager over here.'

'Okay,' Maya responded slowly.

'She said we can't continue to provide the phlebotomy nurses with the kits for blood draw, even though we agreed with your help at the start of the contract we would need to provide them separately for the patients to be able to use the service.'

'I remember,' Maya confirmed. 'What reason is she giving for saying we can't?'

'I don't know exactly. She said that Gary said it was a breach of some rule in the standard legal operating procedures of the company and that you were responsible for ensuring all the clauses were followed.'

'But I amended that clause,' Maya countered, feeling frustration and anger rising up. 'And it was signed off by Elijah as no increased risk to patients, which there isn't, for God's sake. Whether it's a sterile needle being delivered by the National Health Service or a sterile needle delivered by a company, it's still bloody sterile.'

'I know, I know,' Scott answered, clearly feeling as frustrated as she was. 'But I'm being told I have to let the consultant know we won't be doing the bloods of his thirty patients on our drug this week. He's going to go nuts, because if the bloods are wrong and we miss any signals for autoimmune disease, the patient could die without treatment.'

Right, Maya thought bitterly, because that amounts to what the company thinks. Maybe some side effects but nothing to worry about, compared to the chance of living a normal life— that was what they'd been trained to say, wasn't it? It was even quoted in the literature. Maya seethed inwardly at how much the damn company understated the risks of this drug.

'Jesus,' she said, sitting back in her seat and trying to ignore her bladder's response to the extra pressure.

'This is insane. We set them up with a service designed to ease their load and protect their patients and then because of some line in the procedures, and not an actual risk, we're now saying we can't do it and leaving them stranded and in danger of actually causing harm to patients!' she fumed. 'I'm sorry, Scott, I don't feel great. Can I ring you back?'

'Sure thing,' he responded.

The phone clicked off and Maya sat staring at the handset. 'What the actual...?'

She screwed her eyes up, rubbing the front of her head before deciding this breakdown would need to wait until after she'd been to the toilet because a wet seat would likely push her over the edge.

After relieving herself and buying four packets of seaweed because, weirdly, that's all she wanted to eat right now, she walked back to the car in a daze and slid into the driver's seat.

She sat for a minute and watched cars coming and going, most with suited and booted men and women scurrying like ants while staring at their phones and ignoring cars that could clearly hit them, assuming instead that everything and everyone would stop for them to cross the road.

Maya tossed the phone down on the passenger seat and pushed her head back on the headrest. She'd been sitting in the motorway services for half an hour, trying to sort out the issue, which had ended with Gary telling her that if she'd set things up properly this wouldn't have happened. Which was simply not true—how could she have known the guidelines would change three times since the set-up? And she was magically supposed to know what those changes would be and how to find an answer before they happened?

She was half convinced he had even re-written the

guidelines just to cause her problems, which ultimately affected the company's reputation, so it was actually counterproductive and stupid. Yet only Maya and Scott seemed to be able to see this.

The phone rang again; it was home. She sighed and picked it up.

'Hello,' Jacob chirped over the line. 'How are you?'

'Don't ask,' Maya answered, stifling a sob that was rising up in her chest, driven by pure frustration and loathing of the situation she now found herself in.

'What's happened?' he sang quietly. 'Come on, tell me. Did you drink too much champagne again?'

Maya rolled her eyes but a tiny smile came to her lips. 'No, Jacob. I told you I don't actually do that,' she replied.

'Apart from when you're flying First Class to Vancouver,' he reminded her.

'Well, yes, apart from that,' she laughed.

She told Jacob the whole story, which then spewed out into much more, giving him full visibility of what had been happening to her at work and just how much on the edge she was. She finished by explaining, in between tears, that she'd just checked their bank account and found only forty pounds available in their overdraft until she gets paid in nine days. She paused, trying to collect herself.

'Maya,' Jacob started with a seriousness in his tone. 'When you earned thirty thousand we spent it and more. When you earned fifty thousand, we spent it and more. Now you earn more than that—I don't even know how much,' he muttered, 'we *still* spend it and more. Maya, it'll never be enough. You have an issue with money—an unhealthy view, most likely born from your parents.'

Jacob paused, waiting for Maya to explode as she normally did when he mentioned money, but it never came. That's a first, he thought to himself.

'Maya, are you still there?'

'I can't do this any more, Jacob. I just can't.'

'Okay,' he said, pausing before clearly having a lightbulb moment.

'Maya, get to the airport, call in sick and get on a plane to the island. There's one that goes in a few hours. Pick up the keys to the house and get yourself over there on your own for a few days.'

'I can't,' she said.

'Can't? Or won't, Maya? Please,' he whispered. 'I'm worried about you.'

Maya sat back and rubbed her eyes. She needed it, she knew that, and she could have a session with Lesley out there which would be amazing. But she just couldn't. If she wasn't at work, she should be at home with her children and her husband. Taking some time on her own would be very selfish. Wouldn't it?

'MAYA!' Jacob shouted down the line. 'I know what rubbish is running through your head right now. I'm overriding it. You're going to hang up, ring your boss, call in sick and get on that plane.'

'But I'm not sick!' she rebuffed.

'Not true,' he countered. 'You have an infected tooth and it's flared up again.'

'It's not *that* bad,' she replied.

'It will be when I punch it, Maya. Do it now!'

As the conversation between Jacob and Maya raged on, above the car three dark, persuasive Demons, accompanied by swirls of negative energy, filled her head with guilt and fear.

That's how we keep control and keep them small, they cackled nervously, peeking over their shoulder every now and then to throw a glance at Tal, who stood back from the scene unfolding in front of him.

He couldn't interfere. She needed to learn this for herself. She was never going to ascend out of polarity and ego without doing some of the work to understand exactly what was really going on in the energetic field. He sent a touch of love through their telepathic bond and continued to watch from afar.

Maya sighed as the phone went dead. Jacob clearly had nothing else to say on the matter. She took a moment to clear her thoughts and then smiled for the first time in long time. In fact, she started giggling when she realised it felt so foreign to her.

Wow, when did everything get so serious? she mused.

She felt something shift again as she recalled the love and determination in Jacob's voice. To tell her to put herself first when all he probably wanted was some peace from the kids was evidence of his love too.

She absent-mindedly stroked the steering wheel and looked out the window. She needed to decide fast. Suddenly something flicked into life, like a piece which had been out of reach now appearing through the veil. Her hands scooped the phone off the passenger seat and, without hesitation, she called Anna, leaving a voice message announcing she was ill and needed to go home. Then she sent an email to the estate agents to say she would be picking up the keys today and would they be open until five thirty for her to be able to do that? Following that, she searched online for a hire company on the island and rang them to book a small rental car. She then texted Scott to let him know her plans had changed, and finally Lesley to ask if she'd have time this evening for a quick call.

Releasing the handbrake, she turned the car north. It was like she was on autopilot, but, for the first time in years, in a good way. She felt excited at the prospect of the next few days—scared but excited, like maybe there was a way forward that didn't involve suffering and frustration. I mean, she had no idea how, but it was there, like the irresistible flow of the river during a rain storm—you just had to go with the flow.

The Demons scurried away, moaning and spitting in Tal's direction. He stood firm, allowing his light to shine so bright they had to divert their path to keep their darkness intact.

You see, that's the thing, he whispered. *Light will always find a way through. Like a cave that's been in darkness for decades and then suddenly a brick falls in and floods it with light. It will always find a way through.*

✳

The small plane rattled down the runway and leapt off the ground. Maya gripped the armrest tightly as the plane banked right and straightened up on its journey north. She felt herself relax. She always felt calmest when heading north. It was like her spiritual self belonged north, whatever that meant. She knew intuitively she'd had many lives in Scotland, and it held a special place in her heart, but every time she travelled north, she couldn't grasp where this sense of returning home came from. The memory somehow felt close to the surface of her consciousness, but not close enough to reach.

She gave up and closed her eyes, turning her thoughts to how thirsty she was. The bang of the tiny refreshments trolley heralded the arrival of drinks and, after a cup of tea and a wafer, she was feeling decidedly better.

The flight was short and, after dozing for what seemed like just a few minutes, she felt the plane start to descend. As it cleared the layer of cloud, the island came into view. Out of the window to the left she saw the endless blue-grey of the sea. It was rough today and the huge white waves crashed upon the rocks that lined the shore. The sea met the land on a long, thin, bright yellow beach that seemed to stretch on forever.

Maya daydreamed as to what it would feel like to gallop the length of that beach on a horse, and smiled at the thought. The sand dunes behind it seemed to dance in the wind, long reeds lashing to and fro.

As the plane pulled onto the tarmac, Maya was overcome by the change in energy. Clambering down the steps, the earth beneath somehow felt alive, somehow calmer than the mainland. It was like the interference had been turned down on the radio, or at least that was the only way she could describe it to herself.

She walked into the airport building, picked up her bag and collected the keys to the hire car. On leaving the terminal, she noticed the taxi drivers standing outside, chatting cheerfully about the weather. A few of them were speaking in a dialect that felt familiar, but she couldn't understand it and guessed it must be Gaelic.

She stopped abruptly on scanning the cars and finding the right registration that matched the key fob. She'd been furnished with a small, bright green bubble car. Maya laughed out loud, feeling it right down into her chest. Well, she said to herself, that's pretty perfect.

After trying to squeeze her suitcase into the pocket-sized boot, and giving up, she hauled it onto the back seat, before manoeuvring herself into the driver's seat.

'Geesh!' she moaned out loud. How do really fat people get in here?

Maya set the car in motion and pulled into the first fuel station she came across to pick up some supplies for her short stay. As she walked towards the entrance to the shop, her eyes rested on the sacks of coal and kindling for sale in the forecourt.

Perfect, she thought, as she remembered the small fireplace in the front room, deciding to take some with her.

After collecting the house keys from the estate agent, she made her way out of the small town and onto the open moor road. She giggled to herself at how it reminded her of a scene from Lord of the Rings and how she may never be seen again.

She passed by a group of young stags stood proudly on a rock just above the road and marvelled at their auras, as bright as the sun setting behind them. Then the car crossed a small bridge and Maya realised she was almost there. Her stomach flipped for some reason. She felt nervous and a bit light-headed. It was so out-of-character to do something like this, both buy the house in the first place, and then drop everything and come out here for a few days. The guilt started to creep back in and she thought of Faith having to get the horses in by herself again.

Stop, she told herself. You need this. You know you do.

She did. She really did, she agreed from her heart, while her head continued to battle.

Maya swung into the parking space in front of the house and turned off the engine. She looked out over the sea loch and gazed in awe at the view, feeling even more excited when she realised this was the same view that she would see from the kitchen and lounge tomorrow morning.

The sun was now below the horizon and she moved quickly to get her things indoors before the light faded completely. The key turned stiffly in the lock. The house had not been lived in for a few years since the previous owner had died, visited only a few times by her daughters before they put it on the market.

The house smelled of damp and dust and, as she brought

her suitcase inside, she considered opening all the windows to let in some air. She decided it would be best to wait until tomorrow, as it was getting cold and dark and the wind was picking up.

She dropped the sacks of coal and kindling in the hallway and looked around. A sense of peace washed over her. It was so very quiet. Outside, she could sense the roar of the sea as the wind whipped up the waves out past the point where the loch met the open ocean, but in here it was barely audible. The silence seemed to hold her and she felt an instant affinity with the house.

She locked the door behind her. The house looked tired, not having really been upgraded since the 1970s. The sellers had agreed to leave some of the lounge furniture, having no need for them, and Maya thankfully sat down on an old, comfortable sofa. For the bedroom, she'd brought the blow-up bed and sleeping bag which was always in the back of the car. Although she tended to roll her eyes at Jacob's 'Zombie Apocalypse' habit of having everything you could ever need with you at all times, she was pretty grateful for his preparedness now.

The light disappeared behind the horizon and the water danced out on the loch under the darkening sky. She breathed deeply and noticed how it felt—raw, like she'd not used those parts of her lungs for quite some time. She went into the kitchen and was met by a bottle of champagne and a card.

What a lovely thought! she smiled, opening the card and reading the well wishes of the women who had been born and brought up here and who had now moved on to different phases of their lives.

She used one of the pans left on the cooker to boil some water and made a cup of milky tea, taking it back to the sofa in the lounge. Setting it on the small shelf by the window she became distracted, lighting the fire and preparing for her session with Lesley, and ended up with a lukewarm drink, which she quickly gulped down as she powered up her laptop and connected the call.

Maya sat in silence, waiting until Lesley's smiling face came into view. 'Hey, gorgeous!' she exclaimed. 'How are you?' Then, after a short pause, 'Where are you?'

'I'm on the island,' Maya replied shyly.

'Oh my God, no way!' Lesley cried. 'That's awesome. Are you on your own?'

'Yep,' Maya confirmed, twiddling with her earphones. 'It feels weird, but nice,' she added.

'This is amazing! Oh honey, I can feel the energy from here. So, what are you going to do? How long are you there?'

'Well, I want to try some meditation again,' Maya replied. 'I've never been able to do it on my own. And I'd like to visit the Standing Stones. I've seen pictures of them and they call to me. I don't think they're far from here. And, well, I guess I'll just chill. I'm only here three days so I'm sure it'll fly by.'

'Perfect,' Lesley responded.

The two women spent some time exploring Maya's childhood again, and Lesley helped her to sit with the things that had cause her grief and upset.

'Remember, you were doing the best you could in that moment. Be kind to yourself. Tell your younger self it's okay and move on. By leaving the conditioned behaviours and beliefs that don't serve us, we open our heart space for those that do to come in,' she explained.

'Yes, I get that,' Maya agreed. 'But it's hard.'

'It's as hard as you want to make it,' Lesley replied.

Maya didn't quite get what she meant by that.

'Shall we finish with a meditation?' Lesley asked, cutting through her confused thoughts.

'Sure,' Maya said, tensely. She struggled with the meditations, often allowing her mind to wander to the washing and other mundane topics, while scolding herself for not concentrating on Lesley's voice.

'We're going to try something a little different tonight,' Lesley announced.

She produced a large Native American looking drum from somewhere off camera and began to beat it rhythmically. Maya closed her eyes and was instantly transported back to the vision of the past lives she had experienced before. Yet this time she could hear the thoughts of the perpetrator that had hurt her and her companions.

'This doesn't seem right,' he mumbled in his head. 'They don't seem like savages. But I have to feed my family.'

He was anxious and thoughts raced around his head. Maya felt the pain in his heart, as if it were her own.

Behind the scene playing out, she saw a tall man standing on a hill watching the events. He seemed almost transcendent, like he was a ghost. He wore a large headdress of colourful feathers and he raised his stick to the skies, holding out both hands and praying to Almighty Mother Earth and Father Sky for mercy for his people.

The scene changed and Maya could see impressive stones arranged in a circle, each one unique. She felt as though she was sitting with her back to one but she wasn't able to see herself. At each stone around the circle was a different animal, all looking at her. The wolf three stones round from her held her in a stare with piercing yellow eyes. As she stared back, she saw a young wolf playing in the trees with a teenage boy. He was tall with dark hair and she guessed he must be about seventeen. The young wolf squealed with delight as the boy rolled him around in the snow and chased him in and out of the trees.

Suddenly a shot rang out and the wolf fell to the ground. The boy clambered to his side and wept uncontrollably over the lifeless corpse. Maya felt emotions rise in her, the anger was almost too much, the grief at what it felt like to witness this, this past incarnation which she started to compute was likely to be her.

She was brought back to the yellow eyes of the first wolf, as a tall Native American man entered the circle. She recognised him as the man from the hill.

'We are all one,' he spoke clearly into her mind. 'We are all here to have experiences, to help us learn and grow under the watch of the Great Creator.'

Maya looked again at the wolf, who had now been joined by a whole pack. Despite the presence of nine large, menacing looking canines, the deer, rabbits and other animals standing at the stones did not back away. They appeared to welcome their companions, accepting their great role in the circle of life.

Maya felt a huge wave of emotion as tears streamed down her face and she heard the last words the man uttered as a question.

'What things do you not say yes to because of fear?'

As she slowly came back to an awareness of the present, she realised Lesley had stopped beating her drum and had fixed her eyes on her.

'Sooo, what was going on there, then?' she asked, coyly smiling. 'You were proper gone, Mrs I-can't-meditate. Yeah, whatever.'

Maya cleared her throat, hoping it still functioned well enough to allow her to speak. She recounted the experience to Lesley, who listened intently and finished the session by telling her to get herself to those Stones tomorrow.

Maya flipped the screen shut and stood up, stiff and in need of a warm drink. After a few minutes of fiddling, she managed to work out the heating and hot water, and headed to the bedroom to make up the blow-up bed. She punched her pillow to make it comfy and laid her head down.

As soon as she closed her eyes she heard Tal's voice as clear as day in her head.

Light is knowledge is truth. Darkness is lack of knowledge, or untruth. If humans tell themselves stories enough, they will believe them equally. If someone is told often enough that something is true, and they don't have the discernment of the light—because they are in fear—then it will become their truth, even though it's not the actual truth. Do you see?

She nodded, dazed and unable to process the words further, other than a fleeting understanding of what Tal was trying to tell her. Promising herself she would think more on it tomorrow, she fell into a deep sleep as the moon beamed in through the curtain-less window.

11

Jacob sighed as he scooped up Zidan's socks from the bathroom floor and held them up for inspection. Yep, rock solid with mud. He knew why—trying to get Zidan to wear shoes outside was painful; the kid had insisted many times that he didn't in fact need shoes and that socks sufficed just fine, thank you, Dad. He seemed completely oblivious to the fact that he was trailing mud through the house every time he ran in and out with just socks on.

Jacob tossed them in the laundry and shouted down to Amy it was time for her bath.

'Dad,' Aurora yelled up the stairs. 'I think Faith's fallen off the horse. Pilot's running loose by the gate with his tack on.'

Jacob's blood ran cold. He dropped the shampoo bottle and barked at Aurora to put her little sister in the bath and not leave her. He raced out round the house and to the back gate in his slippers looking for signs of Faith laid out on the field.

On first look he couldn't see her anywhere. The horse, bored now with the drama, had started munching on the grass, his reins trailing behind him. Jacob scanned the field again and saw Faith sitting down in front of the stone wall at the far end. As he got closer, he was relieved to see there were no bits hanging off her, but she was holding her stomach and tears tracked down her face.

'What happened?' he asked sympathetically, hauling her up and checking her over himself.

'He just tanked off and bucked! Bloody idiot horse. He's such a twat for me sometimes, but he's always good for Mum.'

'Well, Mum doesn't gallop him round the field. And she's bigger than you. You need to be careful, Faith. Why were you riding your Mum's horse anyway?'

'I just wanted to exercise him,' she responded miserably. 'I think he misses her. He needs work. He's going to get laminitis.'

Jacob put his arm round her and led her back towards the gate. 'Do you want me to have a look at your stomach?' he asked.

'No!' she shrieked, recoiling from him. 'It's just a scratch.'

'Okay, okay,' Jacob answered, holding his hands up in surrender. 'Yesh, Faith. Chill out.'

'I'm just fed up,' she sniffed between tears. 'I never feel like I do anything right and all my friends are so good at everything and I get so angry a lot of the time. I don't mean to,' she said, sobbing again. 'I just get overwhelmed and I don't know whether I want all this responsibility of the horses. No one helps me when Mum's not here. You won't let the kids help because you think they'll get hurt. That's not fair on me!' she swung round, voice almost at a shout again.

'Faith, they're young and they don't know much about

horses, right? I don't want them handling them. I told your mother that leaving you to do the horses was a bad idea, but she doesn't want to sell them and she's away a lot of the time. I mean, what are we supposed to do?' He wrung his hands in exasperation.

Pilot, having decided the commotion with the humans was more entertaining than the grass, had started walking over to them, accidentally stepping into his trailing reins and making half rearing gestures in an attempt to get free.

'Oh, for God's sake, Pilot,' Faith fumed, stomping over towards him and releasing the buckle at the end of the rein to free him.

'Come on,' Jacob said, opening the gate. 'Let's get him put away.'

They walked into the stable yard, Faith dragging a reluctant Pilot who would have preferred to stay in the field. 'You haven't brought the horse feed I asked for. What am I supposed to feed them?' she ranted, but Jacob had already closed the stable door and her voice was just a muffle inside.

He sat down on a bale of straw in the lean-to at the side of the stable, retrieving a cigarette he had rolled earlier and reaching into his pocket to find his lighter.

You see, this is the thing, he told himself. We've built this life for our children, trying to give them a free and varied upbringing in a good part of the country with a nice house but, truth be told, in order to give them this, Maya's selling her freedom and her energy and, potentially one day, her soul.

He kicked at the dirt. Maya was always the one that had pushed for the horses. She had ridden as a child and had continued all her adult life. She'd had horses when Jacob met her and, since they got married, the animals had been a non-negotiable part of their monthly budget. He wondered how much of it was actually because of a true passion for riding, and how much was simply something she'd been programmed to do as a middle class pastime when she was younger.

He rubbed his head, successfully singeing one of his eyebrows with his cigarette and frantically rubbing it for a few seconds to ensure it was out, after which he continued his trail of thought. He knew how much horses meant to Maya— he could see it when she was with them. It was like she could talk to them, and their understanding of her gave her a sense of peace. But he couldn't help thinking that perhaps all this riding and taxiing Faith to pony club and keeping horses in small paddocks was a toxic energy for both the horse *and* Faith, and it was actually causing more pressure than benefit. Faith seemed as overwhelmed as Maya, he reflected.

'Dad,' Faith shouted, jolting him out of his thoughts. 'What the hell are you doing? You'll set fire to the stables!'

'No, I won't,' he scowled.

'Really?' she shot back, closing Pilot's stable door behind her and putting her hands on her hips.

'How do you explain the singed eyebrow then, if you're so good with things that might burn other things down?' she spat, tripping over her words. 'For God's sake, you silly old git,' she ranted, stomping off in the direction of the hay shed.

Silly old git, he fumed quietly. That girl is so bloody rude most of the time. She needs a reality check. He tried to gather his frustration, remembering what Maya had said about being more tolerant and less confrontational, and that the kids took his gruff ways to heart. He sighed, fighting between good old-fashioned discipline and trying to ensure his temper didn't make the situation worse, giving Faith even more reason to hate him.

He stubbed his cigarette out in the dirt and started back towards the house, remembering that Amy was in the bath and hoping that, for once, Aurora hadn't chosen to ignore his instructions and leave her little sister to drown.

✳

'Aurora. Aurora,' Jacob yelled, taking the staircase two at a time. He stopped at the door to the bathroom, being met by the scene of bubbles everywhere and Aurora playing with a rubber duck at one end of the bath while Amy shrieked with laughter at the other.

Jacob leaned his head on the door frame.

'Thank you, Aurora,' he smiled. Then, directing his gaze at the little girl laughing and throwing bubbles towards him, he said, 'Make sure you dry yourself off well, Amy, and get your pyjamas on.'

'Okay,' she said, standing up and reaching for the towel Aurora passed to her.

Jacob wandered out of the bathroom. Free of needing to react to whatever the kids were getting up to, he remembered that he'd set out his clippers to shave off his now very long and irritating beard.

Time for a fresh crop, he thought, entering the bedroom and picking up the clippers laid on the side.

He managed to get halfway through transforming his overgrown bush to a grizzly stubble when he heard an almighty crash and a loud scream from the kitchen, heralding the next trauma to be dealt with.

Zidan had beaten him down the stairs and was standing in the entrance to the kitchen, shouting at Faith. Jacob stepped around him and surveyed the broken plates and cups all over the floor.

'Sorry,' Faith mumbled apologetically. 'I was trying to put them away and start the dinner but I tripped.'

Jacob sighed. 'Well, at least you were being useful for once,' he grumbled, starting to clean up the mess while Faith put some frozen pizzas into the oven.

Twenty minutes later they sat down to eat, squabbling over the pieces that had the most cheese on them. Silence descended while they tucked in and then Jacob noticed the sniggers and giggles.

'Kids,' he snapped. 'I'm not in the mood.'

'Dad,' Faith explained calmly. 'It's kind of hard not to laugh when you're sitting there looking like you've been attacked by a Viking with a blunt axe.'

Jacob crossed the room to look in the mirror by the door. He tried not to laugh but the kid's giggles were spreading like an infectious wave and they *did* have a point—he looked ridiculous.

He sat back down, enjoying the joviality at the table before a wave of sadness came over him. Maya should be here. This is what family is really about. This is what *life* is about.

He sighed, acknowledging that while they had a huge rent and bills to pay, none of that was real. They had created the comfortableness of privilege that comes with living in a large house in the country with horses. It meant, however, that the children didn't have the stability of two parents at home and the one thing money can't buy: time. Time to be together while they were all still young. Even if Jacob were to switch places with Maya and go out to work, it wouldn't be any different, not if they wanted a better future together. There was no question about it—they were going to have to swap material goods for that valuable energy called time.

12

Maya blinked her eyes open, aware of the immense light streaming into them. She rubbed them and looked around, forgetting for a second where she was. The sun had risen above the horizon and was flooding into the window, casting light across the walls, so bright that she struggled to see. Sitting up on her makeshift bed, she remembered where she was and smiled, flopping back down again.

The bed wasn't hugely uncomfortable, although getting up out of it may be an issue for her since it was only about ten inches off the ground. She lay for a few minutes, listening to the sound of silence. Occasionally a sheep bleated or a seagull cried, but in between it was the kind of silence that appeared loud. It was exactly what she needed, although a part of her felt nervous and stripped bare, like there was nowhere to hide, like a screen was about to start playing of her life and she had to watch it even though this wasn't the moment before death. It was a crossroads she had come to pause at and was forced to choose the path forward from here.

After a while she stretched and got up, padding over to the

window. The heather was brown, devoid of life after the long winter, but the grasses had started to peep through, rendering the landscape various shades of green and brown.

In the distance, on the loch, Maya spotted a small fishing vessel chugging through the water, presumably heading out to open seas in search of a catch. Overhead, the seagulls fought over the remains of a fish, snapping at each other in mid-air, while a row of starlings sat on a single electrical wire and watched.

Maya soaked in the view and surroundings before making her way to the kitchen to boil up some water for a fresh cup of tea and to open one of the packets of biscuits she'd bought the evening before.

Once her makeshift breakfast was prepared, she took it to the chair in front of the large window and relaxed back into it, cradling her tea as she continued to observe the scene outside.

In the meadow opposite, newborn lambs were playing with each other, running around and jumping from the small rocks that dotted the landscape. She soon found herself in stitches at their antics and she felt as though, if she could just stay here, everything might be okay. True, she'd soon get hungry and miss her family, she figured, but some time, just to sort out her jumbled head would be great, she told herself. The thing was, she knew a few days wasn't going to cut it. She had a lot of internal work to do if she was going to get to the other side of the hill called anxiety and overwhelm.

After what seemed like a few minutes but was actually nearer two hours, Maya peeled herself out of the seat, desperate for the toilet, and then got dressed. She decided to head out to look for the Standing Stones she had mentioned to Lesley last night. It was an overcast day but not raining, thankfully. She remembered the beach she'd gone to with Jacob and made a mental note to herself where she'd need to turn on her way back so she could visit that too.

After following the snaking, single track roads for around half an hour, regularly checking the signposts and the map on her phone, she pulled into a car park and from there was able to see the Stones on the top of a nearby hill.

Maya locked the car doors and made her way up the winding path towards the Stones. There was a busload of tourists just coming down the other way but otherwise it seemed quiet. Good timing, she thought to herself.

She opened the gate sectioning the Stones off from the open moor and walked towards the large information board. She paused, starting to read it but then decided she'd rather see what the Stones themselves had to tell her instead.

They were arranged in the shape of a large Celtic cross, with thirteen large stones of different shapes creating a circle in the middle. A larger centre piece stood opposite an area which had at one time perhaps been a type of altar, with four corner supporting beams, worn down by the weather and devoid now of the altar centrepiece that may have lain on top of it.

Maya noticed that the colour of the grass outside the circle was different to that inside and, as she walked to the middle of it and stood in front of the large headstone, a vision of the night before came to her.

This was where I was last night when I saw the wolves,

she realised, her hand involuntarily moving over her mouth in shock.

She bent then, removing her shoes and socks and touching her hands to the earth in front of the Stones. At first, she was aware of the cold ground biting at her toes and felt a bit self-conscious, but as she persisted she saw visions of ancient times flash across her mind's eye, celebrations with children singing and laughing, huge baskets of fruits and vegetables being offered to the Gods at harvest. The people wore bright, light clothes and the long-skirted women looked on as the children played. The energy felt light; it felt happy.

The vision changed then, the feeling becoming dense and heavy. Maya felt the terror and sadness before the images came, first of still-life, then of movement, of people being dragged into the stone circle, being offered as sacrifices on the slab at the head of the circle where she now stood. The pain and blood from these poor, innocent souls, mainly young women, dripped into the soil, blocking the beautiful ley lines she had observed in the previous vision.

Then came visions without people, and of a time where the earth covered the Stones high, and they were forgotten and left to fall into ruin.

The visions stopped then and she came back to her surroundings, aware that a couple had just entered the gate with their small dog and were making their way over. Feeling a wave of self-consciousness come over her again, she put her shoes and socks back on and wandered around the other parts of the site, observing the energy at different points. She felt like she couldn't stay too long. It was like this place needed to be visited regularly, but in short bursts, as the energy was so strong, a mixture of both light and dark, which made her feel dizzy.

As she left, she noticed that two rows of stones ran from the main block pointing north. So many references to north in my life, she thought to herself, smiling and turning back towards the direction she'd come.

She mused some more on that as she wandered through the ancient stones and acknowledged a deep feeling that there was clearly more to understand about the significance of heading north.

Maya headed back towards the information board, interested to know what it said about the Stones. She let out a small laugh as she read how the Stones had been found recently buried under mounds of soil and peat, and been restored by the local community.

She left the site and wandered back down the path, stopping at the small gift shop to buy a few bits for the kids and grab a coffee and cake.

＊

She drove back along the road towards home. Home. She liked that. The house already felt like home, even if they weren't going to be living in it full-time. She stopped once to admire the seals laid out on a rock about twenty metres from the shore. Getting out of the car and scrambling down the rocky escarpment to get a better view, she noticed a baby seal lying next to its mum and wished she had binoculars to get a better look. Be grateful for what you have in the moment, not what you don't, she chided herself, making her way back up to the road.

She returned to the house via the beach she'd visited with Jacob the last time they were here. As she walked across the sand and felt the wind blowing through her hair, she considered the colossal feeling of the land she was immersed in. For the first time, she understood what people meant when they said they could feel the land in them. There was an ancient calling here, memories bubbling below the surface that, on the mainland, could not be heard for the hustle and bustle of the cities and technology.

She sat on the grass, wiggling her toes among the different blades and small flowers just starting to bud, and watching the huge waves crash on the rocky island that stood proudly out to sea. She suddenly remembered that one of the ladies who'd sold them the house had said smugglers used to use this beach, and wondered how they landed their boats without them being smashed to pieces on the jagged rocks.

Pulling her phone out of her pocket to call Jacob, she realised there was no signal and found that surprisingly comforting. Ah, work couldn't reach me here, she laughed out loud.

'Where the hell is she, useless woman?' she imagined Anna exclaiming in a posh English accent.

I just don't fit into that world, she thought.

But I need to. I mean, how can I provide for my family if I can't earn a good living? And nowadays it's all about getting a good job, or working hard at a manual job with low pay until you're too knackered to continue. Mind you, she added to herself, manual jobs knacker you physically—the job she did, well, some days it felt like it was trying to rob her of her soul. It's a mental toll, she realised. And it's a trap. So much of her energy could be put to better use.

As the sun began to lower in the sky and a chill crept into the air, Maya walked back to the car and drove the short distance to the house. She couldn't help but feel a process had been kicked into motion and a huge change was coming. She just had to hold onto the hand rail of the train and wish for the best.

It's happening for your highest good, Tal reassured her as she drove back, blinking back tears and feeling like this island was where she had come to heal.

And heal you must, he told her. Not only for her sake, but for the sake of her children, who would continue with the same old overwhelming conditioning and trauma unless she broke the pattern and set them all free.

The next day flew by far too quickly for Maya. When she spoke with Jacob and told him what she had been up to she couldn't really recount anything on the second day. It was like time had stood still. But as she packed her few possessions to leave, she felt a heavy ache in her heart. She didn't want to go back to work, she didn't want to go back to the way things were at home. She'd been holding on so tight, just keeping things together, and now it felt like the cord had been pulled and she was unravelling at an alarming rate. She wanted more than anything to go home, fix the problems at work, prove she could do all that was required of her and keep earning lots of money for the next ten years to ensure her kids had a good start in life. But she didn't know if she could. Her spirit was too strong, her sense of what's right and what's wrong—it felt like her days of being polite and of conforming were over. A huge wave was bursting up within her and she just couldn't play along any more.

Oh, God, she thought, shutting the car door and setting off to the airport. She could feel the lionheart in her stir into life, and that didn't bode well for the fragile balance of pretence she wore like a mask most of the time.

The plane bumped down on the tarmac and, after navigating through the hustle of the airport, Maya made it to her car and drove homewards. As she pulled up on the drive, she noticed Amy hanging upside down in a tree in the garden. She cut the engine and gathered her things, walking round to the door and, as she did, a scream rang out from round the corner.

Maya raced round just as Jacob appeared out of the back door in time to see Amy hanging by her ripped pants three feet from the ground. She was half laughing, half crying and Maya dropped her bags and ran to her rescue, while Jacob watched on in fits of laughter.

'Dad's laughing at me,' she cried, as Maya unhooked her and lifted her down.

'Well, it *was* a bit funny,' Maya responded, hiding her face in Amy's shoulder so she couldn't see that she too was having a hard time not laughing.

'I was rushing to see you,' Amy said sadly.

'I know, princess,' Maya reassured her. 'And here I am. Come on, let's go inside. You can tell me all about what you've been up to.'

'Okay,' Amy said, grabbing her hand. 'I've made cupcakes!' she squealed, as she dragged Maya to the door, allowing her a brief kiss with Jacob and a rushed hello. 'Look, Mum,' she said, proudly producing a plate of cupcakes with watery icing dripping off the sides.

'Lovely,' said Maya. 'I'll just make a cup of tea to go with them, shall I?'

'Okay, but only if I can have juice,' Amy responded, wagging her finger, with her other hand on her hip.

'Chip off the old block, that one,' Jacob commented, as he passed through the kitchen, winking at her.

✳

After Maya had spent time with each of the children and then flopped down beside Jacob in their large bed, she allowed herself to think back to the last few days.

'So,' Jacob started, turning to face her with one eyebrow raised, as he tucked the edge of the pillow over on itself to get his head comfy. 'How was it?'

'It was… it was amazing,' Maya smiled. 'It felt weird being on my own, but after a day I started to love the space and freedom. I thought I would be doing a lot of thinking, but actually it wasn't like that.'

Jacob snorted and barked out between laughter, 'So you just sat there mute? I can see it now, just sat there staring into space for three days, like she finally *has* lost it,' he continued between chuckles.

'Shut up,' she squealed, throwing the nearest spare pillow at him. 'Not like that. It's hard to explain.'

'There's something about that place, isn't there?' he said, his tone growing serious.

'Yeah,' Maya agreed. 'There sure is. It feels like the path to a new life. Scary, but needed,' she concluded, but, in his usual fashion, Jacob had fallen asleep mid-sentence and had shifted into his pre-snore breathing rhythm.

Maya sighed, rolling over to reach for her earplugs before the soft vibrations became a roaring hippo and she wouldn't be able to get off to sleep.

✳

It felt like only two minutes since she had snuggled down to sleep when Maya was shaken awake.

'Mum, I've been sick,' Amy cried, standing next to the bed, covered in vomit.

'Brilliant,' Maya groaned, rolling out of bed and steering Amy to the bathroom. Vomit trailed the walls from her room to Amy's.

'Like, couldn't you stand still while you were doing it?' Maya reprimanded, feeling queasy herself.

She'd never been very good with vomit but, luckily for her, kid puke seemed to affect her far less than what the dogs spewed up. That was always left to Jacob to clean up, otherwise Maya ended up hurling alongside the dogs.

After cleaning Amy up and giving her a small bath and clean pyjamas, and tucking her up between her and Jacob, with a bowl at the side of the bed, she finally lay back down. Glancing at the clock, she sighed to herself when she saw she only had fifty minutes before she'd have to get up at five a.m. and leave for work.

She rested as well as a Mum with a vomiting child could for the remaining time and then got up and dressed, gathering her things quietly. Amy had fallen asleep again and was now sprawled across her side of the bed, still looking rather green round the gills. She figured there was no point in waking a grumpy Jacob to tell him what had happened.

He might just get the same surprise I got when I woke up, she thought, smiling to herself as she went down the stairs and out to the car to drive south.

The traffic was quiet and Maya was making good time. After travelling for around three hours, she stopped to grab a coffee and a croissant. The sun was coming up behind the line of trees outside the motorway service station as she made her way back to the car, coffee in hand.

It was a pleasant morning, but Maya couldn't shake the feeling of dread in her stomach. She was becoming tired of trying to convince herself it wasn't there and that everything was fine and work wasn't that bad. She was getting weary of trying to tell herself that it wasn't that corrupt and messed up in the corporate world now, and that they still did make a difference and saved people's lives. It's true that sometimes they did, but it felt like only once in a blue moon these days. It had all got lost in this bigger monster of money, half-truths and greed, and the whole thing felt tacky and wrong to her.

She considered as she drove south how simple things must have been three hundred years ago when, if you were ill, you either died or got better from a combination of herbs and your own natural healing methods. Nowadays, how do you know what makes you ill and what cures you? From stress to EMF radiation to an array of pharmaceutical drugs, it was hard to isolate the good from the bad. It all just felt grey and tangled. The energetic feeling of modern-day medicine wasn't a good one, she concluded, as she swung the car into the company's parking lot and dusted remnants of croissant off her blouse.

Ben was already at his desk when she walked in. 'Hi, Maya, how are you feeling? Are you on this workshop thing today?' he enquired, lifting his head above the computer to get a better look at her.

'Better, thanks. And yes, I am, for my sins,' she answered, sitting down and opening her laptop, not really feeling like engaging.

Ruth came round the corner a minute later and, straight away, Maya could detect the panic in her.

'You okay?' Maya asked.

'Erm, can we talk in one of the offices?' Ruth answered, looking nervously around her.

'Sure,' Maya replied, shutting her laptop lid and leading her into the nearest room. 'What's up?' she enquired, closing the door behind Ruth.

'Well, you know how we set up the contracts in a certain way because we couldn't just stop the services to patients or their blood would be lost to follow-up and it would be dangerous and make everyone at the hospital go mental?'

'Yes,' Maya answered, noticing a tingling feeling run down her spine.

'Well, the new Medical Director says we've breached all sorts of stuff and he's saying that we've put the wrong things in the literature too and that you aren't fit to manage all this stuff. Sorry, Maya, I thought you should know. And Anna just lets him talk about you like she doesn't care. While you were off I tried to talk to your old boss, you know, the one that signed it all off? But she clearly doesn't want to support us now she's moved on and got her promotion and, well, it's so unfair and it's not right you should take the blame for delivering almost the impossible and everyone else is just basking in the glory and now it's old news and the work actually needs doing and there's problems—'

'Ruth,' Maya cut in, touching her arm. 'Breathe. It's okay, I'm a big girl. I will handle it. But thank you for your honesty and your concern,' she smiled.

'What if they fire you?' she said, blinking back tears.

'What if they fire me?' Maya returned. 'We were just trying to do the right thing, being put in difficult positions by those higher up not wanting to take responsibility and... Ruth, I know, I know. It's okay. Go and take a breath. Why don't you go for that walk you enjoy round the block? Just centre yourself before we go to the workshop,' Maya said, more calmly than she felt.

'Okay, yes, good idea. Sorry, I'm not normally like this,' Ruth responded nervously.

'I know,' Maya confirmed, smiling. 'You're one of the best members of the team and I'm sorry it's stressing you out so much. Go and have a walk. We can talk more later.'

'Okay,' Ruth sniffed, picking up her bag and leaving the office, moving quickly down the corridor to the exit, clearly not wanting to bump into anyone in case she needed to explain her state.

Maya sat back, fighting the urge to scream. Was there anyone in this company not willing to tread on someone else to get up the ladder? That isn't even the craziest thing, she thought. What's crazier is they actually convince themselves that they aren't treading on anybody and come up with delusional stories about how people were just not cut out for the job, or it was for their own good, or through character assassination they're neatly put into a box of 'Oh, we were just different people.' The lies they told themselves were insane, yet they seemed to truly believe it.

The devil is very sly and convincing, Tal offered her as she calmed her breathing.

'Isn't he just?' she snarled, getting up, determined to stand her ground. Well, not on my watch, she thought, angrily banging open the door and stomping back to her desk.

Ben looked up and pushed back his chair. He walked over to Maya. 'Maybe you should have stayed off sick,' he whispered. 'Maya, don't make yourself ill. It's not worth it.'

Maya huffed, looking at him through glazed eyes. 'So I'm the talk of the office, then? You don't even need to ask what's wrong. You've already heard the stories, I'm guessing?'

'I told you to be careful,' Ben sniped back. 'You know what it's like if you get on the wrong side of the wrong people.'

Maya abruptly put her hand up in front of his face. 'Stop!' she barked. 'Stop talking like that's okay. It's not. Look at all this Human Resources policy bullshit,' she exclaimed, grabbing the thick manual from her desk. 'Yet really, none of it matters. It can all be spun a certain way if needs be, as long the person spinning it has the talent of the Devil in them.'

'Maya,' Ben grimaced, glancing around, aware that people were starting to look at them. 'Don't get all biblical on me,' he groaned. 'Come on, let's get a coffee before the workshop from hell starts.'

'No, thanks,' Maya said bitterly, staring back at her laptop.

'Maya, come on. I *do* care. It's—'

'It's what, Ben? You only care to the point that it doesn't affect your job or your reputation. You're not willing to stand up for what's actually right. No one is. It doesn't matter... What if it had been *your* wife that had died?' she asked, staring up at him.

His eyes flickered like he was pretending he didn't know what Maya was referring to, but then he hung his head slightly. 'Well, she wouldn't have taken it. I would have told her not to. Too much risk,' he said quietly.

Maya's mouth dropped open as she processed what she'd just heard.

'Right,' she said slowly. 'Yet they're giving them out like candy at the hospital and that's okay? And *you're* one of the good guys in here by comparison!' she snorted, pushing past him towards the toilets.

Maya spent the afternoon standing on the outside of groups, avoiding eye contact with Anna who had made some loud remark about Maya's mood to the group. She clung to each shallow breath, willing herself not to cry or to allow the emotions bubbling inside her to come to the surface. It felt like she was drowning, suppressing all her true self to fit into a box of conformity. Why couldn't she just perform like a robot and go home like most of the people here? Why did she care so much? Why were the emotions so raw and so real?

There had been a time that she'd felt nothing and, in some ways, it was peaceful. Numb but peaceful. Now this raging storm was awake inside of her and, no matter the fear of what may happen, she couldn't toe the line, couldn't put her inner fire back to sleep. It wasn't going to work.

Maya could feel people looking at her. Some were sending waves of sympathy, others judgement, and a few were clearly wondering if her job was about to come up and whether they could get it. Nobody really got it, she thought to herself, sighing internally. She felt she would burst with frustration; she just didn't fit anywhere.

Four o'clock came around and the last group presented their findings. Maya turned on her heel as soon as the last clap had finished and bolted out the door. She went upstairs, gathered her things and walked out of the office to her car without a backward glance. As she roared out of the car park, she felt eyes from the top window on her and, glancing up, she saw the smug face of Anna looking down at her from the corner office.

Maya's tears blinded her as she sped north, not stopping until she reached home as the clock hit midnight. She tried the door, finding it unlocked and Jacob standing behind it with outstretched arms.

'I felt you coming,' he said, smiling as Maya's stream of tears turned into a raging torrent. She fell into his arms and cried until she couldn't see for the swelling in her eyes.

He guided her up to bed, tucking her under the blankets

and kissing the top of her head. Maya felt the warmth of the blankets and the protection of Jacob's love, and fell into one of the deepest sleeps she'd ever experienced.

There were voices calling to her in that time between sleep and awakening. They told her it would be okay, that she would find her true north. They told her not to give up or turn back, but as her eyes blinked open she felt a huge wave of fear grip her stomach.

What had she done? How would they feed themselves? What if they got kicked out of their home or couldn't pay the mortgage on the island house? What would the kids think? What would Jacob think?

She couldn't do this. She needed to drive back down there and go back into work. She needed to say sorry to Anna and agree to the retraining she was no doubt going to suggest and maybe a sidestep into something else.

Maya sobbed into the pillow, wrestling with the feeling of fear consuming her. She felt so alone, so tired and alone. In a house full of five other people, she had never felt so isolated.

Angry thoughts arose then, like fuel on a fire. It burned hotter. She stoked the flames as she thought about how Jacob never brought much money in and begrudged looking after the children, how he judged her for every penny they didn't have but didn't contribute fully to the bills, how he constantly moaned that the kids were a twenty-four hour job, then fell asleep on the sofa in the middle of the afternoon, leaving them to feed themselves some days.

She sobbed harder, trying to turn her thoughts more positive. She could feel the negative energy swirling round her and suddenly had the thought to ask for help. 'Tal,' she cried quietly between sobs. 'Please help me. I don't know what to do.'

Maya remembered reading about angelic protection and how, due to Earth being a free will planet, you need to ask for their help. They couldn't give it without your permission, unless it was a split-second decision that would deviate you from your purpose in this life.

She felt the air around her lift almost immediately and was aware of some kind of unseen tussle of energies that lasted only a few seconds. The intensity lifted enough for her to get control of her breathing and calm herself down.

Above her, beyond the veil of the 3D world, Tal batted the Demons away as they scurried around him, his companion that had been watching from afar swooping into the fight and pulling two by their wings.

It would be a lot easier, he stated while wrestling the snarling creatures, *if she understood she needs to tell these buggers they don't have permission to be in her auric field.*

I know, I know, Tal groaned, watching more Demons circling above them. *She doesn't realise this*, he said and then stopped, cocking his head to the side. *But then where's the fun in that?*

He barked out a laugh as he shot vertical in a stream of

light, knocking them all outwards. The other Angel shook his head, remaining more serious.

We're behind schedule. Humanity is not waking up quickly enough and understanding the real game and what's at stake. What if they fail?

They won't, Tal pressed into his consciousness. *We'll help enough to reach critical vibration. Just keep believing and assisting. The Fallen One is hoping to take a great many. So many have succumbed to his deceptions and whispers of inversions of the truth, but it won't be enough to claim his victory, not when there's fight left in me,* Tal finished.

Mmm, agreed his companion, smiling and feeling the love-light shining through him, seeing Maya's calmness and watching a string of light as he hoped to connect into the Earth grid.

She's growing stronger and finding her way back. She just needs to lose those Demons from her thoughts, he said, casting an eye at the herd of them, ogling her now from a distance, wary of the Angel's blinding light and the permissions Maya had given them.

Jacob touched Maya's shoulder lightly and she sprang awake.

'What,' she groaned. Then, sitting bolt upright, she turned and looked at Jacob. 'Did I fall back asleep?'

'I don't know. When did you wake up the first time?' he

asked, passing her a cup of tea. 'The kids are away to school. I didn't tell them you were here. No one found you, then?'

'No, I guess not,' she shrugged. 'Wait, Jacob, wouldn't they have seen my car?'

'You think our kids are that observant first thing in the morning?' he snorted, sitting down on the end of the bed.

Maya smiled, in spite of how she felt. 'Yeah, fair point, but Faith would have been out to the horses?'

'Yeah, but she's too freaked out by the fox that's been calling for a mate in the dark to notice anything else at the moment. You should see the speed she runs back to the house,' he laughed.

'Jacob, that's mean! Why don't you go out with her, make her feel more safe?' Maya scolded.

'Why, Maya? She *is* safe. I know where she is. Why turn her into a wuss?'

'Oh, for goodness' sake, whatever,' Maya sighed, taking a sip of her tea. 'You could be a bit more compassionate, you know,' she said after a pause.

'Maya, don't start on *me* to detract from *your* issues. What's happened then? At work, I mean?'

Maya's mouth went dry. She didn't feel like she could even voice the words. Her pride felt wounded and she didn't want Jacob to know, didn't want to feel useless and stupid, didn't want him to ask the same question she was asking herself: why couldn't she just shut her mouth and get on with it?

'Maya,' he tried again in a raised voice. 'Tell me what happened.'

Jacob was never good at the more subtle ways of caring,

would never understand that right now putting an arm around her and holding her would help her talk. No, he was going to continue sitting at the end of the bed staring at her and demanding a response even though her tears had started flowing again.

Maya took a deep breath and pushed down all the egoistic things that wanted to come up, to protect the overwhelming vulnerability she was feeling, and tried to explain what happened.

Twenty minutes later, Jacob stood up from the bed and stared out the window for a few seconds before turning back to her. 'Right, let's just move to the island,' he sputtered out.

'What?' Maya cried, screwing up her face. 'We can't! The kids' school, my job, it's—'

'Maya,' he boomed, silencing her. 'I want you alive. This stress and conflict, it's driving you mad and making you and everyone around you unhappy. You can't carry on like this and we never have any money left at the end of the month anyway, paying a huge rent all the time. Just let go. The kids will understand in time. They're not going to have a Mum if you carry on like this. You're exhausted, you look ill and miserable, you don't even feel like my wife recently. You work seventy hours a week and they don't appreciate you. Do you really think people lying on their death beds had wished they'd worked more? Do you really think they wouldn't replace you at the drop of a hat if you weren't here any more?' he demanded, pacing the room.

'But *we* wouldn't—your family, the ones that never see you. Work gets most of your time and energy and attention, Maya.

Just stop!' he pleaded, staring at her as she rubbed her face furiously, knowing that Jacob was right, knowing that striking out and telling him that if he earned a good wage she wouldn't have to shoulder all this would get her nowhere.

The kids' faces passed through her mind and fear jolted through her. 'We can't move them again.'

'MAYA!' he yelled, now getting close to her face. 'They need a *Mum*, not a money factory. I'm struggling. I'm sick of looking after them all the time on my own. I'm tired and grumpy with them most of the time. We need to bring our life back into balance.'

She knew he was right, knew she didn't have the strength to cope any more, but she didn't want to let her kids down. She had built a life for them that, in truth, they couldn't really afford. Now they would hate her forever because she was going to take it all away.

'MAYA!' Jacob yelled at her again, trying to calm her and get her attention. 'You're going to the doctor's. You need to get signed off,' he huffed, stomping out of the bedroom and returning with the phone.

Four hours later, Maya had visited the doctor and got signed off for two weeks with stress and anxiety. She was sitting in bed, staring out of the window, unable to process what was happening. It felt like her world had cracked and water was flowing in uncontrollably, like something had been set in motion that she couldn't stop.

Underneath, and through her connection with Tal, she could feel that it would take time and it was a long journey, but it would end somewhere better. She felt like a young eagle taking its first steps to flying, by beating its wings and finding it could only do it a few times before feeling tired and defeated, but knowing that one day it *would* fly, one day it *would* soar and that staying in the nest forever would no longer be an option, despite being safe and familiar and warm.

Great, she rolled her eyes, staring at the sheep moving slowly across the field outside the window. I'm an eagle, and a baby eagle at that.

'Oh my God, get a grip, woman,' she groaned as the phone lit up, announcing the presence of her Mum and interrupting her somewhat crazy thoughts.

✴

In her bedroom, Faith listened through the wall as her Mum chatted to her Grandma about being off work and needing to rest. She didn't sound particularly sick, Faith huffed, turning her music up on her mobile phone to drown out the noise.

She didn't really get this life, she decided, moving the chair to cover up the area of carpet her hamster had chewed through the previous evening. She had everything a girl should want—a good group of friends, horses, a nice school to go to, but it just didn't feel right. At the same time, she didn't want it to be taken away.

'I mean, what's with that?' she said out loud to herself. To be worried that something will end, but then not being sure you even liked it in the first place?

Faith sighed, picking her nails and pondering whether she'd taken an incorrect turn at the birth canal and ended up on the wrong planet. Everyone here annoyed her, particularly her Dad. He was the worst.

'Big boss man,' she growled, kicking the corner of her wardrobe. She turned her music down again, but Maya had finished her call and all was silent. Faith felt a surge of fear. Something wasn't right with Mum and Dad and things were changing. She could feel it. She knew her Mum wasn't coping —that was evident from her mini-breakdowns, but she didn't want things to change. She finally felt a sense of some kind of stability. Faith often felt angry or upset for no reason, but this was deeper, like a part of her wasn't there. It was unreachable; it felt wrong and she didn't know how to make it better.

The unseen Demons were there, swirling around her energetic field and her Higher Self could feel them, but Faith continued her day, unaware of their effects, as they picked at her confidence and light one thread at a time. Sometimes she would almost grasp their presence, lashing out with her hand or fist at something, but never being able to understand what was driving it.

Tal stood back, knowing her road was long and she wasn't even at the starting blocks yet. But if Maya could master the journey somewhat, then the children could surely follow.

Jacob swilled the water around the washing bowl before letting it out of the sink and hanging the sponge to dry over the tap. He sighed as he turned his mind to Maya. She was adamant she was going to take a break and then go back fighting, that she had to keep going as they didn't have any spare money and that she could talk Human Resources into understanding that what was happening was wrong. The whole organisation wasn't corrupt, she had assured him, just Anna.

Jacob's heart knew otherwise. Sure, most people do good things in the company Maya works for, and they would be horrified if they thought they were helping to push an agenda where profits and control went before patients' health and well-being. But that didn't mean it wasn't happening.

Jacob felt there was much that drove humans that were not of a true and pure nature, but it was slippery and hard to get hold of to explain. He had tried with Maya, but she just didn't seem to see the bigger picture, stuck in her way of seeing the world, of what made her successful and how money would keep them safe and fed. She had, since early childhood, been told that what job you do and how much money you earn were important, and she was struggling to break free from this. He knew her family regarded him as disappointing for not earning a huge wage and conforming as society expected him to, and sometimes he wondered if he was wrong not to play that role. But deep inside there was a greater meaning to all this, a greater path for them all, and working fifty hours a week so he could burn out too wasn't the answer.

Since the early days of their marriage, he had suggested they live off-grid somewhere quiet, lead a simple life and homeschool the children. Over the years, Maya had gone from horrified to mildly interested in the idea, but she didn't see the advantages in the same way Jacob did. He chuckled as he recounted her face when he had described how to build a composting toilet. Yet living here in this big house with all the modern comforts was leading to spoilt kids and a wife in self-destruct.

He sighed again, rubbing his eyes. He knew one thing—he would rather die standing after a good life than live on his knees, and that felt very ancient for him, like it had been his motto in many past lives. Still, he couldn't work out where it fit in this society now. It felt so complicated and interwoven, it was hard to know which thread to start unpicking first to get to the real truth of things. He headed upstairs, deciding that rubbing Maya's feet always chilled her out and might help her think a little clearer.

✳

Maya tossed and turned as visions ran through her mind. She was in that place between awake and asleep again. Women kept appearing and disappearing from her mind. Some were happy, powerful, grounded, knowing who they were and in control of their energy. Others were distraught, sad and captured in chains. Maya's visions slowed to focus on a black-haired woman in a long dress, crying and wailing on the floor.

'You told me they would be safe,' she was sobbing over and over.

Behind her, a man bounced a ball on top of an oil drum, looking bored. 'I lied,' he said, turning and looking straight at what felt like Maya. 'We lie about everything. You're living in an inversion. WAKE UP!'

Maya bolted upright, breathing heavily. The vision faded but the message hammered like a drum on her heart. If the pharmaceutical industry wasn't all that it seemed, what else wasn't as she thought it was? How could she get more control over her life and feel less like she was being tossed about in the middle of the North Sea?

Breathe, a simple word whispered in her consciousness. *Breathe and remember who you really are.*

Maya felt a spark of something rising within her, starting at the base of her spine and flowing up to her head. It wasn't an unpleasant feeling but it sure was strange. She felt a sense of calm wash over her, followed by a surge of determination.

Who the hell does Anna think she is? Who the hell do they *all* think they are? To take my confidence, make me feel like I'm losing it, make me feel like I should just get on with it like everyone else. Do what's right, don't cause a fuss, it'll just go bad for you if you try to stand up. Just sit down and carry on. Who's running my life anyway? she growled to herself. Enough! I'm taking my life and my energy back, she decided, and in so doing she would show her kids how to live like a lion, not a hamster on a wheel.

It sounded great, but how did she do it? she pondered. She felt so tangled in a mess, like a huge ball of wool tightly knotted with no end in sight. Maybe it's too late. Maybe she'd just have to stay on the path she had forged, the bed she had made.

It would be easier, a voice offered. *But no*, it reassured her, *staying where you are leads to rot and decay and suffering. You're done with that story. It's never too late to call back all the energy that's ever been stolen from you. Stand up, get rooted and move forward. You can do this.*

I can, she said through tear-filled eyes. I can.

Jacob pushed on the door as she wiped her face. Wordlessly, he sat down on the bed and started rubbing her feet. Okay, so far so good, she laughed to herself, relaxing back and closing her eyes.

After a few minutes she opened her eyes and looked straight at Jacob, who was studying her curiously. She leaned forward, put a hand either side of his face and gave him a single, loving kiss.

'Okay,' she said, as she pulled back, still looking into his eyes. 'Let's do it. Let's go to the island. All of us.'

He smiled, winking at her as she sat back. 'Now you're talking! There's my Maya, the crazy lady I married,' he chuckled, getting up and punching the air.

13

Jacob sat on his usual rock at the top of the hill behind the house. From here he could see the other hills beyond, littered with wind turbines, the cows and sheep grazing below, and the comings and goings of the road connecting the two villages that sat to the east and west of the farm. He watched as the dogs ran around a nearby bush, blissfully unaware of the churning chaos in the world. He often admired the ability of dogs to be utterly in the present. They really had that off to a tee—maybe that's why Maya so often got frustrated with them. They didn't adhere to time or stress. They just existed in the now.

He turned again, watching the landlord's car speed along the road before him, and wondered what business deal he was hurrying to now. When he first met Richard, he was encouraged by the discussion which centred around his belief that he was a caretaker of the land and was here to look after it for future generations. This claim, however, was not supported by his actions. During his brief stint of working for him last summer, Jacob had been asked to fumigate and kill just about every nettle and so-called weed that existed, and he had to endure endless conversations about money and buying more farms. The man was drunk with ambition and the greed to own more and more, while his wife became sad and lonely and his son learned that to get his father's attention, he had to work all hours of the day and look down on anyone who didn't have money. He had trained him well—the little blighter clearly looked down on Jacob's girls at school and reminded them often they're living in his house and that he'll be moving into it the minute he turns eighteen.

He sighed as the huge four by four disappeared around the bend. Jacob got so triggered when people looked down on him. It had always felt like they were literally stabbing him in the gut. Fundamentally, he mused, it's because of how we measure success on this planet—it's all screwed up and upside down.

He heard a shriek and turned his gaze to the stable yard below, where Faith was chasing after a loose horse. Bloody horses, he muttered, half amused at the show unfolding. Maya was trying to block the horse's escape route, which was easily ten metres across, and Shadow merely dodged round her and into the front garden, where the lush grass was waiting patiently to be strimmed.

Jacob rose from his sitting position, stiff from perching on the edge of the rock, and stretched out his lower back before setting off down the hill, dogs in tow. By the time he entered the yard through the back gate, things had calmed down and Maya was throwing saddles into the back of the car.

'Where are you off to?' he enquired. 'You're on sick leave

and supposed to be resting,' he persisted when Maya ignored him, continuing to rush around, picking things up and throwing them into the boot of the car.

'Taking Faith and Amy to pony club,' she answered, stuffing into her mouth a sweet she'd just extracted from her pocket, which to Jacob's eyes was covered in dirt. If Maya had registered this, her face didn't give it away and she kept on chewing loudly, sending his nerves to the edge of the abyss.

'Maya,' he barked, pacing behind her. 'Why? We agreed we're going to talk to the kids tonight and it can't involve the horses. Why are you rushing to take them to that bloody place?'

Jacob had taken the kids to pony club twice when Maya was working and vowed he wouldn't do it again. The energy at the club had been very low and he'd recognised immediately that most of the kids and ponies didn't want to be there. No, this was much more about unhealed middle-aged women filling themselves with self-importance and forcing their children into something considered to be exclusive.

He sighed again, rubbing his face and trying not to explode. 'Maya,' he tried once more, grabbing her arm and spinning her towards him.

She stopped then, mainly out of shock but also slight dizziness at the speed he had whirled her around.

'Stop. Slow down. Rushing around, doing things you think will make them happy. Being manic and trying to block out what you know we need to do for us and this family, no matter how hard it will be, is only going to exhaust you further.'

'It's not that,' she said, shrugging free of his arm, irritated. 'You wouldn't understand. You never understand.'

'Maya,' he growled. 'You can love horses and have a connection with them without owning a herd and trailering them to a field to look pretty and jump fences, which, by the way, they told me they don't really want to do.'

He deadpanned at the last statement and stood back, watching the boiling pot start to emit steam. A jettison of abuse followed, but he had already tracked back towards the house, knowing he needed to remove himself before he erupted as well.

Maya slammed the trailer shut behind the loaded horses, yelled at the girls to get in the car and pulled herself into the front seat. She slammed the door and tried to get a hold of the frustration bubbling in her chest. Waves of anxiety beat through her, as visions of being fired, having no home or money, letting the children down, and the hurt she and Jacob would cause them by moving house, rushed through her again.

They only want me for the money, she seethed, wondering if she would be better to just do away with herself and let them have the massive life insurance payment the company so gracefully offered. She couldn't catch her breath and could feel the swirling darkness around and in her, but this time it seemed to be clinging tighter than ever, almost a desperate and insistent feeling.

She closed her eyes and concentrated on her breathing, feeling herself ordering the senses into that familiar place, the numb place where she could cope, where she was on autopilot.

By the time the children had climbed into the car, she was calm enough to enquire if they had their hard hats with them, and they set off down the road.

'Hey, Dad,' Zidan chimed as Jacob entered the kitchen. 'What's going on?'

Jacob grunted at him and passed through into the lounge, throwing himself on the sofa. He watched though the reflection on the window as the car and trailer drove off down the lane, and he could almost see the dark cloud swirling above the car, Maya's ego and her Demons desperately trying to keep her trapped and small.

He closed his eyes and settled down to have a nap. Despite everyone around him thinking he was lazy, naps helped him cope. They were an escape from the harsh energies of reality and the constant bombardment of challenges that life seemed to throw at him. They were a place where the kids didn't need something, a place where he couldn't hear their arguing and often where his dreams were about being free and fleeing to beautiful lands. It was hard waking up some days. Yes, sleep was his refuge, he concluded, as he fell into a slumber, unaware of the lonely child stood in the kitchen, wondering what Mum and Dad had been arguing about now.

Zidan fiddled with his toy at the table. It had at some point been a Transformer but was now missing most of the parts. He liked it, though. It kind of looked like an ET Alien with half of its limbs missing. He thought about going upstairs and setting up his Star Wars toys. There wasn't much else to do, as Aurora had her nose in a book, as usual, and Mum was away with the horses again, as usual. Then he thought better of it. There was something odd about his bedroom, the large old wardrobe that had been there when the family had moved in. He didn't like it. At night he could swear he felt monsters moving around in there. It had a bad energy. Something had happened in there, he reasoned. He didn't want it in his room any more. He had told both his parents but they didn't listen. Mum had pointed out it was an expensive piece of furniture and Dad had scoffed at her, telling her to listen to the boy, but then, like most times, he hadn't done anything about it.

He decided to go out to the pond and throw rocks instead. Perhaps he could catch a few more tadpoles for his own mini-pond in the garden. He rose and stomped back out of the door, leaving muddy bootprints under the table for his Dad to find later. Ah, he thought, shutting the door, at least I have three sisters to blame. He picked up a stick and wandered across the lane, reflecting that things could be worse—it could be a school day.

Zidan didn't feel like he fitted in at school. He couldn't understand the bitchiness of the girls, or the boys that were his friend one day and not the next. Why would kids act like that? It didn't make sense to him. Sure, he saw his sisters do the same thing—it was like everyone got programmed to be horrible to each other, yet all the teachers and parents say is that we should be nice and be friends. It didn't make sense why the opposite happened. Come to think of it, it happened to all the adults, too. They're always saying they should treat each other with respect, but he constantly saw the opposite happening in all areas of his life. His Mum had told him once that people often said one thing and did the other, lying to themselves about their behaviour. He figured that was a pretty good description of the state of his school.

After a while of digging around in the dirt and the edge of the pond, and finding two small frogs but no tadpoles, Aurora wandered over to join him.

'Did you find some more?' she enquired, knowing without asking what he was doing.

'Nah,' he replied, sitting down by the water's edge and immediately wishing he hadn't, as the midges were in full force at this level.

'I've finished my book,' she declared. 'It was really good,' she added, looking at him hunched over, rubbing his eyes to try to ward off the biting midges.

'What's up?' she asked after a pause, poking him with one of the smaller sticks she'd found by the edge of the water.

'I heard Mum and Dad talking last night,' he said, looking at her. 'They were talking about moving again, about how Mum's ill from all the travelling and stress and she needs a break and they need less outgoings to be able for her to have a break, or something like that.'

'What?' Aurora exclaimed, taking a step forward. 'No, you must have heard wrong. I'm not going anywhere. I've finally got a few friends and, apart from my older sister being horrid, things are going okay. I'm not leaving. I like my room.'

Zidan lowered his head, regretting awakening the beast. Aurora was kind and fun, but she could also be stubborn. He knew better than to anger her further.

'Okay, whatever,' he said, standing and wandering off down the lane, leaving Aurora staring behind him, processing the implications of what another one of Mum and Dad's crazy adventures might mean for her.

Maya battled with the two horses in her hand, the smaller pony trying to pull in the opposite direction to the larger one, as both had decided the grass was probably sweeter on the other side of her. She had sent Faith and Amy off five minutes ago to find out what groups they were in and they hadn't returned yet. One of the other parents was eyeing her from across the parking area with discontent, having tied her child's pony to the large horsebox they had, and was sitting calmly drinking a cup of steaming tea. Maya found it both upsetting and frustrating—upsetting that she was being judged, frustrating that she didn't have that cup of tea in her hand. She was parched.

Where are those bloody kids? she thought, yanking the reins of the smaller pony in an attempt to pull it back towards her.

'Mum!' Faith shrieked, coming round the side of the trailer at last. 'Why have you let her eat grass? She's going to have green goo on everything now. Thanks a lot!' she scowled, ripping the reins out of Maya's hand.

Amy appeared from the other side of trailer.

'I don't want to ride today,' she said, sitting down. 'I'm tired and so is Burt.'

'I don't care,' Maya mumbled, fastening the girth of the

smaller pony, now that Faith had relieved her of the other one. 'You are riding. Get up.'

'No,' Amy pouted, looking out across the field. 'It's stupid. I'm not doing it.'

'Amy, get your hat from the car and get back here right now. I'm not in the mood,' Maya answered quickly, and in such a manner that sent Amy off to find her hat and comply with the instructions.

Faith was still ranting about green goo while attempting to mount her pony from the side of the trailer ramp.

'Faith, wait!' Maya shouted a second too late, as the saddle slipped and Faith fell back onto the ramp. A couple of passing girls the same age as Faith giggled and started whispering as they carried on walking to their ponies.

'Mum!' Faith yelled at her, tearing up. 'Why didn't you do up the girth? That's great. Now they think I'm an idiot!' she wailed, silent tears falling down her cheeks.

Maya observed the girl in front of her like she was seeing her for the first time. She didn't want to be doing this, not really. She was an Empath too—she could feel every judgement projected onto her, and this was a very judgemental place to be. But through encouragement from Maya, and because of the upbringing Maya had had with ponies, it had become some kind of ancestral torture ritual. Maya wanted to laugh out loud for the absurdity of it, but caught herself in time, knowing there was no way Faith would understand.

'I'm sorry,' Maya began and then instantly scolded herself for apologising. Why was she sorry? Her daughter knew very well that one of the most basic rules before getting on a horse is to check the girth.

Faith had scrambled off the ramp, wiping the tears away and yanking up the girth. Maya handed Burt's reins to Amy and came over to help, but Faith snarled her lip at her and told her she'd helped enough. After a few more tries, she successfully mounted and rode off to find her group.

Maya sighed and turned back to Amy to find she had shimmied up the side of the trailer and somehow pulled herself onto Burt, while being completely oblivious to the fact that Burt had his reins wrapped round his legs and was almost falling over from the downward position his head was in due to the tangled reins. Amy then proceeded to shout at him to get his head up and Maya swore she saw the pony literally roll his eyes while continuing to remain calm in his trapped state until Maya rescued him.

'I love you,' she said, pressing a kiss to his soft muzzle. 'You are so patient with kids.'

He looked at her and, for a moment, she wondered, Why? Why do animals offer so much unconditional love and help to humans, and yet we call them an inferior intelligence? That was another thing very wrong with the world, she noted, and hurried to encourage Amy to walk on, realising they were now late for the start of the lesson.

While the instructor lectured the children on rising trot and got them to practise as the parents held their ponies, Maya had a few minutes to observe the scenes around her. She could see Faith in the distance, warming up for a jumping lesson and all seemed calm. Relaxing her eyes, she scanned over the ponies and their riders, watching the mums that rushed to and fro, always busy.

On the surface, it looked like everyone was having a good time, but underneath, an anxious manic feeling came over her. Many of these people were just going through the motions of a life they'd been told they should live. Beneath the surface, exhaustion, pain, financial difficulties, born from keeping up with the Joneses, came up. The overall feeling was one of trying to swim upstream, and it wasn't lost on Maya—this was often how she felt too. Feeling deeper, she became aware of the parents' guilt for forcing their children to ride, watching them snap at their offspring and thrust them on ponies while, at the same time, feeling resentment for doing so.

Maya sighed, turning back to Amy. So strange, we humans. We must be the only species that make ourselves do things, while simultaneously feeling guilty about doing it.

Centuries of conditioning, Tal supplied, appearing at her right side.

What do you mean? she asked, after a short pause to check in with his energy and make sure it was him and not those pesky Demons that seemed to be very present at the moment.

For centuries the Dark Ones have infiltrated everything, layer upon layer of conditioning about who we are, what we want, why we're here, what's important, what's not. The common theme? Money, of course, he sighed. *Money is just an energy, but it's been weaponised over the centuries and is now entangled with fear and guilt, but also with happiness and success. Much has been inverted but, in a nutshell, most of humanity have so many conditioned layers, it's almost impossible for them to pull them apart and sort them into truth and good versus pain, fear and bad.*

Mmm, Maya agreed. On a deep level this resonated and she needed to come back to it later for further inspection.

She felt Amy topple forward onto the pony's neck and turned to look at her, smiling while her daughter found the loss of balance gave her a good excuse to wrap her arms round Burt and give his neck a squeeze.

'Right, Mums stand to the side. Let's see what these little ones have learned.'

Maya pulled back, unclipping the lead rein, and Amy commenced flapping her legs and loudly shouting at Burt to walk on. Maya laughed. Amy wasn't the most subtle or gentle rider but Burt, God bless him, took it all in his stride.

Maya continued to watch as she become aware of Patricia stomping up to meet her. Patricia had taken over as the Pony Club District Commissioner a few months ago when the last one retired. Clearly, Maya had observed, she takes her role very seriously and lived and breathed the pony club. While Maya admired her dedication and, in truth, had not had much to do with her, she often felt a strange energy around her.

She turned to look at Patricia as she arrived by her side, panting with the exertion. Her face looked swollen and red and she took a moment to catch her breath before speaking.

'Hello,' she started. 'You're Faith's Mum, right?' she all but barked at Maya.

Taken aback by her approach, Maya took a step back and nodded.

'Okay, well, I'm afraid I need to pull her up on her dress

code. I've told her but I'm telling you as well. Her shirt must be tucked in and she's not wearing a hairnet.'

Patricia finished talking and put her hands on her hips, clearly waiting for some kind of apologetic response from Maya, to which she duly complied.

'Oh, okay. Right, sorry,' she answered.

Seemingly satisfied, Patricia stomped off and Maya watched in a haze, quietly observing a swirling darkness around the woman that seemed to move into different shapes as she walked.

Why? Maya's mind immediately whipped at her. Why the hell did you apologise for that? She felt anger rising from her throat, making it feel constricted. What just happened? Maya wondered, trying to process how she was feeling. She felt like she was eight years old again and her father had just berated her for something, making her feel small and unworthy. Maya wiped her eyes. Come on, get a grip, she told herself.

Why did she let that demon-possessed egoistic woman just talk to her like that and make her feel so insignificant? What was wrong with her? Tal was back at her side and offered an explanation.

You have conditioning of unworthiness and bowing to authority, which makes you give people the energy that is rightly yours. You give control to others, and the reaction you are feeling is actually sadness for not being your whole self, and for not being in control of yourself and your reactions. The more that others are like that, the more unhappy they are with who they are. This, in turn, allows lower entities and Demons to come in and influence them further, leading them down a path of hate and jealousy and a false sense of importance.

Tal felt Maya's confusion and tried a different way.

The more aggressive and condescending a person is, the less they love and honour themselves. To fill the gap in them, they take—and abuse—others' control and energy, not realising they themselves are often being controlled by demonic forces. You gave away your control and handed it to that woman when you apologised for something you didn't believe you or Faith had done wrong.

Okay, Maya said slowly to herself, looking at the floor. She didn't really understand how she had given control to Patricia but, like earlier, the concept didn't feel wrong so she let it sit.

Looking up, Maya watched as Amy trotted round on Burt, her hands held too high, her heels pointing up instead of down and her legs too far back on the pony's side, but she was managing the up-and-down of the trot, and Maya smiled at the small progress she had made since last time. While she was silently praising Amy, she heard the teacher starting to instruct her.

'Heels down, Amy. Hands down. You'll pull his mouth. Your legs are too far back on the girth.'

Too much, too quick, Maya fumed in her mind, watching Amy try to execute all the commands at once, lose her balance and fall forward.

Amy regained her position after a few strides and tried again. Her hands were lower and, more importantly, her heels were now level rather than pointing up. Great, Maya thought. They're on the way to pointing down, at least.

The teacher, however, had other ideas and kept barking instructions until Amy decided she'd had enough. She sat still, pulling Burt to a walk. Maya took a stride forward, then stopped herself. Wait, her gut told her. Just observe.

The instructor came over and started lecturing Amy. Maya watched in horror as she saw Amy's confidence literally flow out of her in a dark cloud. Her lip started trembling and she burst out crying, throwing the reins at Burt's head.

'I don't want to ride any more,' she sobbed. 'I'm not doing it.'

'Pick up your reins,' the instructor barked at her and proceeded to tell her how dangerous she was acting and how the pony could gallop off and hurt her or someone else. Maya stepped forward, trying to keep her cool.

'She's five,' she growled, over-pronouncing the 'five', as she eyeballed the instructor. 'It's too much for her to take in.'

'Well, the other children seem to manage,' the instructor snapped back, looking at Maya.

'Okay,' Maya said, wanting to put distance between her child and the rest of the class before more damage was done to her confidence. 'I'll take her out and calm her down.'

Maya led Burt away. Her initial feelings had been to tell Amy off. It was, after all, a fair point that throwing the reins down could have resulted in all kinds of hazardous outcomes for Amy and her pony, and the fear in Maya wanted to tell her that. The Maya of two months ago would have shouted just that at her. Something had shifted, though. Today she could see what actually happened in that lesson and she wanted to comfort and support her child and take her out of the dense, harsh energy she had put her in in the first place.

They walked back to the trailer in silence, Burt trying to snatch mouthfuls of long grass as they went. Amy was still crying and she seemed frustrated and angry now. Maya reached up and lifted her down holding her close.

'It's okay,' Maya soothed in her ear.

'It's not fair. I can't do it!' she sobbed. 'Why can't I do it?'

'Amy, it takes time to learn to ride. Remember the old saying I shared with you—it takes seven falls to make a good rider?' she joked, tickling her arm.

But Amy wasn't in a playful mood and slowly walked over to the car, throwing her hat into the boot and fishing out a packet of crisps. She climbed into the back seat and shut the door.

Maya sighed. Maybe Jacob was right. They didn't have the right relationship with horses any more. At the end of the day, Amy didn't spend time bonding or connecting with her horse. She just showed up to ride, expecting Maya and Faith to muck out, tack up and manage the day-to-day care. How could she build a relationship if she just turned up and expected the horse to do want she wanted?

To be honest, it was much the same with Faith. She resented doing the mucking out and feeding, and she scattered food everywhere so that the rats came, and left manure piled in the field. Yes, she confirmed to herself. Faith had fallen into the same trap they all had. The true meaning of relating to horses, of using intuition and connection through means other than words, learning discipline and patience and hard work—it had all been lost. All that was left were the negative traits of using horses to have fun, racing and jumping them, often against their will, while pompous, stuck-up humans bounced around on their backs. That's what was actually going on here. There was no sense of community and growth at this place. It was a place of judgement, envy and ego, a place where ego could grow or under-confidence could blossom—neither were traits the human population needed any more of, thank you very much.

Maya untacked Burt while she thought and then turned to look for Faith, noticing that the other lessons had finished and the riders were making their way back across the fields. She could see Faith struggling with an over-excited Zara, who was swinging her rear end into the other horses, looking round and neighing for Burt, having only just realised he was missing from her side.

Faith look flustered and the riders around her were glaring at her. There were at least five parents between Maya and Faith and not one stepped forward to help calm Faith's horse and take the reins to walk her back. They just stared in judgement.

Maya set off across the field and met them halfway, by which time Faith was visibly upset and Zara was sweating, still dancing on the spot.

'Where were you?' Faith hissed at her. 'You're useless, Mum. You're never here when I need you. Just leave me alone. I can cope by myself,' she continued, her voice breaking at the end as she rode past.

For some reason the 'You're useless' accusation rolled off Maya's back, but the charge 'You're never here' hit her like a bolt of lightning. It was true. I mean, not in this particular instance—how was she supposed to know the horse would suddenly act up? But more widely, she was right. Maya was never there. She was always out earning money so she could pay for this lifestyle, the one she'd just identified was actually causing the kids harm and breeding self-doubt and egoistic behaviours. All to produce another couple of people to add to the world population of adults that were messed up and worshipped the false idols of money and ego. Jesus, Maya thought. What a mess.

She shook her head and trailed after Faith and her prancing horse, vowing no matter how hard it would be, things were going to change.

The ride back in the car was sullen until Maya pulled into Tesco's and handed the girls a fiver to buy some ice-cream. From there the mood lightened somewhat and they managed to unload and sort out the horses without further problems.

After taking the dogs for a short walk in the woods, and after four attempts at reversing the trailer into its spot at the side of the house, she made her way inside. She found everyone gathered in the kitchen, eating beans on toast and arguing over the last of the grated cheese. Apparently, the cheese made the difference between it being a horrid meal and the best meal ever. Maya flopped down in the chair and looked up at Jacob.

'Where's mine?' she asked, raising an eyebrow to indicate she wasn't about to throw one of her 'You're the parent at home—you should cook' moments, and that she was in fact having a rare moment of light-heartedness.

Jacob looked up from shovelling beans into his face to

explore her expression and, visibly softening from his original tense stance, signalled to the bread bin and the cupboard with an outstretched hand.

'Never mind,' she groaned, pulling herself up. 'I'll have a salad.'

'Brilliant,' he quipped back. 'And then moan in half an hour that you're still hungry. I can't wait for that.'

Zidan pulled a face at the mention of salad. 'I only like cucumber,' he announced. 'And peas in the pod,' he added quickly.

'Yes, we know,' the family chorused, on account of the stripped pea plants outside that no one else got a look into.

The mood quietened again as Maya went about making a salad. It was Aurora who ventured to ask the question on everyone's mind.

'Please tell me we aren't moving again?'

Maya and Jacob looked at each other. Then Jacob took a deep breath and answered with a resounding, 'Yes. We are.'

Brilliant, Maya thought, seconds before the kitchen erupted. So empathic and gentle as always. What is *wrong* with this man? Now she was going to have to patch up the bluntness and soothe the chaos.

'Shh,' she stood up, waving her hands to calm the kids down one at a time.

'We moved, like, a year ago,' Zidan moaned.

'I know, but that was because we should never have moved out of the house in Northumberland in the first place. We should have never moved south and so we took the first house that came up in the north.'

'Mum,' Faith said with exasperation. 'It wasn't south, it was just a little more south than Scotland, for God's sake.'

'Yes, well, we hated it. Too busy, too polluted. You saw how we and the horses were affected by the spraying,' she defended their decision, lowering her voice at the end to try to soothe everyone's nerves.

'They spray up north, too,' Faith stated, deadpan.

'Okay, yes, I get that, but it wasn't the right place or environment for us. I should never have given in to the demands of my nagging mother.'

'Okay, so now what?' Aurora chimed in, throwing her hands in the air. 'What's the problem now? I love my room, I love it here and I've finally met some nice friends at school.'

Maya froze in place. How could they hurt them like this again? But then they couldn't see the bigger picture, could never understand what it was like living a lie just to pay for a big house and a so-called good life. They could never understand the things she did, and nor should they at their age. How did she protect them while creating enough change for her and Jacob so that they didn't split up or go insane or worse, die because her soul was withering and the stress was playing havoc with her physically. The fight inside her between her soul's wants and needs and her ego was raging and threatening to tear her apart, and now the most potent of energies had joined it: a mother's love for her children, wanting to protect them and give them what they wanted, not to cause them pain or hurt. The voice in her heart cut in below her whirling thoughts, softer and deeper with a clear message.

But if you stay they'll follow the societal mould and become 'successful and prosperous', chasing false idols and losing their souls' connection in the process, just like you now. If *you're* able to fight to free yourself, then perhaps you can help show *them* a better way. They won't see that if you stay working for a corrupt, unethical, soulless organisation. They'll think they have to follow that path and do the exact same thing. You'll have failed in one of your soul's life missions—to raise children to be free and creative and sovereign.

Wow, okay, she noted. That was new. Since when was that my soul mission? It makes sense, though, why I feel the way I do.

'MAYA!' Jacob roared, bringing her back into the room. 'HELLO,' he waved a hand in front of her face. 'Are you actually with us?'

Maya came back to the present and looked around at the scowling faces of the children.

'I'm SO done!' Faith yelled, standing up and throwing the chair to the floor, making the other kids jump as she stormed out of the room.

Jacob rose to go after her and Maya grabbed his arm. 'Leave her, she's upset.'

'Upset or not, Maya, it's not okay to act like that, to throw and break our furniture whenever she feels like it. And, by sticking up for her, you're reaffirming to her that it *is* okay. Which, by the way,' he added over his shoulder, 'will one day come back to bite you on the ass.'

'You shouldn't let him talk to you like that,' Aurora piped up. 'He's an idiot. Maybe if he got a full-time job we could afford to stay here. I mean, that's why you want to move, isn't it? For money?'

'Not exactly,' Maya replied. 'It's complicated, it's right—'

'Yeah, course it is,' Aurora interrupted, getting up and leaving the room.

Amy and Zidan stood up and came to hug either side of Maya's shoulders as she sat looking into her lap. 'It's okay, Mummy,' Amy said.

'Yeah, it's okay,' Zidan echoed, laying his head on her shoulder.

Maya felt the sweetness and innocence from her younger children wrap round her like a soft, comforting blanket. They had not yet been fully programmed into mobile phones and schools and the world of the ego, and there was still part of them connected to the place before they came to Planet Earth in their bags of muscle, bone and goo, that only knew peace and love.

'Home is where the heart is,' Amy spoke softly to her ear, and as long as they were all together everything was going to be okay. Maya smiled, tears blurring her eyes.

'That's what your Dad always says,' she answered, patting Amy's hand. Yet as she said that, she could hear Jacob and Faith going at each other with malice and hate in the corridor.

She put her head in her hands and cried, not because she thought it was okay for the kids to see but because she could no longer shield them from the pain and hurt in her heart. She had to get real with each member of the family as to where she really was. Exhausted, broken, tired of giving her energy to a company that represented all the things she didn't want in the world, tired of giving all of her free time to things that were not in alignment with what she wanted to feel and get from life. Physically, she was still broken from four caesarian sections without any rest. All she had left was to be honest with herself and with others about where she truly was. She was wrong—she wasn't a robot, she wasn't invincible and she couldn't just keep coping. She was falling and the bottom of the cliff was fast approaching.

She cried and cried, sitting at the table with the two smaller kids comforting her, rubbing her shoulders while casting worried looks at each other, until they took themselves to bed, scooting around a still arguing Jacob and Faith on the stairs.

Strange, Maya thought as she woke groggily, her head and arms hanging off the kitchen table, legs stiff from being in an uncomfortable position for a long time. She stood and stretched, looking around.

What was strange? she asked herself, mentally catching up. Oh yes, strange that things seemed to fall apart just as, on a physical, material level, it should be a happy time. I mean, look at this house. It's beautiful. The tall ceilings with fine detail showing the grandeur of its age. It's a dream house for so many, yet for us, ever since we moved in here, it feels like life has become everything I don't want.

You won't find happiness in money, she remembered her Granny saying. Your Mother puts too much emphasis on that False God, so you listen here, lassie, she had said. That's not your path.

Maya felt like it was important for her to recall her grandmother's advice right now. It seemed very pertinent. She registered it in her mind and crawled upstairs, throwing her-self into bed.

The other side was empty, of course. Jacob was sleeping on the sofa and had been for a few days now. Their relationship felt like a roller-coaster with no stop or off button. There's got to be a reason for all this, she pondered as she fell into a deep sleep.

*

The next morning the children had already gone to school when she emerged from the bedroom. Jacob had been up for hours and Maya could hear him whistling in the outhouse as she went downstairs in search of caffeine.

A short while later he entered the kitchen as Maya was tak-ing a rare moment to drink her tea without doing five other things at once. He acknowledged her with a nod and headed to the kettle, picking the coffee jar off the side as he went. Maya watched him fill the kettle and switch it on. He seemed relaxed in his face and movements, but when she observed closer, she could see the tension carried in his back and the lines on his forehead. She could tell there was so much he wanted to say, but getting Jacob to actually say it had always been one of the big battles in their marriage.

'Are you going to talk?' Maya enquired.

He carried on stirring the cup in front of him, saying noth-ing at first and then turning and shrugging his shoulders.

'What's the point?' he asked, looking at her directly in the eyes, in a way that Maya knew he wasn't being difficult. He genuinely, from his side, couldn't see the point in talking.

'Why would it be pointless?' Maya answered, noting the bright green hues in his eyes, highlighted by the dancing light flooding in through the kitchen window onto his face. Jacob's eyes, in the right light, looked dragon-like and something that by far fitted a more vibrant, mysterious, powerful, dragon-filled world than this crazy one.

Maya sighed and left the room to put the washing on. It all felt too messy and too big to deal with. One foot in front of the other, she reminded herself.

Tal watched the scene before him. Above, the hackling Demons circled Faith's room, still alight with the chaos they caused in the poor girl's mind during the night. The first step was for Maya and Jacob to create space and time in their own lives before they could even begin to work through and heal the multitude of traumas, fears and conditioning that existed in the wider family. It was a long road but, like other souls scattered in bodies across the globe, this is what they'd signed up for. Whether they completed their journey, well, that was always up to them.

He looked skywards, his mind floating to the souls working hard in other areas to help bring Earth back into an energy that would serve her, the energy that she used to have before the Fall, as they called it, the infiltration of Satan and his minions.

Still, he held respect for the Main Man of Evil. After all, how would souls learn and grow if they were not influenced by both the dark *and* the light, the good *and* the bad? His very favourite human quote, 'How would you see the stars if there was no darkness?' sprang to mind.

Yes, he mused, like us the Big Bad Demon has his purpose. But right now he needed Maya and Jacob to see the Demons and ask them to leave. For being embattled with them would keep their energy low and their progress slow.

Maya swung the car into the car park. It was small and already jammed with cars. Great, two minutes until my appointment, she mumbled, searching frantically for a space and identifying one at the far end that she might just be able to squeeze into.

'Mum, I thought we were going to Tesco's to look at toys,' Amy asked quizzically.

'Yes, in a minute,' she answered, trying to grab her phone from the floor while manoeuvring into a spot.

'You only have ten pounds,' Zidan shouted at her. 'I've told you it won't buy what you want. Mum, tell her.'

'Oh, shut up!' Amy screamed, pouting her lip and throwing the blanket she was clutching at her brother, whipping it past his face and invoking a squealing high-pitched voice that ran right though Maya.

'KIDS, please. For the love of God,' she shouted, feeling pure overwhelm, as if someone was actually sitting on her lungs. 'I'm late for my appointment. I'm super stressed. Please just try not to bloody argue.'

She finished parking and squeezed out the door, trying not to hit the car next to her.

'Out!' she barked at the still arguing kids.

'Die!' Zidan screamed at Amy, while climbing out of the car and banging the neighbouring car in the process. Maya had to breathe deeply to save herself from hanging him up by his trousers on the nearest tree.

'I'm staying in the car,' Amy announced, crossing her arms and nestling into her seat in the back. 'I'm not going anywhere with him.'

'Get out!' Maya shouted at her. 'I am not leaving you in the car for some pedo to grab you. OUT!' she bellowed, opening the door and wondering if either her car or the one next to her had any paint left on it.

'Some what?' Zidan asked, calming down a little and looking at her, puzzled.

'Oh, never mind. Get in the doctor's and sit quietly before I kill myself and you will have no Mother.'

The two kids, momentarily a little taken back by Maya's statement, shuffled behind her, taking swipes at each other on the way up the ramp to the surgery. Maya ushered them inside and pointed to the play area before rushing up to the desk.

'I'm sorry I'm—'

'Late,' the receptionist finished for her, looking up from behind her glasses. 'You will have to wait until we can fit you in. Luckily the lady due after you was EARLY,' she emphasised, 'so she went in and shouldn't be long.'

Maya bit back the temptation to sarcastically praise the wonder-lady, who probably had a rich husband, no kids and loads of stress-free time, on being the saviour of humanity, but the woman behind the desk, who looked like she'd eaten pretty much all of Tesco's, didn't appear to have a sense of humour.

Jesus, Maya thought, flopping into a chair. I'm getting bitchy in my old age, even if it *is* just in my head.

She felt her phone vibrate and pulled it out of her pocket. Ben's name flashed up on the screen. She couldn't talk to him. He wouldn't understand. Besides, she thought miserably, he's probably just going to be reporting back to Anna.

After about twenty minutes, a slim, older lady came out of Room 5 and called her name. Maya's heart sank when she realised it wasn't the same doctor she'd seen when she was first signed off sick. She reluctantly followed the lady into the room, after throwing a sideways glance at the children to check they were at least not breaking anything or pulling each other's hair out.

The lady introduced herself as Dr Bartle and sat down, scrolling through the computer screen in front of her.

'So,' she said, then paused again, reading.

Maya shuffled in her chair, feeling like a lab specimen, and decided to offer a human, rather than computer, explanation as to why she was there.

'I was in a few weeks ago,' she said.

'Yes. With depression,' the doctor stated, swivelling her chair around to face Maya, her gold bracelets jingling on her arm in the process. The awards around her desk referred to the pharmaceutical industry and a 'Sponsored by' notepad lay at the side.

'Something like that,' Maya muttered. Okay, this one clearly thinks I'm a fake, she thought to herself. I'm not being very vulnerable here.

'So do you feel like you're ready to go back to work?' Dr Bartle enquired, turning back to her computer and picking up her prescription pad, clearly keen to write something on it, any number of drugs to shove at Maya and get her out of the consulting room.

Maya said nothing. How could she explain to someone who clearly was trapped in an egoistic society, idolizing herself as some False God, that she was having issues fitting in there herself.

'I'm not sure,' Maya eventually answered truthfully. 'I mean, I need to for the money and I don't want to waste the career I've built up there, but I feel anxious just thinking about going back.'

'Who do you work for?' the doctor enquired.

When Maya told her, the doctor then spent the next five minutes informing her that her brother-in-law was high up in their Mumbai office and that they had an excellent global counselling and occupational referral system and that she would write her another two-week sick note on the agreement that Maya contacted her Human Resources department and sent through a request to refer her to occupational health and phased return.

'Okay,' Maya sighed, standing up.

'Hang on,' the doctor said, scribbling on her pad and tearing the top sheet off. 'Something to calm you and lift your mood.'

Maya glanced down at the prescription sheet and noted the three drugs written on it.

'Any side effects?' she asked.

'No, not really. Just possibly a little nausea but it'll pass,' the doctor smiled at her.

Maya turned and planted her feet in the ground, taking a deep breath and resigning herself to the fact that yep, this rant in her head was really going to come out and she had no way of stopping it.

'Dr Bartle, might I suggest you review and refresh your knowledge on those drugs. This one,' Maya pointed to the top one on the sheet, 'has links with suicidal tendencies, as listed on the black triangle warning on the product characteristics. The bottom one has been linked in three papers to cancer, and all of them have heavy side effects for some people, of which you have no idea if I am going to turn out to be one of those people, nor did you ask me if I was taking contraception or had any past episodes of bipolar, immune function disorder or stomach ulcers. You took an oath to do no harm. I would expect you to at least share the possible downsides with me and give me the information I need to make an informed risk/ benefit decision about my treatment. After all,' Maya finished, pointing at the latest GP marketing posters on the wall, 'you and I are supposed to be a team, right?'

Dr Bartle's mouth opened and closed without a sound and Maya didn't wait for the steam timer to go off. She dropped the prescription on the desk, snatched up the sick note and left, shutting the door behind her.

'Kids,' she shouted, striding through the waiting area. 'We're leaving.'

The kids dutifully dropped the toys they were playing with and followed Maya through the door and into the car park. She hauled herself into the driver's seat and tried to slow her racing heart.

You go, girl! Lesley would have been proud of her. If only I could do that all the time.

But she could. Why couldn't she? Why couldn't she take all that assertiveness training they drilled into her at work and use it to benefit herself instead of someone else?

'Now there's an idea,' she said out loud, drawing more Mum's-going-bonkers looks from the kids as she pulled out of the car park.

14

Maya dragged herself off the bed, where she'd been packing her makeup and hair accessories into a box, and readied her computer for the Human Resources call scheduled for eleven a.m. Things had moved pretty quickly over the last two weeks since she'd returned from the doctor's with another sick note in her hand. Jacob had already informed the landlord that the family were moving out and had started packing the first box. That's the thing about Jacob, she smiled. Once he gets behind something, he doesn't hang around.

She sighed, thinking back to her call with Lesley last night. It had felt so uplifting and powerful, unlike now when she'd been summoned to a meeting with HR. Anna had wanted to be present but Maya had refused, citing that Anna was a large part of the problem and that her presence would make her anxious. It was true, but Maya also wanted to talk to HR about what she had seen, what was really going on. The HR manager assigned to the meeting was someone she'd always got on with when recruiting new members to her team or dealing with issues, and she was hopeful that maybe she'd be open and would listen. We'll see, she sighed again to herself, joining the meeting.

Mary's face came up onto the screen.

'Maya!' she exclaimed. 'How's it going?'

'I'm okay,' Maya responded, giving Mary a brief smile and feeling far from it underneath.

'I'm sorry to hear you've been poorly,' Mary said, then paused, clearly waiting for Maya to lead the conversation.

'I assume you have a copy of the occupational report that the company requested?' Maya began.

The Occupational Assessment was not something she'd been looking forward to but, actually, when a copy came back and Maya read through it, it concluded Maya had been the victim of bullying and intimidation and had been burned out with little to no support. It was grim reading for the company, but it made Maya feel a bit more confident that perhaps she was in the right not to tolerate the way she had been treated by Anna and others. However, the hope that HR may see this point of view quickly evaporated, as the conversation with Mary continued.

Having heard Maya's side of the story, where she detailed three clear instances of bullying and explained the corrupt cover-up of the death of a patient and the three internal breaches of the company's own procedural rules, Mary was pushing towards a conclusion that sometimes manager and employee just didn't get on. These things happened and the main thing was what they were going to do about it.

'You're not well, Maya,' she finished, staring at her with pity.

'I'm not well because of what I've been through! Even Occupational Health can see that.'

'Well, yes. It *is* only one view, though'.

One view, Maya snorted internally. That's not what you said when we were working to remove an employee that had a drinking problem. You said it was the final word!

Maya tried to calm herself. The injustice, the fact that HR was not independent, was not non-biased. It clearly, like everyone else, had an agenda, so out with it, Maya thought. What is the agenda here?

'Maya,' Mary said, as if talking to a small, scared child.

Admittedly, Maya could feel tears welling up in her eyes, but they were tears of frustration and anger. How dare they treat her like this after everything she'd done?

'You know, Mary,' Maya cut in. 'I've read Anna's report and she cites that I live too far away to do my job properly. Yet I haven't missed one important meeting and, in fact, one of my colleagues has missed many, on account of lack of child-care and other such things, and they only live an hour away. My husband stays at home so that I can give work one hundred per cent, and I've worked long hours for years. Anna's statement contains lies and I can prove it. So, whatever you're about to say, please say it with conviction.'

A look of fear passed over Mary's face and Maya felt an immense boost in confidence for finally standing up for herself.

'Well, being off sick long term is no good for everyone.'

'It's just fine for me at the moment,' Maya said. 'I don't know whether I'll get better or not, but I know I'm well within my rights to be off sick for a much longer period of time in order to find out, and you're not allowed to harass me.'

'Maya,' Mary started again. 'I know you're emotional and upset. Please be assured I wasn't trying to rush you into a decision.'

Like hell you weren't, Maya seethed in her mind.

'You could apply for another Sales Manager role in a different department, but there's no guarantee you would get it.'

Maya tried to suppress more tears of anger but they spilled over anyway.

'So I'm being offered a demotion that I might not get?' she blurted out, her voice slightly shaking.

Holy crap, she thought to herself, trying to hold it together. She thought back to other managers that had been through what she was now going through. She remembered how they had acted and what they had tried to tell her, but she believed her bosses' versions about the reasons they had left, and just figured the job wasn't for them any more. Now she realised this is probably exactly how they'd felt, pushed out for having a different opinion. Was this the reason why they were being bombarded with messages about needing to have a diverse workforce? Was it really just to cover up the bullying and intimidation inflicted on those who didn't conform?

Maya felt sick to her stomach. Why had she not offered her colleagues more support? She let the familiar feelings of unworthiness, failure and victimhood wash over her, but this time a resistance seemed to rise up to meet them.

No! she yelled in her mind, which came out as a series of

coughs. No, I'm better than that. They don't deserve me. This is ridiculous.

Once the coughing subsided, Maya realised Mary had stopped talking and was staring at her.

'Mary,' she started. 'I'm not sure what HR manual you have in front of you, but you seem to be completely ignoring my Occupational Report and the Grievance Report I submitted. Irrelevant of who has told you what they want as an outcome in this situation, I will hold *you* personally accountable for any breaches of HR or the organisation's responsibilities regarding employee health.'

Maya knew she wasn't going to get anywhere with the corrupt and disgusting way the company operated, and it wouldn't bring back the young woman who had died, or indeed ones that would likely die in the future because the risk/benefit hadn't been fully explained to them. But it *would* make a stand for what she was willing to tolerate, and she vowed in that moment that she would help to halt and heal everything that was being done wrong in this industry. She would. But right now she needed money and she needed to take back her power and she knew what would help her do that.

'I'm not applying for a demotion. I'm ill and I refuse to be bullied. I note you call my issues with Anna 'a difference of personality'—I call it bullying, plain and simple.'

Mary stared at her, blinking rapidly.

'Okay, well, I need to get back to you with options on next steps. Can we reconvene next week at the same time?'

'Sure,' Maya responded, 'I'll look out for the invite.'

She flicked the button to end the call before Mary had the chance to sign off herself.

Okay, well, that was a bit rude to end it so abruptly but seriously, I can't take that woman's energy any more, she told herself, rubbing her head before standing up and making her way over to the bed, flinging herself dramatically onto her back.

Jacob entered the room a short while later and saw her laid out like a starfish, staring at the ceiling.

'It went well, then?' he enquired, physically moving her body to make room for him to lie next to her.

'Mmm,' Maya groaned, debating whether to still be angry with him, but deciding a foot rub would be more conducive to her mood. She wiggled into his stomach, letting him pull her into his arms and start using his heels and toes to rub her feet.

'That's nice,' she murmured, thinking that, actually, if she just did this with him all the time they probably wouldn't argue at all. 'I stood up for myself,' she offered, after a few minutes.

'Good,' he whispered into her ear and started roaming her body with his hands.

'Jacob, really. It's one p.m. and—'

He interrupted, biting her neck gently. 'Go on, live dangerously,' he suggested, starting to tickle her gently.

'Okay, okay, stop,' she laughed, wiggling around and, in doing so, left him in no doubt she was up for what he wanted. I suppose this is better than packing and wondering if we're making the worst mistake of our life so far, she mused, as he pulled the covers over their head and started removing her clothes, while kissing her in a way that reminded her of when they were much younger and more carefree.

Later, as Jacob slept next to her, Maya dozed in and out of sleep. She was aware that her Guides were there. It wasn't like voices, more like an energy wrapping around her, reassuring her that it would be okay, that, despite the three dimensional perspective of her life, which many would say was all falling apart, she was in fact on the right path and needed to listen to her guidance, her knowing to keep going north, in order to find her One True North.

The next few days went by in a blur. Faith admitted reluctantly that maybe it was time to have a break from horses, that she had grown out of the ponies they currently had and it was time to find them new homes. Strangely, as soon as they had made that decision, homes just seemed to appear, and by the end of the week, they had either gone to their new abodes or had places agreed for them.

Similarly, the extra geese and chickens they had intended to leave behind found a home with the neighbours, and everything just seemed to be falling into place. Everything, that was, apart from the landlord. Clearly rattled by losing a substantial rental income each month, he'd become increasingly difficult and was being very rigid on the move date.

The next few days, as Jacob watched Maya and Faith pack

up the horse bits that had been washed and spread out in the yard to dry, a panic started to stir in his gut. How were they going to get everything packed up and, more to the point, how was it all going to fit in a trailer and the hired lorry?

Maya and he had discussed engaging a removal company but, after looking at a few quotes, quickly realised they couldn't afford it. They were just going to have to make it work, he had reassured Maya, but now he wasn't so sure what made him so confident. Oh, great, he groaned, rubbing his eyes and finding yet again he was in charge of moving them with too much stuff and too little time to get it done. Right, well, he told himself, standing up and stretching. We need to get rid of some stuff, some of the material bollocks we've outgrown, his mind whispered to him, making him chuckle.

'Zidan, bring me the chairs from the kitchen,' he shouted, turning his head towards the house.

By the time Maya had made her way over to the house for a cup of tea, a fire had been started with the chairs from the kitchen, and Jacob was now throwing dismantled bedroom drawers onto the growing flames. Maya stopped when she caught sight of the fire and saw Jacob tossing one of the drawer inserts into the blaze.

'What the hell are you doing?' she shrieked. 'Have you lost the plot?'

She looked around at several items clearly waiting for their turn to be incinerated.

'Oh my God,' she continued. 'You've lost the plot. You have actually lost the plot.'

She paced back and forth by the fire.

'Why are Amy's knickers in there?' she yelled, stopping her pacing briefly to point at the pink underwear in the middle of the flames.

Jacob shrugged. 'She said they were too small,' he answered, taking a swig of the beer in his hand.

'What the hell are you losers doing now?' Faith demanded, joining them both by the edge of the fire.

'Your Dad appears to be burning the house. I think he's lost it. Zidan, why are you assisting in this madness?'

Maya threw her hands up in exasperation as the boy dragged another chair past her. 'Seriously, Jacob!'

She swung round, staring at Jacob as he calmly leaned back on the rock near the side of the garden gate.

'Maya, we don't have room to take everything. I'm just ridding us of some deadwood. Literally,' he added, laughing and winking at Zidan who began giggling. 'You need to really strip out what we're planning on taking. There's a lot that we can't fit in,' he continued, grabbing a wooden bowl from Aurora and standing up to throw it in the fire.

'No!' Maya screamed. 'Not that. I like that. Give it here,' she said crossly.

Aurora reluctantly handed it back to her.

'It's awful, Mum. It looks like something out of the Last Supper from the time of Jesus.'

'I like it,' Maya seethed, storming inside clutching her bowl.

Maya stood inside the kitchen, feeling sick. There *was* a lot of stuff and she realised Jacob was right. They were going to have to give a lot away to charity. She sat down at the table and looked around. There was stuff tied to events or energies that she felt were no longer helpful, like that small table over there in the corner, she thought. Half broken, it had been left in the house they moved into after Aurora was born and it never had a great feel. Jacob had kicked it during one of their arguments and then glued it back together. These things felt like they needed to stay here, to be committed to the past so they could step into the future, lighter and clearer.

Tal listened to her thoughts showing as colourful energy stripes snaking around her head in beautiful patterns.

She's getting it, he thought. *They're far too weighted down with material things. Lightening the load will free a lot of dense energy in the living space around them.*

He watched as Maya stood again, joining in with the children collecting items in the house that no longer served them, and taking them outside to be part of the cleansing ritual Jacob had started.

Maya woke early the next morning. She immediately felt something was off and opened her eyes to see shadows moving across the opposite wall. She had worked late into the night, packing and worrying while she did. She knew she was getting worn down by everything, but she kept moving forward, eventually falling into bed at one a.m. Now, in the early morning light, she felt like something had accessed her that was less than positive. Her throat felt dry and sore and her limbs heavy. She could feel the bones in her toes, and her head hurt.

'No, no,' she said out loud, sitting up. 'I don't have time for this.'

'What?' Jacob jerked upright. 'What's wrong?'

'I don't feel right,' Maya said, holding her throat. It felt like she had a noose around it, loose but it was still there, applying pressure at the front of her windpipe.

'Yeah, okay,' he said, patting her leg and falling back to sleep.

Maya sat, eyes darting around her room. Breathe, just breathe, she said to herself. It's okay. She reached to feel for Tal, for any of her Guides, but was met by a cold, dark presence that seemed to surround her. She lay back down, curling into a ball and hoping that, if she fell back to sleep, she would wake feeling much better.

Tal watched from a distance as the large Demons swirled around the bed Maya and Jacob shared.

How is he so close? his companion enquired, alighting next to him.

She has a tear in her aura due to chronic tiredness and worry. He's found his way in while her immunity and mood are down.

We need to help, came the desperate reply.

Tal reached out and placed his hand on his friend's shoulder.

We can't. She has to get through this herself. It's part of the Dark Night of the Soul for her. She's on the bottom physically. It's her choice whether to stay there or whether to push through the cracks to the light.

Can't we at least tell her we're here? the other Angel persisted with concern.

No. The Demon is there by consent, despite her not realising it. We have to wait for her to ask him to leave herself. All we can do is wait and continue to protect the others in our care. You know how this works, Machie, he said, turning to his companion again. *This is a planet of free will, a planet where everything is an experience and humans choose their own paths.*

But she's come so far, Machie argued.

Yes, and Creator willing, she'll shake this off and continue her journey in the right direction, Tal finished sternly, taking flight away from the house and towards other souls in need.

Maya awoke again sometime later. The awful feeling was still with her, dark and desperate with aches deep in her bones. She coughed and sneezed her way to the bathroom, tears blurring her eyes, and tried to blow her nose. She was so blocked up she had to breathe through her mouth and she leaned on the door, feeling light-headed.

'Mum,' Amy said, worried. 'Are you okay?'

'Yes, just a bug, sweetheart,' she said, kissing the top of Amy's head. 'You go get breakfast.'

'Okay,' Amy replied, still looking concerned with big wide

eyes. 'I'm going to have Weetabix. Three Weetabix with milk and golden syrup,' she sang, skipping down the stairs.

Maya closed her eyes for a second before re- grouping her strength and making her way back to the bedroom to get dressed. This didn't feel like a bug, she thought to herself slowly, dressing and feeling like every movement was a chore. It felt like something was dragging her down. It was hard to keep her thoughts positive. She felt anxieties skipping quickly through her head, concerns about lack of money and frustration and not owning this house so they could just stay here. She tried to stop the thoughts but it felt hopeless.

God, I feel so ill, she said to herself, making her way slowly downstairs. Visions of a car crash on the way to the island flashed through her head, the trailer turned over, boxes everywhere, and a cold shiver of fear ran through her. Something isn't right, she told herself again. That's not what's going to happen. Everything is going to be okay.

No, it's not, a voice supplied into her head.

That's not Tal, she instantly recognised, but then she paused, holding her stomach as a sharp pain went through her. She sat down, trying to work out if she was going to be sick.

Faith clumped into the kitchen and kicked off her filthy shoes, spreading mud everywhere. Jesus, I must be ill, Maya thought. I don't even have the energy to shout at her. Faith looked her up and down and then left the room without another word. She seemed unaffected by Maya's state and almost oblivious to her feeling ill.

Maya stood up and went in search of the hot lemon drinks in the pantry, only to find they had, of course, been packed up. Sighing, she scribbled a note to Jacob to say she was going to get some from the supermarket, and reached for her keys on the ledge by the door. As she left the house, she was met by Julie, the landlord's wife.

'Ah, morning,' she started. 'I'm just coming to warn you I'll be performing the marching out meeting tonight,' she announced.

'Marching out meeting?' Maya mumbled, staring at her.

'Yes, you know, I'll be checking for damages and charges.'

Stupid egoistic woman, Maya thought, walking past her to the car.

'I'm not well,' she threw back over her shoulder, not bothering to wait for the sympathy that would never come. 'Knock yourself out, but we may not be done packing tonight.'

'Well,' Julie laughed sarcastically. 'You best be. You're out tomorrow,' she snapped, storming back to her brand new Discovery parked like it was in a showroom in the middle of the yard.

Maya bit back tears and climbed into the car. She wasn't sure how she managed to drive herself into town and shop for basic First Aid supplies and milk and drag herself back into the car, but the next thing she knew, she was sitting in the driver's seat, staring out at the rain without a shred of energy left to even lift her arms to turn the key.

As she sat there feeling too ill to even cry or groan, she felt herself metaphorically hit the bottom. The ground was hard and dark and cold. Her chest was so tight she felt she may not be able to breathe for much longer. She felt like the tubes were closing up. The cold spread through her bones and she stared at the wall in front of her. What do I do now? she said to herself. She felt trapped between a conscious and unconscious state. Visions flashed across her mind.

'I'm not here,' she said out loud. 'I'm not meant to be here. I'm meant to be on the ledge far above, near the top where the sun shines and the flowers grow. I'm not staying here. You don't have permission to stay here and be this,' she told herself crossly.

She sensed something clawing at her heart and she felt like an elephant was sitting on her chest.

'No, I'm not leaving. I'm not going that way with you.'

She took a deep breath in, struggling against the fluid and constriction in her chest.

'Help me,' she whispered through the tears. 'Please help me.'

Maya had no idea who she was talking to, but she hoped they heard.

'You must leave now. I don't want you here with me,' she said again out loud and with more confidence this time. 'Leave me alone. You have no power here, Demon.'

She was talking but it was coming from some higher place. Her brain wasn't thinking it; this was coming from her gut. She couldn't quite explain it, but as she said the last words something shifted. The colour behind her closed eyelids became lighter and the feeling of heaviness on her chest lifted slightly, enabling her to breathe a little better, not much but enough to feel like she could use her arms again and drive home without passing out. The dark feeling seemed to have lessened as she struggled to stay on the road, and she felt closer to something familiar again that didn't make her run cold with fear.

It's going to be okay, she told herself over and over as she drove home. You're going to make it; everything is going to be okay.

She pulled up on the drive and Jacob came out and opened the car door.

'Jesus, Maya, you look awful!' he exclaimed.

Wow, I must look bad, Maya thought. Jacob usually told her she was faking it but now he looked genuinely concerned.

He helped her into the house and instructed her to lie down on the couch by the fire so he could pack up the bedroom. Maya lay staring into the hearth, trying to draw energy from the flames. She had to get better. She couldn't be like this. She had to drive the car and trailer tomorrow.

Rest, a voice quietly whispered.

Maya didn't recognise it, but it felt kind. It felt like love, like genuine help. She trusted it. She felt hands on her head, and energy flowing through her, starting at her crown and eventually reaching her toes. Warmth started spreading into her cold body and the aching lessened a little. That's the last she remembered until Jacob shook her awake.

'Maya,' he whispered, his face very close and his breath on her nose. He's just had a cigarette, was her first thought, followed by the realisation that she could actually smell again.

'Maya,' he said again, and she opened her eyes, sticky from sleep. 'Are you okay?'

'Yes, I think so,' Maya croaked. 'I feel a bit better.'

'Maya, you've been asleep for seventeen hours straight.'

'What?!' she said, sitting up. 'What time is it?'

'It's three in the morning,' he answered, and Maya had the

chance to really look at him. He had deep, dark shadows under his eyes and, as the light from the flames of the dying coal fire flicked cross his face, Maya noticed how pale he was.

'Jacob, you need to get to sleep,' she said.

'I'll sleep when we've moved,' he answered, standing up. 'There's still a lot to do, and we can't miss the ferry tomorrow afternoon.'

Maya moved to get up.

'No. Rest,' Jacob said, pushing her gently back down. 'I need you to drive a car and trailer for seven hours in the morning. Rest.'

Maya lay down and, before she knew it, she was asleep again.

15

Maya pulled forward carefully and tested the brakes on the car. Okay, so it stopped, and the trailer was following her. That's a good start.

She looked over at Jacob, who pulled alongside her in the rented van with Amy and Aurora next to him in the front seat. Aurora had her hamster perched on her lap in a cage and was waving at Maya. She smiled back, catching Jacob's eye as she did so. She lingered a second trying to read his expression. It was one of grit and determination, like they were setting off on an adventure their souls were longing for but their minds were terrified of.

She broke eye contact and turned to Faith and Zidan in the back of the car.

'Are you ready?'

Faith said nothing and stared out the window. Zidan gave her the thumbs up and continued playing with Speckles, his favourite ever dinosaur.

'Okay,' she said, mainly to herself. Releasing the handbrake, she followed Jacob down the drive for the last time. She was too ill and too tired to know how she felt about leaving, but she could feel the sadness in the children and guilt spiked through her. God, she hoped they were doing the right thing, maybe not for them right now, but the right thing that would help them lead amazing lives eventually.

When they reached the end of the drive, Maya noticed Richard sitting on his quad by the side of the road, phone in hand. Even before she looked up, she could feel the negative waves coming off him. Dark clouds seemed to swirl around him and he ignored both vehicles as they turned onto the road. He's up to no good, thought Maya, wondering just what nastiness he was trying to spread, and imagining into existence a shield around the people in both vehicles.

The Demons around his head cackled and laughed.

She didn't shield the actual vehicles, just the people, they danced and chanted, while egging on the man, completely trapped in their control, having long since sold his soul for money and possessions, and was therefore very easy to manipulate.

'Hi, is that the police?' he bellowed into the phone. 'I'd like to report an overloaded vehicle.'

As they made their way north on the dual carriageway, for the first time Maya felt the density of the area. There was so much greed here; people that had made their money and moved north so they could buy bigger houses and nicer cars and live the country dream. Except they weren't. Some of them at least were serving Satan, miserable inside, yet their ego wouldn't let them acknowledge that; they were too proud to ask it to step aside in order to reconnect with their true selves. The truth is, we've all taken wrong paths and done things that don't align with what we want to be. But the beauty lies in self-forgiveness, in knowing that, no matter what, it's never too late to have a conversation with your true self and start over. She smiled to herself, feeling that this thought was very apt for her and Jacob at the moment. Ahead, the van bumped along and Maya concentrated on keeping the trailer behind her steady and not too close to the huge wagon that was over-taking at speed.

After a few hours they hit a major town and slowed down as they approached a large roundabout on the outskirts. As they did so, the space between Maya and Jacob expanded, large enough for the police car sitting at the side of the road to slip into and put its lights on.

'Bugger,' Maya said out loud. 'They're after Jacob.'

She watched as Jacob pulled over and, having no room to stop, she went round the roundabout and stopped next to one of the exits to wait for him. She sat patiently, trying to feel into the energy, while calming the kids in the back who were becoming increasingly distressed.

After a short time, Jacob reappeared, being followed by the police car. He flashed at her. He was heading into the direction of town. She knew he wanted her to follow him, but something told her not to. Instead, Maya pulled out and left the roundabout in the opposite direction.

'Mum, where are you going?' Faith yelled from the back seat. 'We need to go with Dad.'

'No, we don't,' she said. 'Just trust me.'

She pulled into a shopping centre car park and found a space at the far end among some low hanging trees.

'Oh my God, Mum, this isn't a movie. What the hell are you doing?'

'Come on,' she announced, opening the door and swinging her legs onto the ground, stretching as she went. 'Let's get a coffee while we wait. We're ahead of time for the ferry.'

With that, both kids quietened immediately and raced over to the coffee shop to order their favourite chocolate delight. They chose a window seat and Maya brought the drinks and some muffins over. As she sipped her tea and stared out the window, she saw a police car drive past slowly, make a turn at the end and then drive round to the other part of the shopping complex.

I knew it, she thought to herself. They're looking for us. The trailer's probably overloaded if it got weighed as well. While she had no contact with Jacob, she knew that was the reason he was pulled over and that their landlord had phoned ahead and tipped them off. Slimy rat, she thought, wrinkling up her nose.

'What's wrong with you?' Faith said, poking her in the arm. 'You're so weird. You're a weird mum,' she continued.

Zidan piped up, 'She isn't a weird mum.'

'Right, yes. Brilliant,' Maya answered, waving a hand at them. 'Come on, let's get on the road. We'll keep heading north. Hopefully we'll hear from Dad soon,' she said, checking her phone.

Meanwhile, across town Jacob sat outside a transport depot. The police officer, having softened considerably when he saw Aurora's cute face, clutching her hamster on her knee and looking terrified, was explaining that he would let Jacob off with some of the charges, on account he didn't realise how heavy the internal lift on the van was, but that the overall overload charge needed to stay and that he couldn't let him drive any further without offloading the excess baggage. The man, in his mid-forties with silver hair, leaned in a little closer through the window after checking over his shoulder.

'Your wife's a smart cookie,' he said quietly. 'She had disappeared when they went back to look for her. You've avoided another overload charge for that trailer, for sure. Three police cars are looking for her,' he laughed. 'It's a quiet day,' he added quickly, becoming serious again, as if to justify the ridiculous notion of three cars looking for an overloaded family trailer instead of actually catching criminals.

'The police aren't the organisation they used to be, are they?' Jacob answered, fixing him with his green-eyed stare but meaning no malice. 'You know, when the bobby on the beat did the job the public paid him to do.'

'I know,' the officer responded, looking sad for a second, before signalling for Jacob to back the vehicle up to the depot drop-off point. 'These boys will pallet your stuff and deliver them to the island for you in a few days. There's no promise things won't get broken, so keep the most delicate stuff with you,' he advised.

As he walked off, his thoughts remained on Jacob. An unusual encounter in his job—he felt different to most other people. Not once did the man get defensive or rude. He clearly didn't feel threatened by the uniform. If anything, he felt Jacob pitied him. The man had an energy about him—he knew who he was. He wanted to stay and chat with him more, but duty called and the radio pulled him away to a two-car collision out on the motorway.

Jacob unloaded items as quickly as possible and, when the load was finally deemed the correct weight, he set off again.

'Okay,' Jacob said to a slightly traumatised Aurora and Amy. 'We should still make it. Aurora, ring your Mum. I don't want to get pulled for phoning while driving by the other three shark cars swimming about,' he said, rolling his eyes.

Faith picked up immediately.

'Dad!' she shouted into the phone. 'Are you okay?'

'Yeah, yeah, fine. We've had to send some of our stuff another way, but it's all good. You're a clever one Missus,' he shouted at his wife over the loudspeaker.

'Yes, I know,' she responded. 'Why on earth were you trying to get me to follow you, you muppet?' she laughed.

'I wasn't thinking,' he admitted.

Maya thought about bringing up the question of how the police had known they would be there, but decided against it. She knew Jacob was thinking the same thing and it would only sour the mood.

'Are you going to make it, Dad?' Faith asked, panic clearly evident in her voice. 'We're nearly there.'

'Yes, should do,' he said. 'Just let the ferry guys know we'll be right up against the check-in time.'

'Okay,' she responded and clicked the phone off.

'What a couple of idiots you and Dad are,' Faith started rambling. 'Why didn't you check and see it was overloaded?'

'We knew, Faith, but we didn't have the money for removals, and it wasn't actually unsafe.'

'Well, you have a fine coming now,' Faith reminded her.

Yes, well, that's a trauma for another day, she said to herself, trying not to think about their money situation.

The road opened up in the last hour to rolling moorland, mountains and gushing waterfalls. It was beautiful, and Maya stopped for five minutes to take in the clean air and load herself up with paracetamol. While feeling a lot better, she still felt like she had a heavy head cold and was desperate to lay her head down and rest. One day, she thought to herself, climbing back into the car. One day I'll have a proper rest.

What, when you're dead? her mind supplied.

Something like that, she thought, rolling her eyes and pulling back out on the road again.

Half an hour later they began their descent into the port village. The road wove along beside the large loch leading down to the port that sat out on a peninsula where the loch waters began to meet the open sea. The stretch of water between here and the island was often rough, but nothing like the waves of the Atlantic Ocean that bordered the west side of the island.

Maya pulled up at the check-in point and, after a few minutes, the ferry operator flagged her forward to pull into one of the lines waiting to board the ferry. The dogs in the back had started to climb on Faith and Zidan, barking at the ones in the camper van parked next to them and generally causing chaos.

'Okay, okay,' she said to the dogs, applying the handbrake and exhaling deeply. 'Faith, grab their leads. We need to take them out for a pee. God knows how the cats are in the cages in the trailer. I daren't look,' she said to Zidan, who was climbing out the car trailing a duvet with him.

Maya untangled it from his legs and threw it back in, before turning with her arms around his shoulder to follow Faith towards the shore front. Zidan started laughing at the sight of Faith being pulled in different directions by over-excited dogs, and tripping over Harris, the terrier.

'Go and help her,' Maya chided.

'Nah,' he snorted. 'This is way too entertaining,' he said, as Sam, the Golden Retriever, tried to cock his leg on a man standing at the corner.

'Oh my God, that's hilarious!' he howled, as Maya tried to suppress a smile while Faith's face turned crimson and she apologised to the man, babbling something about the dog thinking he was a lamppost.

'Brilliant,' Maya laughed. 'I'm sure he feels better now, knowing he was mistaken for a lamppost,' she said between giggles, as Faith caught up to her. Zidan trailed behind holding his sides.

'Dickheads,' she hissed at them both, failing to see the funny side.

Maya turned her thoughts to Jacob. He should be here soon, by her calculations. He had to make it.

'Twenty minutes left until check-in closes,' she announced, looking at her watch. 'Come on, Jacob,' she whispered. 'You'll make it fine.'

With two minutes to spare, Maya saw the large white van appear in the line to check in as they made their way back to the car with the dogs.

'He's here,' she said, relief filling her and tears springing to her eyes.

Zidan rushed up to the van but Jacob was now embroiled in a heated debate with the check-in operator.

'What's up?' Maya enquired, appearing by the side of them both.

'This guy's saying the van is longer than the checked in length by two metres. Oh, and two inches,' he added sarcastically, throwing a sideways look at the man aggressively flicking the tape measure in his hand.

'Okay,' Maya breathed, then turned to him. 'How much?'

'What?' the operator answered hotly.

'How much extra do I have to pay? It was a mistake.'

'It's not just that, lady. There might not be room on the ferry,' he said, scowling.

Jacob opened his mouth, no doubt to launch some other dripping sarcasm, and Maya shot him the shut-up look.

'Come on,' she said. 'You and I both know it was a mistake.

I'm ill, he's tired, we have our whole lives in these vehicles. How much extra?'

'Go pay the office sixty pounds and I'll let you on,' he said, gruffly handing Jacob a green ticket and walking off.

Jacob made to answer the retreating man but Maya put her hand up in front of his face.

'You're here. We're getting on. That's all that matters,' she said.

Jacob turned, noticing tears in her eyes and softened a little.

'He's still a jerk,' he grumbled.

'And a jerk he can remain,' she laughed. 'I'll go and pay it, you get in line. See you soon,' she said, gently kissing him on the cheek and walking off towards the pay desk, Zidan in hot pursuit chirping about salty chips.

✦

Once they had boarded the ferry and settled the dogs and kids with food and juice, Maya and Jacob made their way up towards the outside deck to watch the boat leave the port.

'I'll meet you there,' he said turning back as they reached the doors to the deck. 'Two minutes,' and he disappeared back down the stairs.

'Okay,' Maya said, moving to find a quiet corner at the back of the deck overlooking the port.

She sighed, letting the tension of the last few days ebb from her a little, and watched the seagulls dancing and playing in the skies around the boat. People scurried back and forth on the road below, but it was a more leisurely pace than what she was used to, a little less manic and little more heartfelt, she thought, smiling. The thing is, everyone goes on holiday to get away from their lives. Life should be like a permanent holiday, she concluded. Then you wouldn't have to snatch a week or two to feel happy. It's crazy really what humans tolerate and yet we think we're free.

As the thoughts swirled around her mind, she swore she heard Tal laughing.

Exactly! Now you're starting to see the truth, he chuckled and she smiled affectionately.

Yep, I've still got a lot to learn, she thought.

Before she could ponder just what that was, Jacob appeared beside her with two glasses of Prosecco.

'Here's to our new start,' he smiled, staring into her eyes and handing one of the glasses to her.

Emotion bubbled up from deep inside. All the pain, the trauma, the fights, but also the love, the passion, the hope, seemed to merge in the pit of her stomach and form a knot behind her throat. She couldn't speak, she could only nod in agreement and reach out to hug him.

They stayed, arms wrapped around each other for several minutes, unaware of anything else, until she heard a huge, 'Yuck! Don't make people look at that crap,' as Faith came across the deck.

'Can I have some more money please?' she said. 'We need chocolate.'

Jacob rolled his eyes and handed her a fiver out of his pocket.

'Go on, bugger off,' he said kindly, waving his hand after her.

Maya had turned back to watch as the ferry started to pull out of the port.

'Were you worried you wouldn't make it?' she asked Jacob, who had snuggled in behind her after taking a sip of his drink.

'Yes, especially when I hit those traffic lights at the road-works about fourteen miles out,' he admitted.

'Yeah, I know the ones,' she replied. 'I guess that would have been about twenty minutes before you arrived, right?'

'Uh huh,' Jacob said, moving her hair aside to rest his head on her shoulder.

'That was when I knew you would make it,' she said, squeezing the hand holding his glass and resting on the railing in front of her.

'Ah, my lucky charm,' he said, pressing her close. They watched in silence as the port slowly disappeared and the ferry sailed through the mouth of the loch and out into the open sea.

'Can you feel that?' he asked.

'Feel what?' she said, somewhat sleepily and a little dizzy after finishing her drink.

'The sound of freedom. The leaving behind of all the crap. It's alright for you, I hear you say, you don't have to head back there, but the thing is, Maya, neither do you. We have a choice. It might not be an easy one, but we always have a choice. Let go of what you think you need to be, and allow yourself to be who you're supposed to be.'

'Wow,' Maya mocked fake shock. 'You're quite the spiritual teacher! Okay, oh wise one,' she smiled, pulling him close again and enjoying the feeling of freedom and love, as the wind whipped her hair around her face and the warmth of Jacob's body soaked through to hers.

✦

'DAD!' Amy squealed in his ear abruptly, bringing Jacob back from a very enjoyable dream involving a mouse, an elephant and a magician, in which he would have preferred to have stayed.

'What?' he croaked.

'Time to get off the ferry,' she said excitedly, waving her soft toy pony around in front of him.

'Okay, okay.' He stretched, sitting up and seeing that passengers were already heading down the stairwell to the car deck. 'Where's Mum?'

'Toilet, of course,' Aurora answered, pulling her coat on.

'Of course,' Jacob echoed, rolling his eyes.

Within a few minutes, the doors had opened and they were rolling off the ferry onto the island terminal. They passed through the small port town and followed the road out over the open moor.

'Brilliant,' Faith grumbled from the back, pulling the hood

of her sweater up over her head. 'You brought us to Turd Island.'

'What?' Maya exclaimed, staring at her in the rear view mirror, perplexed.

'T...U...R...D... Island, Mum,' she punctuated.

'What? Like poo?' Maya asked, raising an eyebrow.

'Yes, Mum, it looks like a giant turd. It's all brown.'

Maya scoffed. 'It's just the time of year, Faith. It's beautiful.

'Whatever,' Faith mumbled, shutting her eyes.

Maya fumed silently. Turd Island, she muttered to herself, trying to ignore the fact that Zidan had indeed found it very funny but was trying to hide his giggles on account of his Mum's feelings.

After another half an hour of travelling, they pulled up at the house. As they rounded the corner past the giant Scots pine tree Maya remembered from her last trip, she felt the familiar sensation of tears welling up. It felt like freedom and healing.

In the van behind her, Aurora was chatting to Jacob about how she thought the house looked Spanish because of the veranda, and maybe it would be quite nice, and she wanted to choose her bedroom.

'It's already been chosen,' Jacob cut in quickly, unwilling to entertain another 'That's my room', 'No, it's not' argument.

Aurora huffed and pouted quietly, shuffling to adjust the

position of the hamster cage on her lap, which awoke Amy. Jacob swung the van in behind the car and trailer. Maya jumped out, opening the boot and letting the dogs run into the garden. Everyone piled up the steps and through the door.

As she dropped her handbag on the floor, she felt like she had dropped a bag of bricks. The kids ran around looking in rooms and complaining about the dank smell that comes with a house by the sea sitting empty for a while.

'Maya,' Jacob said, grabbing her arm and steering her towards the bedroom at the end of the hallway, which they had claimed as theirs. 'Get into bed. Don't even think about unpacking tonight. I'll settle the animals and get the kids the blow-up mattresses. We'll do everything else tomorrow.'

Maya opened her mouth, then shut it again and kicked off her shoes. He was right—she was exhausted. She crawled under the duvet on top of her makeshift bed and fell asleep to the sound of the waves crashing on the rocks below. The wind was whipping up into quite a storm, she noted, but they were here, they were safe and they were together. And that's all that mattered.

16

Maya smiled as she stepped barefoot onto the sand. The tide was out, leaving a large expansive beach that was a perfect playing ground for four children and two dogs. She closed her eyes for a second and listened to the squeals of delight from Amy as she chased Harris around. When she opened them again she watched Faith play tug of war with Sam, putting her weight behind the large chunk of kelp they were wrestling that had been brought up by the recent storm. Zidan was in the rock pools, no doubt looking for crabs, and Aurora was drawing with a stick in the sand.

She looked around for Jacob and found him by following the line of rocks bordering the beach. He was half way along, sitting upon a particularly large rock, his back straight, his eyes closed and his head tilted up to the sun, meditating. She smiled, thinking how blessed they were with the weather today. They were the only people on the beach and were treated to the now familiar sight of a sea eagle flying up over the moorland behind the ridge of the first hill next to the beach.

'Mum!' Amy shrieked, being the first of the kids to spot the majestic bird. 'Look!'

'I know,' Maya smiled. 'Beautiful.'

Maya had seen this eagle several times over the last few weeks. When out walking the dogs, it would appear and then disappear just as quickly, but it was always high in the sky and always coasting on the breeze. She took it as a sign to show her it didn't always need to be a struggle, that sometimes it was okay just to coast and rest our wings.

Doers, Tal called humans. *Always doing,* he said. *Try just being. You'll be far more successful.*

It still seemed an alien concept to Maya but then, things that had seemed an alien concept only a short time ago were now feeling just right, so maybe in the future she could be a 'just being' rather than a 'just doing' soul.

There was hope for her yet, Tal had told her and she smiled at the memory.

It had been two weeks to the day since they had arrived. Maya had spoken with HR last week and again yesterday, and finally came to an agreement to leave with nine months' salary. At first, she had felt like she'd been beaten, like she'd given up but, as Jacob had said, what are you fighting against? You won't win—save your strength for another day.

He was right. The money was much needed and would give her the chance to regroup. She filed away the corruption and unfairness in her head, ready for when her strength returned, because she wasn't going to let it go. She felt strongly about this, about bringing injustice to light and helping build a holistic and fair healthcare system where people could be held, heard and healed, without money being the driver. But, for now, she needed to heal herself.

She turned as she reached the end of the beach, climbing up the grass and rocks at the far side. She kept climbing, wanting to reach the summit of the hill where the cairns of the village elders still dotted the landscape. Her breathing became laboured, but she pushed on, thinking back to the kids' first days at their new schools.

Faith and Aurora had come home saying it was terrible and their classmates were all, in Faith's tactical way of describing people, 'goons'. She had listened patiently, trying to offer words of encouragement. She knew the school wasn't as good as their last one—it had been one of the considerations—but she found herself that evening sitting in the dark, visualizing the energy of the school lifting as more and more kids like Faith and Aurora came into this place.

The whole island sat on huge chunks of clear quartz—it should be a beacon of vitality. Over time, Tal had shown her that dark power, and witchcraft of a less than positive nature, had brought denser energy in, but all it needed was a tipping of the energies to bring the positivity back and recharge the crystals. Maya smiled, thinking of how she was going to enjoy learning more about how to work with the land to raise the vibration. It felt like the start of something exciting.

She stopped to catch her breath and turned to look down at the beach. The aquamarine water sparkled in the sunshine and spots of seaweed were dotted along the large expanse of sand. The sea was easily ten metres deep below the point where she was standing, yet she could see clearly all the way to the bottom. It was cold but she was desperate to get in. Maybe get a wetsuit first, she thought, turning to climb the last bit to the top.

Once there, she rested on a rock for a few minutes, taking in the view and breathing the fresh air from the breeze that whipped through her hair. From here, standing on the thin strip of headland, Maya had almost a 360° view of the water around her.

To the east was another small island, separated by a small slip of water flowing quickly though the gap as the tide was going out. Looking straight out, before the ocean became a vast expanse, she marvelled at the small rocky island that rose from the water in a horseshoe shape. She'd learned that smugglers had once lived there and it was already her favourite of the little islands around the place.

Over to the west, the ocean grew lighter, where rocks were concealed just below the surface, and then darker again before disappearing into the great blue abyss. It was strange to think that, if she set off, she would eventually reach Canada, although she might need a rather sturdy boat. Even from where she was standing, Maya could feel the mighty roar of the Atlantic—its beauty and its warning blending into a single sound.

She turned her head, observing the cairn situated a few feet from where she was sitting. The pile of stones was covered in moss and Maya imagined the type of man that lay under them and what his life must have been like. Tough but free, she concluded.

She could envisage the small boats rowing out to sea, hoping to catch the masses of fish still available in those times. Others would have stayed on land, cutting the peat and bringing it down to the blackhouses to keep the fires going, for smoking the fish and for cooking and keeping warm. Simple. She would like to find her way to a simpler life, one that leaves room for new adventures.

Maya felt a chill tingle down her back and became aware of a subtle singing on the wind. It wasn't in English—the words sounded like an ancient dialogue as she listened further. She knew in her heart it was Gaelic, the local language all but forgotten across most of Scotland but kept alive on the islands.

Maya watched as the woman from her visions appeared beside her and continued to sing. Her long, dark hair fanned behind her in the wind, her shawl and long dress flowing in the breeze. She was dressed the same as in Maya's vision in which the men had drowned her in the pond.

Maya blinked twice. The silhouette of the woman was faint, but it was there, and the presence next to her was huge. She found herself singing along, even though she didn't know a single word of Gaelic. The woman reached the end of the song and looked directly at Maya.

'It's time to heal,' she said, her green eyes glowing like crystals. 'Welcome home.'

Then she was gone as quickly as she had come.

Maya clutched her heart, feeling something leaving her body as her chest became lighter. This was followed by the awareness of the presence of many souls around her, villagers dressed in clothing from long ago, all smiling, all welcoming her back. She found her eyes had welled with tears.

I'm home, she said to herself. And I can remember. I know who I am and where I've been.

She laughed with relief. I'm home. All I need to know now is, how do I go forward from here?

She closed her eyes and took a huge breath. Above her, she felt the Angels flying, swirling around the two eagles that had appeared on the ridge again. She didn't know what was next, and she was aware there was a lot more to heal, but she knew she didn't have to do it alone. She knew her team was with her, both down there on the beach and around her in the ether. If she tapped into who she truly is and welcomed the support of this amazing team, how on Earth could she fail?

About the Author

Georgina Templar is a Psychic Empath, a Medium and a Quantum Energy Coach, on a mission to coach and support the future world's spiritual leaders and healers.

She offers people a bridge between the energies of this polarity planet, helping them transition from the 3D world of fear, compliance and control into the expansive and liberating realm of 5D consciousness.

Georgina lives in Scotland with her family and their herd of various animals. She can be contacted via her website *www.wolfmediumship.com*

One True North is Georgina's first book.

Coming in 2024

POLARITY PLANET

Sequel to ONE TRUE NORTH